mere mortals

To Peggy & Walter

Enjoy

Cam.

mere mortals

Cameron Ghent

Published by Cameron Ghent

ISBN 978-0-9949233-0-1 (pbk.)
ISBN 978-0-9949223-2-5 (mobi)
ISBN 978-0-9949233-1-8 (ePub)

Copyright © Cameron Ghent 2016

Cover art, design: Magdalene Carson / New Leaf Publication Design

Cataloguing in publication data available at Library and Archives Canada

To Leela, Kiran, Vivian, and Greyson.

The propagation of my genes,
for better or for worse,
depends on you.

contents

alphabetical list of characters

Paul Albright, Eric Clouser's defence attorney, Redfern
Dr. Faisal Al-Taqi, ER physician, Beaverbrook Hospital, Redfern
Arnold, a disobedient member of the Turle family
Joel Atherton, sergeant, Forensic ID, Redfern Regional Police Services
Dr. Glenna Bass, intensivist, Beaverbrook Hospital, Redfern
Jim Bimini, sergeant, Redfern Regional Police Services
Al Cahill, fire captain, Redfern Fire Department
Eric Clouser, retailer, Shacletown
Carol Creek, nurse, Intensive Care, Beaverbrook Hospital
Joanna Fisher, judge, Ontario Court of Justice, Elmsville
Inge Glacier, nursing team leader, ICU, Beaverbrook Hospital
Joe Glacier, Inge's husband, liquor store manager
Jim Hendrickson, detective inspector, Redfern Regional Police Services
Mavis Hook, ambulance attendant, Redfern
Paula Kaufman, rookie constable, Redfern Regional Police Services
Dr. Martin Midges, intensivist, Beaverbrook Hospital
John Orvis, ambulance attendant, Redfern
Dr. Winki Pham, surgery trainee, Beaverbrook Hospital ICU
Joe Pickett, detective, Redfern Regional Police Services
Garth Rowley, *Toronto Star* crime reporter, Toronto
Jeff Salmon, Dr. Leslie Turle's attorney, Redfern
Dr. Shanks, psychiatrist, Beaverbrook Hospital
Dr. Ben Speckle, plastic surgeon, Beaverbrook Hospital
Tom Stone, Eric Clouser's partner
Rod Strike, Crown prosecutor, Redfern

Dr. Will Turbot, internist, Beaverbrook Hospital
Dr. Barbara Turle–Knott, Leslie's daughter, philosopher, Baltimore
Isaac Turle, Leslie's son, security technician, Kingston, Ontario
Dr. Leslie Turle, retired intensivist, Redfern
Nancy Turle, Isaac's wife
Velma Turle, dietitian, Leslie Turle's second wife
Dr. Jeff Whitlock, family physician, Timmins
Kevin Wulff, Inge Glacier's son, Catholic priest, St. Catharines

secrets

Police Seek Help to Identify John Doe Found in Park
Garth Rowley, Staff Reporter

The headline on the front page of the GTA section of the Saturday Toronto Star caught Inge Glacier's attention. She looked closely at the photograph of a police sergeant talking to reporters over a police tape with the caption, "Sergeant Jim Bimini of the Redfern Regional Police briefs reporters at possible crime scene in Beaver Park." Inge lived near the park and read on.

Redfern Regional Police are seeking help from the public to identify a man they found naked and unconscious in Beaver Park in Redfern late Friday, in the midst of a snow-storm. After responding to a 911 call, they found the man lying on the bank of the Beaver River with life-threatening injuries. Police suspect foul play and have detained for questioning one man who fled the scene. The victim is listed in critical condition in Beaverbrook Hospital.

The report went on to ask that anyone who may have witnessed any unusual activity in the area or knew of anyone who had gone missing, to contact the Redfern Regional Police or Crime Stoppers.

Inge was intrigued. The unidentified man, if still alive, would be in the Intensive Care Unit when she returned to work there on Monday. It certainly sounded like an interesting case—the lack of identification and the crime implications would be the talk of the staff. At 57, she sometimes found her work as a nursing team leader to be challenging and she would have to assign nurses and monitor them carefully in this situation to make sure they did not get caught up in its sensational side.

She enjoyed her work but reflected that she would miss having Dr. Leslie Turle's insights in this case, although his replacement, Dr. Martin Midges, was certainly competent enough. If it turned out to be a juicy media story—the man was found naked in a public park, after all—Dr. Turle would have had some pithy memorable remarks about it. She found her job to be a challenge, but was determined to do it well for another three years before retiring at age sixty—and caring for John Doe would be a real challenge.

She looked up as the GO Train rattled over the Bronte Creek trestle bridge and was grateful that she had decided not to drive, as all the nearby roads were covered in snow from the previous night's storm. She thought about her upcoming visit with Kevin to celebrate his birthday and reflected how finding him had changed her life. She knew deep down that her marriage to Joe was over in all but name.

For five years, she had dated the entrepreneurial, handsome, and charming Joe Glacier, cautious because her best friend from nursing school at Toronto Western Hospital had warned her with rumours that he had been a heavy drinker and abusive to a previous girlfriend. But Inge had found him to be kind and loving and had never experienced any abuse other than on one occasion when he had gotten quite drunk and had called her an idiot. And on the rare occasions, only after their engagement at her insistence, when she had yielded to his advances, he had been a reasonable lover, although not particularly attentive to her needs. And she was nauseated by the occasional stench of stale cigar smoke on his breath from the fat Robustos that he was fond of smoking. It helped that she was careful to never forget to take her contraceptive pills in spite of the church's policies, and she didn't need to worry about getting pregnant. She was still a devout Catholic at that time and always went to confession after such encounters.

But Joe was well educated and had helped to pay off her student loans and had obtained a secure job as the manager of an LCBO store in Elmsville, north of their separate residences. She knew that her time was running out if she was ever going to have the two children she desperately wanted and was tired of being ribbed about being one of the oldest single women in the ICU. In spite of her reservations about him, when he had proposed to her, she quickly accepted and she was married on her 30th birthday.

In the premarital classes, they had been required to discuss parenthood. Inge insisted that she wanted two children, but Joe had been noncommittal. After the wedding, Inge had remained on the pill for almost two years. But she hadn't told Joe when she stopped, as he still seemed ambivalent about fatherhood. She had reasoned that she could tell him that she had forgotten her pills for a few days when she got pregnant, as she was sure she would. She had even kept the disc of contraceptive pills on the bedside table to deceive him. But after another year, she still was not pregnant, and had told Joe that her doctor had told her to take a pill break. Joe finally reconciled himself with the prospect of fatherhood. After another two unfruitful years, at age 35, she had persuaded Joe to attend a fertility clinic for testing. Inge was found to be fertile—no surprise to her—but Joe was not producing any sperm at all. When they both insisted on finding out why, further testing showed that he carried the gene for cystic fibrosis. *That may explain his frequent colds and cough,* she thought. They were told that there was no possibility that he would ever father a child, as males with that gene mutation are invariably infertile. Joe had refused to consider adoption, artificial insemination, or the newer in vitro fertilization. Changing the diapers of a baby carrying his genes would be bad enough; if the infant was not his own, it would be so much worse. When Inge suggested they could adopt an older child, Joe commented, "We would likely then just be adopting someone else's problems."

Despite her repeated assurances that she could accept being childless, Joe had become increasingly distant and seemed to blame himself for his failure to produce the child she so desperately wanted. But rather than consoling her, he spent more time with his buddies, often drinking far too much. When he arrived home on such occasions, he would be loud and rude, often sarcastically pointing out that her needlecraft and knitting hobbies were a waste of time, as she was never going to have any children or grandchildren to knit clothes for.

After 10 more years of feeling somehow unfulfilled, Inge had found Kevin. At first, she would only visit him on days when Joe was out of town, but after two years she grew careless; Joe seemed to not really care what she did or where she was. But Joe had in fact become increasingly paranoid and suspicious about his beautiful wife's frequent, unexplained absences from home on her days off and on weekends, and had hired a private detective to track her movements. When the detective related that she had spent a day in the home of a parish priest in St. Catharines, Joe exploded, and she had then tearfully confessed to him about her youthful affair and the existence of her son by another man. She had not been visiting a young lover, but her long-lost son. Kevin was the product of an unwanted and unexpected pregnancy, the result of a secret youthful indiscretion when she was seventeen.

When she began her search for her child, with the help from the Ontario Adoption Disclosure Unit, she had been both elated and fearful. *Would he look like her? Would he like her or rebuff her?* When they finally met for the first time, she was overcome with tears of joy. He was 37, tall and handsome, with her piercing blue eyes, her curly hair, and her distinctive gliding gait. But she now had mixed feelings about her decision to find him, although she could not imagine life without him. He was a great source of comfort and joy to her, but she blamed her decision to find him for the ruination of her marriage. She often wondered to herself about which came first. *Did I decide to find him because my marriage was on the rocks, or did my decision to find him lead to the marriage wreckage?*

Joe had been devastated. He could understand youthful flings, as he had had many one-night stands in his university days. However, he applied a double standard when it came to the woman he wanted to live with for the rest of his life. He felt that it was fine that *he* had played the field before marriage, but it was not acceptable for his wife. Mostly, he was alarmed that she had managed to deceive him for more than 20 years, and had undergone fertility testing in a deliberate attempt to deceive him further about her known fertility. He asked her on one occasion "If you can lie to me about something this important, why should I believe anything you say?"

He had tried hard to adjust to the new reality and to be civil to Kevin. But he had somehow let her down; Kevin's pious

Catholicism also irked him. In Joe's world of business the only "isms" he subscribed to were hedonism and materialism. He seldom thought much about religion or any other guiding principle in his life. He told her that she should enjoy life without questioning it's meaning.

On the train, she now pondered the advice a clinical psychologist and marriage counsellor had given her a few months before at an appointment discreetly arranged by the Beaverbrook Hospital's Employee Health Services at her request. Joe had refused to go with her to the appointment. After reviewing her situation, the therapist had told her that she should either end the marriage or return to another appointment with Joe in tow. She had done neither. She would never leave Joe, although she yearned for the intimacy, cuddling, spooning in bed, and small talk that was now gone. But she worried that leaving Joe would ruin her false image of a happily married woman and might even alienate her from her one great source of joy, her son, given his pious belief in the sanctity of marriage. *And I have to be strong,* she told herself.

Her private doubt about her adequacy as a wife was coupled with a public image she cherished as a kind, confident, competent, and caring nurse. Only one co-worker, Carol Creek, knew anything about her domestic turmoil, as well as about Kevin, and she had sworn her to secrecy. *I can solve my problems myself,* she told herself. And she would continue to work for another three years in spite of the security of a good pension from her many years of nursing in the ICU. Work provided her with a sense of worth and a diversion from dealing with her domestic problems.

Three more years, she thought. *That's all I need to get to retirement. Then I can think about what to do about this marriage, if Joe does not kill himself first.*

She smiled to herself as she recalled her chance meeting with Dr. Leslie Turle the day before and his timely rescue of her from the embarrassing encounter with the hospital CEO. She had noted that he had gained weight, looked pale, and had aged significantly since she had last seen him six months earlier, but he had assured her that he was healthy and enjoying retirement. She missed his clinical acumen around the ICU, his wry humour, common sense, and sound judgment. And she loved his hilarious, sometimes a bit embellished tales of risky adventures, even though they contrasted with what she recognized as her excessive need for stability, safety and security. *Opposites attract,* she reflected, *and I worry about him. I guess I really do love him.* His outrageous wardrobe combinations and his frequent politically inappropriate comments were easily forgiven and, unlike other co-workers, she never gossiped about them.

The hospital CEO, Brook Falone, included MBWA (Management by Walking Around) in his routine and often showed up in the cafeteria at irregular hours chatting with anyone he found there, whether cleaning staff, the chief of a department, or a visitor. On that Friday the thirteenth he had eaten lunch and chatted with some nurses. Just as they left, he spotted Inge coming into the cafeteria and motioned for her to join him. He thought it was his lucky day as he was also infatuated with her.

"How are you doing?" Inge asked.

"Mostly without," Brook quipped. "How about you?"

"About the same," Inge replied, not entirely sure what he was referring to.

"Well now, that will never do for a beautiful lady like you. If you are not really out of bounds and ever want to come over to my office after work I would be happy to remedy that deficit in both of us."

She then realized that he was referring to sex, and chastised herself for not catching on earlier. It was, after all, not the first time that he had tried to proposition her.

Unbeknownst to Inge, a fierce battle that had been brewing for a few milliseconds erupted into a full diplomatic firefight somewhere deep within her brain at that moment, aiming their fire at each other at her consciousness. A cluster of neurons led by Vanity on one side sent an army from the land of Ego, arguing to the effect that she should be flattered by his choice to hit on her when he could have been successful with any number of other, and younger, women. Lust's troops from Eros entered the fray, reminding her that she had enjoyed illicit sex years before and that this was an opportunity to do so again—and any sex would be better than none.

The opposing neuronal corps led by Propriety and Disgust pointed out to her that she should be insulted and indignant after his highly inappropriate workplace proposal, and urged her to file a complaint about him. Neither side seemed to win a decisive victory in this short-lived war to gain her attention. She compromised and quickly retorted that he was just another dirty old man and he should not count on that ever happening. *If I were going to have an affair, it would only be with Leslie Turle,* she reflected to herself. But she tolerated the CEO's inappropriate advances in part because she rationalized that he had a lot of control over the budget allocations, including what was designated for ICU staff and equipment. Besides, he chaired the Harassment in the Workplace committee, so any complaint would never be taken seriously. In part, she was determined to find out who had nicknamed her "Out-of-Bounds," a nickname that had somehow stuck to her.

Two different subconscious neuronal armies again opened fire within her head aiming in the same directions, when Leslie Turle asked her why she had insulted Falone, as soon as they were alone. Longing, Love, and Lust all recruited Limerence to tell her that she should confess her deep love for him and indicate that she would welcome an affair with him. Caution said she should just shut up about it. Once again, the battle drew to a stalemate within a second or two, so she compromised. She could not be overt about her feelings, but she could give him some hints and leave it up to him to take further action.

She had to be careful with her self-control around Dr. Turle; she could never give any strong hint about her feelings for him. Besides, he was, as far as she knew, happily married to Velma, the dietitian she had worked with in the ICU. And she assumed that he bought into her carefully nurtured public image as a happily married career woman, even though it was a lie.

On this occasion, after Leslie had seemingly ignored her hints about her feelings for him, they had chatted about the weather, her career, new happenings in the ICU with the nurses' attempts to form a union, and the completely new hospital-wide computer system that allowed them to connect with all of the other hospitals in the area. She secretly prided herself in being able to detect signs of any distress in others and in getting them to confide in her and seek her advice, but she had sensed no distress in him. And she was a bit disappointed that he had ignored the clues she had given about her love for him.

Meeting Dr. Turle had led to yet another ugly confrontation with Joe the evening before. After a largely silent dinner, she had sat down to finish reading a Malcolm Gladwell book while Joe watched the close hockey game on TV with his reprimands of the referee getting louder and more profane with each refill of his glass from the bottle of Bacardi at his side. After the game was over, when his Ottawa Senators team finally won in overtime, he calmed down and quite civilly had asked Inge how her day at work had gone. When she could not resist telling him about the chance meeting with Dr. Turle, as it had been the highlight of her day, he had exploded.

"There's something going on between the two of you, isn't there?"

"Of course not. Don't be ridiculous."

"Dr. Turle this, Dr. Turle that!" he sneered. "You talk about him a lot."

"I worked with him for years. Of course, I talk about him sometimes. Stop being so paranoid! I don't think he even likes me." But she had been blushing, unwilling to admit to him, or even to herself, how close to the truth he had come.

"Listen, if I ever hear you mention him again, I will break your neck!" he had yelled. Then he had slapped her roughly across her face, causing a bruise on her cheek and a nosebleed, and stumbled off to their bedroom, tripping on the stairs. Inge had run to the washroom, locked the door, and applied a cold face cloth to her nose and cheek. She had waited until she heard him snoring, then crawled into the bed in the spare bedroom and cried herself to sleep. Tomorrow would be better, she had thought. Before leaving that morning, she had undertaken the familiar task of covering up the bruises with her best camouflage makeup.

As the train neared the Aldershot station, she checked her makeup in her mirror to make sure Kevin would not see the bruises on her cheek and nose. Then she reflected, not for the first time, that Joe's drinking or drunk driving would likely kill him, and wondered how she would conceal her mixed emotions, mostly relief, at his funeral. She pondered the wording of the obituary she would have to write. *Glacier, Joseph Winston, as a result of liver failure? . . . an accident? . . . Beloved husband and best friend of Inge, and . . .* realizing that mention of Kevin Wulff would raise many eyebrows, and her deep secret would no longer be a secret, she moved on to the wording of the eulogy she would have to give at his funeral. She knew that in the 21st century, admitting to having had a child out of wedlock in the remote past would not make most people think less of her, but she somehow could not let that information become public knowledge. She could avoid mentioning Kevin in the eulogy, and, even though he would attend the funeral, if he attended in his clerical collar, few people would ask about his relationship to the deceased. *The Lord has called home my beloved husband and best friend, but he will be fondly remembered by all who were privileged to have known him.* She continued to rework different versions in her mind after switching to the bus for the last leg of the trip.

When Kevin met her, they planned a busy weekend. They took some food items to an ailing couple from the congregation who had no means of transportation and no family in the area. After Saturday Vigil Mass, with Inge at his side, he proudly introduced her to any new parishioners, as was his habit whenever she visited, to avoid any gossip about a beautiful older woman visiting him frequently. They attended the home of a parishioner for dinner, wine, and a celebration of Kevin's 40th birthday. On Sunday afternoon, they joined another priest in attending a recital of Handel's *Messiah* before she left to return to Redfern. Joe was almost sober when she arrived home and apologetic about his treatment of her the previous Friday, but quickly became defensive when she noted that he was unkind and abusive only when he had been drinking and suggested that he should get some help.

"I know I have a bit too much sometimes," he acknowledged, "but I can cut back on my own."

"You have said that before and nothing changes. I really think you need help."

"You just don't believe me, do you?"

"Joe, I wish you knew how much I'd like to believe you. I'll support you all the way—you know I will."

Inge knew better than to push him any further. She changed the subject and asked if he had heard about the naked man rescued from Beaver Park the previous Friday night. He said the man was still alive and in the ICU. She promised to give him an update when she returned from work the next day, but reminded him that she would be limited by the need to maintain patient confidentiality.

It has been a fun weekend with Kevin, she thought that night. *And the new case sounds like a real challenge to start my workweek.*

2

help!

Velma Turle arrived in Kingston at the home of her stepson, Isaac, his wife, Nancy, and their five-year-old son, Adam, early on the afternoon of that Friday the 13th. Nancy greeted her with her usual warm hug, and Velma carefully explained the reason for her surprise visit. They had often joked and shared stories about their men, those "quirky Turle men," but Nancy soon realized that Velma was very serious about seeking some help on this visit. They strategized and then drove together to pick up Adam from junior kindergarten. The greeting from Isaac when he returned from work was cooler.

"To what do we owe the displeasure of this visit?" he asked, only half in jest.

Nancy intervened to reveal the reason for Velma's visit. "Listen, dear, Velma is worried about your father and wants some help and advice."

"That must be a first," Isaac retorted, then said, "Sorry, I couldn't resist that barb." Theirs was a typical strained stepmother/stepson relationship filled with mutual antagonism and suspicions.

"Come on! Velma's worried about your father and has come to ask for help and you can't even be civil to her? Grow up and listen to what she has to say."

"I invited myself and I will go back home right now if you don't want me here. But I think you should know that your father is very unwell, and I need your suggestions if you can stand my presence."

Isaac relented and apologized for his rudeness, but he still deeply resented what he saw as Velma's role in the alienation of his father from his sister, Barb. He also blamed her for the steady deterioration he had observed in his father's happiness and outlook in the two years since his retirement. He had observed the sarcasm and rudeness she often flung at his father and thought that she was too bossy and domineering. For her part, Velma thought that Isaac's job as an installer for ADT Security Systems was beneath his capabilities, given the scholastic aptitude and brilliant inventiveness she had observed in him during his infrequent visits when he was a teen. *If only he weren't so lazy and applied himself like his father had, he could have done much better*, she thought.

She knew that she had a tendency to try to control the behaviour of others and tried very hard to keep that personality trait in check.

"I know I can be a bossy pain in the neck and I am sorry if I am being one now. Leslie has taken to calling me 'She who must be obeyed' or 'the ruler of heaven and earth.' But a man with my characteristics wouldn't be called a bitch—likely he would be called strong, decisive, and a natural leader. But Isaac, someday I am going to be wrong, and that might be today. And someday someone else is going to be right and that someone might be you and that someday might be today."

She secretly blamed her first husband for having fostered her bossiness. During their marriage, he had become so controlling that he would not even allow her to do the grocery shopping alone, even though she was a nutritionist; meals were planned from a menu he set up, and she had to account for every penny she spent. Sex with him was always in his favourite position, and her back always ached for hours thereafter. When, in desperation, she left him, she told herself that under no circumstances would she ever be controlled or cowed by a man again, or by anyone else.

After her divorce, she had become increasingly attracted to Dr. Leslie Turle, the intensivist who worked in the same ICU that she worked in as a dietitian. He was in many ways the exact opposite of her ex—a natural leader, a listener, and a team player. He took the suggestions of other team members seriously and never argued about the recommendations she made for the diets of the patients they shared. She only learned later that he was surprisingly ignorant and uninterested in any aspects of nutrition. And she loved his jovial, fun-loving, adventurous nature. When she heard through the ICU gossip mill that he was separated from his wife and getting divorced, she made her move before some other lucky lady caught his fancy. He was the catch of the year.

At the dinner table that night, with Adam as a pleasant distraction, Velma began to cautiously lay out her concerns to Isaac and Nancy. She had decided to come for the visit alone because she wanted to discuss what she saw as an accelerating deterioration in her husband 's health, both physically and mentally, and wanted the family to help her to get some help for him. After Adam went to bed, their discussion became much more specific and detailed as it continued late into the evening. Isaac softened, realizing for the first time how much Velma cared and loved "the old man."

"There are a lot of things I am worried about," Velma began again. "Over the last six months, he has aged 10 years. He has slowed down both physically and mentally and he is sleeping a lot more. At times he just sits in his recliner and does nothing for hours at a time. And he pulls the recliner up so close to the fireplace that I am afraid he will burn himself. And he is getting confused. And his old witty comebacks and quips are gone. All of his comments are cynical and negative about almost everything. He hates the cold weather but refuses to consider a trip to Cuba this winter. I think he has Alzheimer's."

"Doesn't sound like Dad, for sure," Isaac said. "Does he still go out for his long walks?"

"He does go on long walks. So far he hasn't gotten lost in the woods behind the house, but I worry about that happening, and he has lost his keys. The other day he got lost when we were shopping at Costco. He has written cheques on the wrong account a couple of times, and he forgets to brush his teeth, take a shower, or use deodorant unless I remind him. I have always had to tell him about deodorant. He says he can't detect body odours or any other odours. One time years ago he had a run-in with a skunk in the park and couldn't understand why I was so upset about the stench on his clothes."

"Chalk that one up as just another of those Turle male quirks—my best perfume is completely wasted on Isaac. I don't think he even notices it," Nancy observed.

"Well, I have to remind him when it is time to go to the barber shop to get a haircut and beard trim. And he seems to have no appetite for, or interest in, any of his hobbies. His bizarre eating habits are an embarrassment. He frequently can't remember the names of people that he talks about, like his former co-workers that he should know well. He doesn't update his bucket list on the computer, let alone try to do any of the stupid things that are on it."

"Maybe he is just depressed," Nancy suggested.

"Listen, I know the symptoms of depression, and he may be depressed, but, if so, it is because he is sick, and somehow knows it," Velma responded. There was a long pause as they each looked at her with a question mark in their gazes. "Okay, you're wondering how I can be so sure. I may as well tell you. I have been in treatment with a psychiatrist for depression for almost fifteen years." It was the first time that she had discussed her struggles with depression with anyone other than Leslie and her Hamilton psychiatrist, Dr. Roy Coachman. Nancy and Isaac were both startled by this revelation, but Isaac still had reservations about her interpretation of the deterioration in Leslie's health.

Nancy prided herself on being blunt and practical. "Let's see," she interjected. "He has lost interest in food, his personal hygiene, and his hobbies and travel. What about sex?"

"Let's not go there," Velma retorted.

"Sorry. I just know that when Isaac gets even a little upset and blue, he loses what little interest he has in—"

"Okay!" Isaac's tone was enough to cut off that avenue of the conversation. "I agree that something is seriously wrong with Dad, and we need to work together on it." He was surprised by how concerned Velma seemed to be. She suddenly seemed to be a different person than the self-centred, cold stepmother he had known for years. But he was also still concerned about her role in Leslie's problems. "We need to get him to see a doctor," he concluded.

"Well, he hasn't had a check-up in five years and doesn't want to go. He has that ugly growth on his neck but he won't even see a dermatologist about it, not that a dermatologist would ever solve any of the other problems."

Late in the evening, they agreed that Isaac would visit his father the following weekend to make some first-hand observations. Then Nancy had a suggestion: "What about your psychiatrist?" she asked Velma. "Would he agree to assess Leslie?"

"That might work," Velma responded "I can make an appointment with him at any time without a referral, and he wouldn't refuse to assess a fellow physician." They worked out the deceptive plan together. She would explain in advance that her depression was getting worse because of having to deal with Leslie's supposed dementia, and Dr. Roy Coachman would have no choice but to do a mental status examination of Leslie. She would insist that Leslie accompany her to the appointment with Dr. Coachman. They congratulated Velma for coming up with this plan, even though Nancy had suggested it first. Velma relaxed for the first time since she had arrived and they planned some activities for the rest of the weekend.

Nancy and Velma went with Isaac to Adam's dance lesson that Saturday morning. The Canadian Broadcasting Corporation news on the car radio caught her attention.

Redfern Regional Police are asking the public to help identify a naked elderly male taken to hospital by ambulance late Friday from Beaver Park in Redfern. An earlier report that the man was dead has not been confirmed, but he is believed to be in critical condition with life-threatening injuries. Police indicate that foul play is suspected and an unidentified man fleeing the scene is being held for questioning.

"That's not far from home," Velma observed. "The neighbourhood's sure gone downhill in the last few years. Les says he saw some gays making out there last summer. I don't care what people do in private, but the rules about public indecency should apply to everyone equally."

Isaac commented, "I doubt that they would be making out there last night, in the middle of a blizzard, and you don't need to single out gays for your scorn. But I agree with you about the rules being applied equally."

"Sounds bizarre; there is something fishy about that story. I'm sure we'll hear more."

They took Adam for a skating lesson on Sunday, and Velma helped him build a snowman in the backyard in the afternoon, surprising herself with the realization that she really enjoyed playing with a 5-year-old. In between the activities, the adults fleshed out a more detailed plan to get Leslie the help they all realized he needed. Isaac would take his father out shopping or for a long walk without Nancy or Velma to get his insight as to what was happening to his body and mind. They forgot about the news until they watched the Sunday evening CBC television news together. The man was apparently still alive and in the ICU at Beaverbrook Hospital, now listed as in critical condition and identified only as "John Doe."

"Too bad Dad is not still working there." Isaac observed. "He would have some cryptic comments about that one."

"And he has some personal experience with the treatment of exposure and hypothermia," Velma added. "But I don't think even a case like that would get him to go back to work. He really isn't interested in doing anything anymore."

While Velma was reading a bedtime story to Adam and tucking him in, Isaac called his sister, Dr. Barb Turle-Knott in Baltimore. "I know you don't care much, but I thought you should know that Dad is not at all well. He seems to be losing it, both physically and mentally."

"Strange that you should call. I have been thinking I should reconnect with him. It has probably been unkind of me to completely avoid him just because of that witch he married."

"Listen. That 'witch' Dad married cares deeply about him and is not the same person that you knew when you were growing up. She came up this weekend to try to get some help in dealing with Dad's problems and got all choked up when she described what he is going through. You might even like her now, and I know Dad misses you terribly."

"Does he ever talk about me?"

"Well, not directly, but he tries to make light of the situation and jokes about it. The very last zinger I heard from him six months ago was about you. He was talking about how he had lost his usefulness since retirement, and said he felt as useless as a barbed wire fence without a barb, and he went all teary-eyed when he said it. I know he cares a lot and would love to see you."

"Well, then. That does it. I'm off for Christmas break at the end of the week. I will plan to come up to visit Mother and you folks, and I think I will surprise Dad with a visit too."

"That would be great. I'm sure he would appreciate it. Keep us informed of your plans. We can maybe pick you up if we know when you are coming and we'll help you to break the barrier between you and Dad—and Velma."

They discussed her recent revelation about her third pregnancy and she assured her brother that she was well, and the pregnancy was apparently normal this time. Isaac suggested that it would be great if the impending arrival could bond with his grandfather sometime before the latter departed this world.

"By the way, what is going on in the old neighbourhood? We in Baltimore don't get much media coverage of Redfern, but the bizarre murder in Beaver Park was all over the news here."

"You mean the naked old geezer last Friday? Well, it wasn't a murder. The dude is still alive and in the ICU where Dad used to work, according to CBC News tonight. But you're right that the park where we used to play has gone downhill. Velma says it is a gay hangout now, but then she is a bit homophobic and sees gays everywhere. My guess is that old man was either a demented escapee from a nursing home or was involved in some kind of drug deal that went sour and got robbed and stripped. There are a lot of geriatric narcotic addicts around now, because they get hooked after a surgeon gives them too much narcotic for postoperative pain."

"I don't understand why the media can never get the story right; they reported here that the guy was dead. And their reporting of things that go on inside the Beltway here is a joke. Lyle works there and gets a lot of the real dirt that is never reported."

"Let us know your plans. We would love to see you and get you back in touch with Dad. Give my regards to Lyle."

"Well, he's in Alaska of all places to do recruiting in the winter, right now, but he'll be home on Tuesday."

3

caught!

Eric Clouser closed up the Hook Line and Sinker tackle shop early that Friday the 13th. It was snowing heavily and there had been only two customers since 1:00 p.m. Besides, his buddy, Tom Stone, at Redfern Transportation and Works had called to ask him to stand by for a call for a stint of snowploughing later that evening. He had been grateful to Tom for getting him that part-time job as a snowplough operator, quite apart from the fact that they had been fishing buddies for the past nine months.

"Want to wet some flies in the Beaver tomorrow?" Eric had asked, noting that the weather was supposed to improve a lot by midmorning, and that he was going to be off work sometime in the middle of the night depending on when he got called in. Tom had indicated that he was off work from the snowplough dispatch center at 5:00 p.m. that Friday.

"Sure, what time?"

"Let's meet in Beaver Park at eleven. The steelhead and salmon season is open all year from there on down to the mouth."

"What flies should I bring? I haven't done much winter fishing."

"Don't worry about flies. I will bring some woolly buggers, stonefly nymphs, sucker spawn imitations, and some small pheasant tail and hare's ear nymphs. And I want to try the roe-caught-in river-snot ones that I've been tying up. Just bring warm clothes and your Orvis eight weight with an extra reel and 2X tippet. You will need 2X for the monster steelhead in there."

Eric had first met Tom while standing in the middle of the Beaver River the previous spring, fly-casting for rainbow trout.

After several outings together, Eric felt Tom patting his butt as they changed out of their waders beside the camper in the park, and Tom commented on his rainbow-coloured boxers. That was enough signalling for the shy Eric to connect, and they shared a kiss. They quickly became lovers as well as fishing buddies. The lovers were oblivious to the other visitors in the park, some of whom were quite shocked by their very public display of affection.

The Hook Line and Sinker tackle shop had not been doing well, and Eric was worried about the bills that were piling up. He had reduced the inventory and moved into the empty tiny three-room apartment over the store to save money, being unable to stand the thought of spending another winter living in his camper. Reluctantly, he had agreed to retail some marijuana that a friend from downtown eastside Vancouver was desperate to dispose of. His friend's inventory had expanded to the point of being dangerous to his freedom if he were ever busted. *I am a natural for this,* he thought. *I know many of the regular users in the gay communities around here and no one will suspect a pot operation run out of a tackle shop.* He was also pleased that the BC Arctic Sun Bud and BC God Bud pot that he was getting was much more potent than he could get from the local growers and smoked it regularly himself. His customers were willing to pay top dollar for it; the mark-up income might stave off foreclosure, even though the street price of all kinds of pot had nosedived recently. He was not sure when this sideline would cease to be profitable. He kept the stash divided between a cupboard upstairs and a fishing rod holder in the back of his old Volkswagen Westphalia camper that he used for deliveries. He received deliveries in carefully sealed packages labelled as fly-tying material. He had recently received far too much to stay under the 30-gram limit that would bring on a charge of trafficking if he were busted, and kept the latest shipment in the camper, hoping to sell some soon in one of the Toronto area hangouts for gays.

The snowploughing sideline also looked promising, and, if the weather co-operated, he might avoid bankruptcy. *Pray for snow and more snow, and yet more snow,* he told everyone.

The call from Tom came at 4:45 p.m., and he drove his old camper over to the snowplough depot to get started. He loved that jalopy and had lived in it for almost two years after moving east to take a job at an automotive parts plant. He hated the assembly line work, but the pay was good, and by living in the cold camper in parking lots and eating in the employee cafeteria, he had saved a good nest egg. When the Hook Line and Sinker went up for sale at foreclosure prices, he took the bait. His dream of spending the rest of his life fishing, talking about fishing, and guiding others in the sport he loved seemed about to come true.

In this his first year with the Transportation and Works Department, he would prove that he could do the job well, but he was also a bit anxious, so on this occasion he picked up his small fly box filled with his personal supply of fine pre-rolled Arctic Bud and slid it into his pocket before leaving. He would smoke one during his break, and then maybe another on the way home after his shift was over. He never sold any pot from the store, but his inventory in the upstairs cupboard was already well over 30 grams, and the combined amount in his cupboard and his camper was dangerously high. And he feared that his supplier, now in Nelson, B.C., would insist on sending some more the next week.

His instructions were to clear Redfern Road first in tandem with another more experienced operator. Then he was to do a second clearing of Highway 5 from one city limit to the other on his own and then radio for further orders; and to return to the depot at 2:45 a.m.

The tandem ploughs cleared Redfern Road quickly, and were finished by 6:45 p.m., and he began his work on Highway 5. This was his first solo assignment, and he was determined to do it well, even though it was a "second run," as the route had been ploughed less than two hours earlier. He was finished by 8:40 p.m., and rather than radio for further orders, he reached under the dash to disable the fleet tracker "black box" in the rig and pulled into Beaver Park to clear a few spots in the parking lot so he and Tom could park there the next morning. He was very fond of that park where he and Tom had first met. He knew he was to stay on the main roads and take his break in the parking lot of a strip mall, but some rules are meant to be broken.

After clearing a few parking spaces, he decided it was time to have one of those reefers before reporting back to the dispatch centre. He stopped his rig and opened the windows. The rules prohibited him from smoking cigarettes in the cab of the truck, and in any case, he had no plans to smoke tobacco. But he had those joints in the plastic fly box and lit one up knowing that he would not get very high, but that the last five hours of his shift would be far more tolerable after this. The storm was already subsiding, and the snowfall had almost stopped when he finished, but the wind was still gusting.

As he turned the rig on to the road out of the park, a most unusual sight in the headlights startled him. A man clad only in a toque and boots was shuffling along the Beaver Trail 50 or 60 metres in front of him. He slammed on the brakes, but the image was now out of view.

"Oh, shit! What was that?" he muttered out loud. His first thought was that the joint had made him hallucinate, but he had never hallucinated on just pot before, even though he had experienced some bad trips when he smoked pot and dropped some acid at the same time. *If I am hallucinating, I shouldn't be driving*, he realized. As he turned the headlights on to high beam, he saw a faint image of a man again but the man seemed to be now sitting on Little Beaver Trail, and then he just disappeared. Frozen in panic, he sat there wondering what to do. His first impulse was to call 911. *But if the police arrive quickly, would they detect the odour of pot? If they did find it, when they interview me they might not take my report seriously. They will probably search the cab of the snowplough and find the pot.* He would certainly lose his job. But he was sure that what he saw had been a real man. He jumped down from the truck and plodded through the snow to where he had last seen the man and came upon an old-style snowshoe hanging on a low tree branch. There were faint tracks coming up to it from the north.

He shouted, "Hello!"

No response.

"Hey, you!" Again, silence, except for the wind howling in the trees.

He decided that he needed a brighter light than the headlights of the plough, and returned to the cab to fetch the emergency searchlight. With this, he looked over the edge of the trail down into the black waters of the Beaver River. There was snow-covered ice adjacent to the shore for about 15 feet, and no tracks or

holes, but when he looked straight down, he saw the webbing of a
second snowshoe, apparently caught on a stout tree branch stick-
ing out from the rocks, halfway between the trail and the river. He
panicked again when he realized that the webbing was attached
to a boot and a man's naked body facing downwards against the
stone wall with its head just inches from the ice. The body was not
moving, and he was sure whoever it was must be dead. He now
knew what he had to do. Running to the plough, he called 911.

"Redfern 911. What is your emergency?"

"Yes, I'm in Beaver Park and have just found a naked man
caught by his snowshoe, lying next to the Beaver River. I think he
just died."

"I will put you over to police."

"Redfern Regional Police. What is your emergency?"

He repeated his report.

"How do you know that he just died?"

"Because I saw him walking along the trail a few minutes ago
and now he's not moving and I think I saw blood when I shone my
flashlight down on him."

"Thank you. We're sending a cruiser. Please stay where you
are. Beaver Park covers a lot of area. Do you have a GPS with you?"

"Yes."

"Can you give us your coordinates?"

Punching the Garmin, Eric gave them the exact coordinates.

"Give me your name, address, and cell phone number."

Thinking about his situation, Eric paused and then, in a panic,
replied. "Allan Closer, A-L-A-N C-L-O-S-E-R." He paused again,
then gave the address and phone number of the Hook Line and
Sinker. As soon as he had said that, he thought, *Shit. Coulda,
shoulda, oughta have given them a fake address and phone number, too.
But if I can get outta here and back to my camper before the police arrive,
I can still get out of this.* But he realized that his days and nights as
a snowplough operator were probably over. *How will I explain this
to Tom?* he wondered.

"Is there anyone with you or in the park?"

"No."

"Do not touch anything at the scene until officers arrive. And
stay on the line. Officers will be there as soon as possible. Stay

where you are." Sergeant Finn would not let the originator of this strange call bolt from the scene; he might be one of the dangerously deranged street people the police often had to deal with, or he might be a true hero, reporting a tragic accident.

Terrible timing, Finn thought. There had just been a 39-car pileup on Huron Street, with serious injuries, and he had dispatched most of the cruisers that were available in the area to that, and there were at least eight ambulances headed there as well. He called EMS dispatch. Then he sent out a coded call on the radio to request cruisers to respond to a 904 in Beaver Park. The cop codes kept changing to keep reporters and snoopers off their trail, but all the police in the area knew that a 904 meant either a murder had been committed or a dead body had been found. He then called the Ontario Provincial Police to assist at the scene of the multiple-vehicle crash to free up officers of the Redfern Regional force to go to Beaver Park. Then he realized that the 911 caller had hung up.

Eric decided that he had best ensure that the cops would not detect his pot. He hung up on the 911 call, opened both doors and turned the truck ninety degrees so that the brisk wind would blow through it and clear the air. He stood in front of it and opened his jacket to ensure there was no odour left on him. He flung the fly box of pot out the window into the snow. Then he decided to bolt. His thinking a bit muddled by the pot, and his heart racing, he was determined to get to his camper and escape detection by the police. He sensed that he was in deep trouble and that his life was about to change forever, but he had no idea what direction it would take.

He looked in his mirror as he turned out of the park and saw the flashing lights of a police cruiser making its way into Beaver Park. Then he turned his persistently ringing cell phone off and threw it out into a snow bank.

4

rescue

Constable Paula Kaufman and Sergeant Jim Bimini were pulling out of a Tim Horton's to race to the accident scene on Huron Street when the dispatcher sent out the second call, and she responded immediately. This one fit perfectly with her sense of adventure, and if the man they were to find was truly dead, one of them would likely get a day off the beat at some point to testify at the inquest; or extra pay for the day at the inquest if they were not on duty. In either case, attending an inquest would be a cushy day's work in the world of law enforcement, and a new experience for her. She was tired of listening to Sergeant Bimini talking about himself and his exploits as an officer and a lothario. And the dispatcher's call had certainly described an unusual situation. Sergeant Finn, checking the big map with all of the cruisers' locations confirmed that they were the closest two-officer cruiser to the scene, and asked them to go to Beaver Park to check it out.

"We have a man in Beaver Park reporting a 904 hanging over the edge of the Beaver Trail by the river." He gave them the GPS coordinates.

Constable Kaufman responded. "We're on our way. Nine minutes," she stated after Sergeant Bimini checked the coordinates in the GPS and switched on the lights and siren.

"Do we have EMS on the way as well?" Bimini asked Sergeant Finn.

"I am sending an ambulance, two more cruisers, FIDO, and Homer Simpson to help you."

Bimini was excited, knowing that "FIDO" stood for Forensic ID Officer, and "Homer Simpson" was police code for a homicide detective. This might be the big case that would let him work with the detectives on a murder investigation and earn him recognition and perhaps the promotion that he so desperately wanted.

Paula Kaufman was also excited—this would be her first experience at a 904, and she was glad she was with a sergeant who would take command of the situation until the detectives arrived. She was less thrilled that it was the arrogant and misogynous Bimini, but at least she would not be alone. She admitted to herself that she was learning a lot from being teamed up with a sergeant in her rookie year on the force. As they turned into Beaver Park, they met a snowplough exiting the park, heading east on Redfern Road. Thinking this was a bit odd, Sergeant Bimini jotted down the number 19 that he noted on the side of the plough. He considered chasing the plough but realized that their instructions were to investigate the 904 in Beaver Park.

When they arrived in the parking lot, there was no one around, but there were foot tracks leading over to the river's edge. Bimini immediately reported to dispatch that there was no one in the park and gave him the number of the snowplough. Sergeant Finn was busy reassigning cruisers to different zones to keep the response times balanced when he was interrupted and had to direct a cruiser to chase down the suspicious snowplough. He called the snowplough dispatch centre and was told that Number 19 had gone off communications—either the tracker had been disabled or it was malfunctioning.

Sergeant Bimini and Constable Kaufman searched the area and followed the tracks in the snow, soon finding the snowshoe and the upside-down naked corpse lying against the bloodstained stone wall.

The EMS coordinating centre responded to the call by dispatching an ambulance from a satellite station closer to the park. "Take along some diving equipment and wet suits—you may get wet," the dispatcher advised. "And you may need the re-warming apparatus that we just did the in-service training on. Do you have anyone there who attended that session?"

"Well, there're two of us here who know how to use that. It's not hard. The only trick's to know when to use it, not how."

The paramedic team of John Orvis and Mavis Hook were on their way, with all the equipment that the dispatcher had advised them to bring.

* * *

It had been a quiet evening for Garth Rowley at the police monitoring desk of the Toronto Star until the call about the 904 in Beaver Park. The storm had kept most motorists off the roads, and there had been surprisingly few accidents and no fatalities. A report of gunfire heard on a back street in Etobicoke earlier in the evening got him excited, but the reporter dispatched to cover it had little of general interest to report for the next day's edition. He had padded the report of the gunfire with speculation about whether or not it involved the gang a local mayor's family had been rumoured to associate with, but was cautious about this. He had already run that story by the senior editor and had it returned with what he thought were the juiciest bits deleted, with no insinuations at all about the mayor or her family. Then, within two minutes, the radio reports of a huge traffic pileup on Huron Street and the report of a 904 found in Beaver Park came in. Just to be sure that he remembered correctly, he checked his iPad notebook for the last 904 code he had recorded and found that it was a call for a newly discovered dead body. He also knew that "Homer Simpson" was cop-speak for homicide detective.

The traffic accident report would have to go to someone else. The prospect of a photo of Redfern regional cops fishing a dead body out of the Beaver River for the front page of the GTA section of the Saturday *Star* seemed to be just what he needed at that point. He called his cameraman/driver, and they headed out toward Beaver Park. The photographer punched "Beaver Park" into the GPS and it reported that they were 24 minutes from the scene.

"There's plenty of time. There will be cops all over this for hours. No need to rush," Rowley told the driver as they narrowly missed having a collision on Redfern Road.

"But the sooner the better. Don't want to get scooped by the Globe. Maybe we can get there before the cops cordon it off," the driver replied.

As they turned in to Beaver Park, they could already see the flashing lights of not one, but three police cruisers and of a large EMS cube van in the parking lot. There was a siren behind them, and they pulled over cautiously into the deep snow to let a speeding fire department heavy rescue truck pass. This seemed like just the story he needed, and he might get it on the front page, if only he could get enough detail by press time. He glanced at his watch: 10:12 p.m.

"Why the ambulance and rescue crew if this is a 904? You said that was a dead body," the cameraman asked.

"Maybe they are just not sure—playing it safe. Or maybe they changed their codes on us."

* * *

"How are we ever going to get this stiff up from there?" asked Constable Kaufman, shining her high-powered searchlight down on the body. "I'm not getting my ass wet in that river to retrieve a dead body."

"He ain't dead till he's warm and dead," retorted Sergeant Bimini, quoting an old adage he had learned from his stint of training in the Canadian Coastguard Search and Rescue training school before being accepted into the Police College.

"Well, I am sure he's dead—look at that face; it's all smashed in," Kaufman retorted, shining her flashlight down on the bloody face against the stone wall. "Do you mean that we have to warm him up before someone can declare him dead? If that is the case, why don't we flip a noose over him and then just haul him up? Then you can warm him up any way you want to, and call the coroner to declare him dead."

"Look! Just get your ass back in the cruiser and call for Fire Rescue. And I want the homicide boys here as well before we move anything. We don't have any clue about who this poor bastard is. This's getting a bit complicated for me—we are going to need to wait for help. And get the tape out. I want the whole area from away up the trail down to the bridge and including that snowplough track taped off—now! I don't want John Q Public or some nosy reporter or TV crew to see this. That's an order!"

"Aye, aye, sir," she replied with a smile. "Consider it done."

Always ready to believe a crime had been committed, it had already occurred to Bimini that perhaps the snowplough operator had lured the man to the park for drugs, robbed him, stripped him, thrown him off the stone trail into the river, and then fled. *But then why had he called 911? Or had someone else made that call?* He was anxious to keep Paula busy and away from the body; this would be *his* crime scene investigation. After Paula completed the cordoning, she returned to Bimini.

"Paula, we have to think of all possibilities here. Thanks for keeping the great unwashed hordes of police chasers and ambulance chasers at bay, but don't be an idiot. Would you now call dispatch and ask them to update us on the snowplough operator who's fled the scene?"

John Orvis and Mavis Hook had arrived just as Constable Kaufman was rolling out the police tape; she pointed them over to Constable Bimini. After cursory introductions, he asked them, "Have you ever seen anything like this?" as he shone his light down on the body. "Do you have wet suits, diving gear, and arbourist's long-handled limb cutters?" Bimini asked.

"Two of the three," replied Mavis Hook. "We're not in the tree trimming business, and I'm not keen on donning a wet suit to retrieve some guy for a mortician. But why do we need the limb cutter?"

"How will we ever get him free of that damned snowshoe caught on the tree branch without cutting him free of it? It looks like it's wedged solidly into that thick branch growing out between the rocks, and that's at least 10 feet below us. We need a remote limb cutter. And I'm still working on the premise that he is alive, and you should be, too. Granted that seems unlikely and no one is going to sell him life insurance. But if we fart around for long, your assumption that he's dead will certainly be true." Bimini glanced at his watch and noted that it was 22:15—10:15 p.m.

A fire department heavy rescue truck and another car soon arrived in the parking lot, and almost all the cleared spaces were now occupied: three cruisers, an ambulance, a fire rescue truck, and a car with *Toronto Star News* emblazoned on its side, with cleared spaces only for two more; the snow in the rest of the park was at least 20 centimetres deep.

Standing on the stone trail above the body, Fire Captain Al Cahill agreed to take over from Jim Bimini to coordinate the rescue or retrieval. Although such situations often lead to squabbles between EMS, police, and firefighters in leading the efforts, everyone seemed pleased that Cahill had taken the lead role, and he quickly devised a plan to get the body up and onto the trail.

"This should not take long," he stated. "Moe, get into the wet suit and diving gear. And get into the rappelling harness and crampons.

"Now get him secured with a piton and belays."

"Ready?"

"I should be downstream side," Moe Washington suggested. "That way, if the ice gives way, the rope won't pull the guy off his precarious perch as I get pulled downstream with the current." They changed to the downstream side and he tested the lines he was attached to and began his descent down the side of the stone wall until he was sitting on the ice, then shuffled across until he was staring at the neck of the naked man. "Give me a little slack, so I can test the ice" Moe suggested.

"Don't plan to plant him yet. He may still be alive," Jim Bimini advised.

"I know, I know. He ain't dead until he is warm and dead," Constable Kaufman repeated, saving Bimini from the need to repeat his favourite adage.

"You fellas should know that, too," Bimini warned the fire crew, doing nothing to relieve the tension. He glanced at his watch and noted that it was now 22:29 or 10:29 p.m. He quickly scribbled a note on his pad and dictated a brief one to his pocket voice recorder.

John Orvis and Mavis Hook brought the stretcher from the ambulance, and Al Cahill barked, "Get that stretcher down to my boy." The team attached long straps and added sections of rope to get it down to Moe Washington just downstream of the corpse and began feeding out line.

"Stretcher is under him now. His head is just touching it. Can we lower the rest of him? The ice seems solid."

John Orvis asked Moe to check for any signs of life as the team waited and he indicated that there was a lot of blood on the stones but nothing oozing, no apparent breathing, and no carotid pulse that he could detect.

"No, Moe. We are not going to lower him. I don't trust the ice that much. We are going to raise the stretcher with him on it. But we need a second man down there, so that when we start to lift him, he can free his foot from that tree stump, and secure the straps around him. The second person should not need to get all the way down—but who's the lightest person here that we can lower at least halfway down in the cage?" They all looked around, and Mavis Hook spoke up.

"Does it have to be a man? I'll bet none of you are less than 110 pounds." The others, glad that she had volunteered, strapped her in to the second climbing harness, secured the ropes to a nearby tree, and started to lower her, securing it when she reported that she was looking straight at the bare butt of the carcass to her right. Two stretcher straps were flung to Moe on the ice and he carefully attached them to the centre side hooks of the stretcher, with one on each side of the body, and strapped them over the chest as tightly as he could.

"Any vital signs from your vantage point?" asked John Orvis, ignoring Washington's precarious position and directing the question to Mavis Hook.

"Nothing really obvious, but I am hardly in the best position to be sure. I'm at crotch level, and not anxious to get too close. This isn't the man of my dreams. Can't we just get him up onto the trail and then check? Can you raise me up two or three feet so I can reach that foot in the snowshoe?"

"Best treat him as though he is alive," Jim Bimini interjected, blowing his police whistle, to everyone's annoyance. "Be as gentle as possible."

"Is everyone ready?" asked Al Cahill, ignoring Bimini.

"Can you toss me a rope so I can tie up the free foot and secure it up there somewhere?" Mavis asked. "Don't want him to slide off the stretcher during the lift."

"Good idea. Let's do that."

After the rope was tied around the right foot above the shoe and secured, Cahill ordered. "Start the lift. If Moe or Mavis hollers, we all stop."

"Halt," Moe shouted two feet into the lift. "I want to tighten the straps. Don't really want this guy to fall off on top of me."

As he stood up on the ice for this manoeuvre, it cracked, and he sank to his waist in the Beaver River, tightening the ropes attached to his harness. This complication was witnessed by the officers above him, who rapidly pulled him back up to the level of the stretcher, which still seemed to be in position under the body.

They asked if he had any injuries from his fall. His reply was not reassuring: "I'm okay. Banged my knee on the edge of the ice. This river's damn cold."

"Halt!" Mavis ordered halfway through the lift. She tightened the stretcher straps around the waist of the body, now at her level, and freed the foot from the snowshoe. "He is secure on the stretcher now, and his foot is free of the stump. Not much of a face left."

The rescue crew set the stretcher down on the path and brought heated blankets from the ambulance and draped them over the cold, blue corpse. John Orvis ran to back the ambulance up to the path on the now well-packed route from the parking lot. Mavis grabbed and applied a cervical collar to stabilize the neck. "Don't want to paralyse him if he has a neck fracture."

"Would anyone up there like to help me get outta here?" Moe hollered, with a hint of desperation. The team had already pulled Mavis Hook, holding the retrieved snowshoe, up over the edge, and she and the rest of the crew had all disappeared from his view.

"Not until you get us a sample of the blood frozen on those rocks," retorted Sergeant Bimini. "We may need that for the forensics boys." He tossed down a standard police evidence kit onto the intact ice beside Washington and ordered him to just scrape a bit of the congealed blood into the tube and bring it up with him. Two officers no longer needed for the rescue or retrieval were dispatched by Sergeant Bimini to begin a search of the cordoned-off area, to report back within 15 minutes, and to leave any evidence they found undisturbed for Forensics to deal with.

Al Cahill looked down at Moe. "Are you going for another swim, or do you want to get outta here?" He tossed a second security rope down and helped Moe as he rappelled, with a limp, up the wall. "I think our work here is done, but you better get out of that gear and into the truck. I still have an interesting report to file before I can go home." He watched as Moe Washington limped, holding his right knee, to the Fire Department rescue truck and checked his watch. It was 22:46.

As soon as the body was secured in the ambulance, Mavis Hook hit the siren and took off slowly and carefully through the deep snow in the parking lot. John Orvis was in the back and could now better check for vital signs and tend to the man they all believed to be dead. Paula Kaufman jumped out of the cruiser to lift the police tape to let her through, just as the forensics ID van met them coming the other way. An unmarked car with two detectives from the homicide division was right behind the forensics van. Bimini glanced at his watch: it was now 22:51.

Sergeant Joel Atherton stopped the forensics identification van and asked Paula Kaufman for details of the situation. "Do we have any idea who the bloke is?" he asked.

"Go ask Sergeant Bimini over there," she replied. "He may have some ideas." Then, almost in a whisper, she added "And he thinks he knows everything."

Bimini told Atherton what he knew, handed him the evidence pack of congealed blood, and wished him luck. Two search officers reported to Bimini that they had found some torn clothes a short distance up the trail. The group of six officers, two detectives, and Joel Atherton all huddled beside a squad car. Three were assigned by the sergeants to begin a further search of the area for evidence.

"Someone may still be trying to finish this guy off. And he ain't dead till he is warm and dead," Sergeant Bimini reminded the remaining officers. He instructed two constables to find out where the ambulance was going and to follow it and guard the victim.

"Well, he is probably just a demented old man who went wandering out of a nursing home," Paula Kaufman commented.

"On snowshoes? I don't think so! That is one of the dumbest suggestions I have ever heard," Bimini commented.

"Well, he could be demented, but coming from a home rather than a nursing home." Hendrickson interjected.

The two homicide detectives, Detective Inspector Jim Hendrickson and Detective Sergeant Joe Pickett, Jim Bimini, Paula Kaufman, and Joel Atherton discussed their next move. Bimini asked Kaufman if she had contacted the snowplough dispatch centre and she said she had simply forgotten to do so, but he knew that dispatch had promised to track it anyway. They all crowded into the forensics ID van to warm up and plan.

Bimini called dispatch to get an update on the errant snowplough.

"The guy running the plough was nabbed at the dispatch centre as he tried to leave in an old camper. They found a pile of 604 in the camper and arrested him. But the 911 call came from an unlisted number, and he had no phone with him. He's here in the cell now. I've sent the officer over to you to give you more details," Sergeant Finn reported.

Bimini reported the arrest to the group. "They are sending the officer who nailed him over here." That officer soon arrived and joined the group.

"Why was John Doe buck naked?" Paula asked.

"Well, that could be just because some people who go hypothermic, get delusional, and they can even take off all their clothes. I've seen that once before. It doesn't necessarily indicate that he was robbed or assaulted. But it does seem odd," answered Detective Inspector Hendrickson.

"And the snowplough guy told me that he was just clearing a spot to park and go fishing tomorrow, but who goes fishing in weather like this?" asked the new arrival who had arrested Eric Clouser.

Bimini responded, "Oh, lotsa crazy coots do. If you cruise by here tomorrow afternoon, you'll see at least a half dozen weekend warriors freezing their butts in the middle of that river, and flailing away like mad. It is kinda like an addiction for some people."

An officer searching the area came over to the van and reported that he had found a clear plastic box containing what looked like pre-rolled marijuana joints, explaining that it was lying in the snow beside the snowplough tracks.

"Ah, it's all coming together; must be a drug deal gone awry, as I thought. You found pot on the guy from the plough and there is some here. He was probably setting up a deal and the old man put up a fight!" Bimini exclaimed.

Inspector Hendrickson instructed, "Don't touch it, but show Joel, here, from Forensics where it is. He may be able to lift some prints off of it right here, once we get out of his way."

Joel Atherton instructed the two other officers reporting the finding of torn clothes a little way up the path. "Take me up to those clothes. And measure the distance from there to where you found the body."

Garth Rowley, standing outside the police tape, asked one of the detectives for a statement. Hendrickson replied that there would be a statement within a few minutes, then left to survey the scene, take photographs, and measure the distances that seemed to be critical. They would get more evidence in daylight and would dispatch police divers and the canine unit in the morning.

Once Joel Atherton had the forensics ID van to himself, he tried to see if he could get any fingerprints off any of the evidence. The detectives would ask for permission from higher up to search and possibly impound the snowplough, and he and Detective Joe Pickett would get an update on the snowplough operator in the lockup and get a statement and prints from him. It was now 23:07.

Once the homicide detectives had left, the officers remaining at the scene were Paula Kaufman, Jim Bimini, three searching officers, and Joel Atherton. They agreed that Sergeant Bimini, as the most senior officer present, would respond to the growing crowd of media people outside the police tape. As he walked over to the reporters, Paula commented to the other officers that Sergeant Bimini had never seen a microphone that he didn't like and that he was also known as "Loose-Lips Bimini," as he was prone to revealing more about an investigation than was prudent.

After relating that an unidentified elderly man had been found dangling over the bank of the Beaver River and had been transported to hospital in critical condition, Bimini became evasive.

"Is this being treated as a crime scene?"

"We are considering it as such at the moment—tentatively."

"Are there any suspects?"

"One man who left here in a snowplough has been detained for questioning."

"Is there any drug gang involvement?"

"It is too early to speculate on that, but we have found some drugs at the scene."

"Do you have any identification of the victim?"

"No. He was naked, and we have no idea who he is. We are calling him 'John Doe' at the moment."

"Is he alive?"

"He has not been declared dead." Bimini refrained from adding his favorite adage, but had an inspiration. "You folk may be able to help us to identify the victim. We are requesting that anyone that may have any relevant information contact the Redfern

Regional Police Services or Redfern Crime Stoppers. That includes anyone who may have been in the park or on the Beaver Trail this evening, or anyone who knows of someone who has gone missing in the last day or two." He indicated that there would likely be no further update from the police department until at least noon, and refused to answer further questions.

After his statement to the media, Bimini was pleased and convinced that he had handled the rescue or retrieval very well. If John Doe actually was alive and survived, he would be the hero of the rescue. He reflected that he now wished the Redfern Regional Police Services Board had sprung for the police body-worn video cameras. He generally thought—rightly—that these were dangerous, as they too often document inappropriate action by officers. But if he had been wearing one on this night, he could have handed the video documentation with his application for a promotion to the staff sergeant and the superintendent.

Garth Rowley was just in time to file his report for the *Toronto Star*, but had a devious idea to ensure that other media outlets would get the story wrong. He inferred from the lights, siren and the speed of the departing ambulance that the victim was alive. Knowing that some other media hounds would intercept it, his first electronic report sent without encryption relayed the false information that the body had been taken to the morgue at Beaverbrook Hospital for identification and a forensic autopsy. Two minutes later he sent the fully encrypted version with the picture. It stated that the man had been taken to hospital with life-threatening injuries.

After the ambulance and fire rescue truck left, Joel Atherton in the forensic identification van reviewed the evidence he had obtained so far, including the box of pot, the torn clothes, the tube of blood scrapings, the snowshoes and hiking boots, and some photos he had taken. He would be getting Eric Clouser's fingerprints from the lockup. Those prints would be sent electronically and analyzed by the Toronto Police Automated Fingerprint Identification System. He asked Sergeant Bimini if they had obtained fingerprints from John Doe, and Bimini replied in his best self-righteous tone that that they had not because their right and proper priorities were rescue and criminal investigation, not identification.

Atherton swore to himself; he would have to get those prints at the hospital. He decided to see if he could find prints on any of the items of evidence.

He dusted the fly box and found no prints on the outside, but on the inside there was a good-quality print on the lid, and he sent this to the Identification Centre electronically. He knew better than to try to get prints from the soaked snowshoes and boots. He got luckier with the clothes. In the inside pocket of the leather jacket he found a dry receipt from Home Depot, with lots of fingerprints on it. He sent these to the ID Centre. Unfortunately, the Home Depot purchase of light bulbs had been paid in cash at the self-checkout counter, so he did not have a credit or debit card account to trace. *That would make it too easy to identify John Doe,* he thought. But if John Doe had ever been fingerprinted anywhere in Canada, there was a good chance that the ID Centre would be able match it up to a print in their system and provide positive identification.

If necessary, he could request that the genetic identification unit do some DNA analysis from material that he could get from the clothes—a few strands of pubic hair would likely suffice, and he already had a tube of blood in any case. But he knew that DNA testing is most useful in *excluding* a suspect and not in identifying someone unless there are two sources for the sample to compare with each other. And all the units were under pressure to reduce costs, so he would not initiate this request as yet; and that request should properly come from a detective in any case. But this case was already so weird that he had to think of all possibilities. *What if the clothes with the prints did not even belong to John Doe?* he thought. *Or perhaps the Home Depot receipt had been planted and did not belong to the victim.*

The two officers assigned to transport Eric Clouser to the Red-fern district station lockup had been very careful to follow protocol and not violate his rights. They advised him of his rights, that he would be allowed to call a lawyer as soon as they arrived, and that anything he said could be used against him at trial.

"You don't have to tell us anything. You should wait until you get advice from your lawyer."

But over and over, Eric repeated a bizarre story about being in the park to clear a few parking spaces to go fishing the next day.

He knew that they had found his sizable stash of pot in the fly rod holder in his camper so he even admitted to being a pot dealer. But he adamantly denied ever having seen John Doe before, and knew that the police would not be able to find any evidence that he had been involved in the man's demise.

When they reached the detention centre, he was given a list of lawyers; he called the first one on the list, Paul Albright. Mr. Albright discussed his rights, and agreed to meet with him at 11 a.m.

Eric reconsidered his situation as he sat in the detention centre cell. He knew the officers would search his tackle shop, so he even gave the guard the keys, confident that they would find nothing that would implicate him in the fate of John Doe. He even asked about the condition of John Doe, and was very concerned about what had happened to him, but the police told him nothing.

* * *

"I presume this fellow will end up at Jacks. Can we send Edgar the bill for this call?" Captain Cahill joked as the fire rescue team left the scene.

"Why Jacks?" Moe asked.

"Jacks Funeral Home is one of the few in the area that will accept unidentified corpses and work with us and the police to dispose of a corpse at the expense of the municipality. The paperwork necessary for this is unbelievably onerous, and most funeral directors refuse to get involved as it is not worth their time, given the puny rates of municipal remuneration and the infrequency of the need. And I know that the last corpse we fished outta this river went there and I don't think it was ever identified."

Detective Inspector Jim Hendrickson had no difficulty that Saturday morning in persuading the justice of the peace to issue a search warrant for the Hook Line and Sinker tackle shop. His Information to Order form included the pot box with Eric Clouser's prints inside it taken from the park, and a large quantity of pot that had been found in his camper. The justice of the peace was skeptical about the charge of attempted murder the detective was making, but the fingerprints were enough evidence of a drug crime to warrant a search of the suspect's shop and home. The warrant had hardly been necessary in any case, as the guard at the detention centre had the keys to the shop. When Paul Albright discussed his situation with Eric he had advised him to give the guards and police nothing whatsoever. However, Eric reckoned that he would be charged with drug offences in any case, and knew that the search would uncover no evidence to support any other charges.

The officers sent by Detective Hendrickson to search the Hook Line and Sinker tackle shop on Saturday morning reported a few things of interest to him. They found and seized a few boxes filled with marijuana in the upstairs cupboard, a set of digital gram scales, and a few old gay porn videos. Someone at headquarters would have to watch the latter to see if there were any children in them, and the detectives could consult together and pick for that task the most prim and proper female rookie whom they least liked. If there were children in the videos, Eric Clouser could be charged with possession of child pornography, but Hendrickson knew that mere possession of adult gay porn was not a crime. And he would have to check to see if the quantity of pot seized was sufficient to lay a charge of possession for the purpose of trafficking; if so, he could press for a long prison sentence. The scales, likely used to weigh out the pot, would help to make the charge of possession with intent to traffic stick; that part of the job appeared to be easy now.

Hendrickson asked Forensic ID to check for fingerprints on the boxes he took to the division station—perhaps Eric's supplier would already have a record in the police files. By late Saturday afternoon, they reported back that there were lots of different prints on the boxes, but none that the computer system had matched to any prints on file anywhere in Canada.

Jim Hendrickson was pleased that Eric Clouser would likely be remanded in custody on the drug trafficking charges at the preliminary hearing on Monday, although he might get out on bail; unlikely, though, since he had already been guilty of fleeing from the scene of a crime the night before. If he was remanded in custody, it would give Hendrickson sufficient time to gather more evidence to support the attempted murder charge. As a bonus, he would be able to do so from the comfort and warmth of his HQ office. *No more visits to a grisly scene in a blizzard for at least a few days,* he thought. By Saturday evening, he was pleased with the progress of the case, and decided to take Sunday off to go to his son's hockey game.

Detective Sergeant Joe Pickett was in charge of identifying John Doe, but didn't know where to start. The fingerprints on the Home Depot receipt had not matched up with any on record, and Eric Clouser insisted that he had never seen John Doe before that fateful night. No one from the public had called with any clues, and he had gotten no further information from the officers searching the scene. He checked with all of the local nursing homes, assisted-living homes, and mental institutions; they reported that no one was missing, and it seemed unlikely that a demented old man would have purchased light bulbs or been out snowshoeing in a blizzard. The officers with the canine unit reported that the dogs sniffing the clothes taken from the trail had gone all over the park but had not led them to anything else. The police divers had made only a cursory search of the river near the scene and had found nothing of relevance, except for a broken human tooth on the ice. Joe decided to take the weekend off and await further information that was sure to come in. And he asked Forensic ID to obtain fingerprints from John Doe at the hospital, just in case they did not match those on the Home Depot receipt.

Joel Atherton had already decided that he needed John Doe's fingerprints and, never one to worry about legal niceties in obtaining evidence, agreed to get those prints. He should be able to intimidate the bedside nurse in the ICU to let him do so, even if it was not strictly legal. But that was not critical and could wait until Monday morning. If John Doe died, the prints would be obtained at the forensic autopsy. He had a lot of Christmas shopping to do and that would keep him busy over the weekend.

* * *

Eric Clouser ate a simple but adequate breakfast on Saturday morning in the station cell, and considered his situation. His cell cot was comfortable and clean, and the only guard seemed to be a pleasant fellow. He confided to the guard that he had made the 911 call, but told no one else. He was sure that he would be convicted of some offence related to his marijuana business, and he might be charged with something relating to the fate of John Doe, but was confident that nobody could make a strong case for any involvement on his part in that. And he would never again be employed as a snowplough operator. The Hook Line and Sinker tackle shop would certainly go bust and his creditors would foreclose on it quickly, so he would also lose his humble abode above it. At least he had a comfortable warm place to live—more comfortable than the cold old camper that he had called home for almost two years, and the police would seize the camper anyway. Free room and board ... things could be a lot worse.

As agreed, Paul Albright arrived precisely at 11 a.m. and reviewed the charges. They discussed his situation and Eric admitted to Paul that he had been running a small marijuana business out of his tackle shop. Paul advised him that with the new minimum sentencing provisions passed by the Harper government in the C-10 omnibus crimes bill, the *Safe Streets and Communities Act*, he would be facing a minimum sentence of two years, and it would likely be in one of the prisons in the Kingston area; Eric seemed perplexingly happy about that news.

When asked why he had been in Beaver Park the previous evening, he reiterated his reason for being there. When asked about relatives who might post bail for him, he indicated that he had no contact with any. When asked about friends who might help, he named Tom at the snowplough dispatch center, who had arranged to go fishing with him at that exact time, and said that Tom was also his gay partner. Paul Albright volunteered to call Tom and ask him to consider posting bail for Eric.

"You have not been charged with anything but possession for the purpose of trafficking. There will be a preliminary hearing on Monday, and I may be able to get you out on bail then."

Eric agreed to let Paul call Tom, but refused to consider even applying for bail. He would prefer to remain comfortable, fed, and warm behind bars rather than to live in his cold camper, or on the street. He was sure the police and his creditors would never let him return to his tiny abode

Paul Albright called Tom from the detention centre and got a voice message. He returned to his home and told his wife about the peculiar client he had just met: a gay snowplough operator who ran a tackle shop and a marijuana business; an eccentric, flawed, but honest and very scared man who had fallen on hard times. *A man worth defending carefully,* he thought. Like his fictional role model, Atticus Finch, he took his job as a poorly-remunerated defender of the downtrodden, the defenceless poor, and the wrongly accused seriously, and considered it to be a noble calling, far more fulfilling than earning money from private clients willing to pay handsomely for his counsel.

5

out cold

Mavis Hook, driving the ambulance, reported their readiness to roll and the patient's "Vital Signs Absent" condition to EMS dispatch.

"Take him to Beaverbrook via whatever route you want, if there is any hope. But Redfern Road has a pileup, and Beaverbrook is the closest hospital with any ICU beds available."

"He ain't dead until he is warm and dead, and right now he is very cold," Mavis Hook responded. "We are on our way."

Then, cursing the Ontario Ministry of Health for providing the Interfleet map system with only their location and their destination, she asked how long it would take to get there, but got no response from the dispatcher. She used the hands-free speaker phone to call the Beaverbrook Hospital Emergency Department and report their pending arrival.

John Orvis in the back of the ambulance now could assess the body more carefully. Airway, breathing, circulation—the ABCs of resuscitation—were second nature to him. He pried the mouth open, noting that the right mandible was badly broken, and managed to place a long, curved, plastic airway over the very swollen tongue and placed the breathing apparatus delivering warmed oxygen over the mangled face. Then he checked for a pulse and respirations and detected none. He was lucky on his first try at finding a vein in John Doe's arm and set up an intravenous line running warm saline from the bag, which was being heated with an electric coil. But the flow was very slow. When he dropped the bag down to the floor, the flow of blood back into the tubing was also slow, but it did not stop—there must be some blood circulating. Turning his attention back to the heart and lungs, he attached three leads for an electrocardiogram and a blood pressure cuff. He leaned in close to see if there was any breathing.

"I smell booze!" he shouted to Mavis. "The guy must have taken a breath. Corpses don't smell like booze."

He checked the electrocardiogram recording. Irregular squiggles on the recording from shivering made it difficult to tell if there was any electrical activity coming from the heart, but there appeared to be an irregular rhythm at about 24 beats per minute. *If he is shivering, he must be alive*, he reasoned. *Shivering is a reflex response to cold, and dead people don't have reflexes.* The blood pressure cuff did not record any measurement at all. He then relayed the updated information via the speaker-phone and awaited instructions from the emergency room.

Dr. Faisal Al Taqi was immediately updated about the impending arrival. "Just get him here as soon as you can. We will be ready for him. And keep him warm and quiet."

John Orvis checked the Garmin GPS Maps that he always had with him to supplement the out-dated Interfleet system. "Nine minutes."

"Please clear Resus Room 2. Cold adult male VSA, arriving in less than ten minutes," the clerk stated over the ER overhead speaker.

Dr. Al Taqi recalled all that he knew about treatment of severe hypothermia. He, one of the other ER doctors, and Dr. Leslie Turle had attended one of the monthly Interhospital Critical Care Grand Rounds at Toronto Western Hospital three years before, and the team there had proudly reviewed their successful resuscitation of a hypothermic homeless woman. She had actually been pronounced dead before she was observed to take a breath while being transported to the morgue. He knew that a cold heart would be irritable and the victim had to be kept still, warmed slowly with fluids administered to the core parts, and protected from any unnecessary painful stimulation. He was ready and confident.

Mavis Hook brought the ambulance to a stop at 23:02 hours, and two attendants promptly whisked the stretcher into Resuscitation Room 2. Once they had transferred John Doe to the ER stretcher, Dr. Al Taqi took over. Moments later, two police officers arrived; they were curtly told by the officious nursing Team

Leader to cool their heels outside the room. Dr. Al Taqi checked for vital signs and found none. He checked the airway, and although it seemed to be a precarious means of ensuring that the man could breathe, it would have to do for now, and he too could smell alcohol, so the man must be breathing. He was not about to call an arrest and have hordes of staff come and do all kinds of invasive stimulating things to his patient.

"That tube will have to do for now for an airway. We can't risk stimulating him or breaking his spinal cord by doing a tracheostomy and we will never get a tube through his mouth or nose." He checked the EKG monitor as a nurse tried to get a blood pressure reading. The monitor clearly now showed that there was heart activity, and it looked like it was a regular rhythm, but at only 22 beats per minute. He asked the others in attendance to draw blood for "everything you can think of, including alcohol and toxicology screen."

"Now get me a two-way catheter so we can irrigate his bladder with warm saline. And make sure the IV and the oxygen he is getting are at least at body temperature."

As he was inserting the urinary catheter, lubricated with anaesthetic gel to avoid stimulation, Doctor Glenna Bass, the ICU physician on duty, the senior ICU nurse, and Dr. Winki Pham, a junior surgery resident from McMaster University Medical School doing an elective rotation in the ICU, all arrived. The emergency room clerk poked her head into the room and asked how they were to register the patient, as the lab would not do any tests without any identification. The team leader curtly ordered her to make up a nameplate.

"Call him John Doe, and if they need a birth date, give them February 30, 1938."

A discussion ensued about the next steps. One of the physicians wanted to do an emergency tracheostomy to establish a means of putting John Doe on a breathing machine. Dr. Al Taqi pointed out that to do so they would need to tip John Doe's head back maximally and doing that would be dangerous—or even fatal if he had an unstable neck fracture. Furthermore, slashing the man's neck would be a strong stimulus that might just trigger a cardiac arrest. He knew that no one would ever get the man back if his heart stopped.

"How cold is he?" someone asked.

"I couldn't get above 26.6 rectally when I checked on the way in," John Orvis responded as he was completing some paperwork in the corner of the room.

"Well, I get 26.1 now," the nurse who had just removed a thermometer probe reported.

Not sure about how much the others present knew about the treatment of severe hypothermia, Dr. Al Taqi launched into a mini-lecture.

"That kind of after-drop is typical when someone with bad hypothermia is starting to be re-warmed. We need to get some warmth to his core, not just to his skin. Warming his skin just sends more relatively warm blood from the heart to the skin and sends colder blood from the skin back to his heart where warmth matters most. He needs warm blood, warm IV fluids, warm oxygen, and warm bladder irrigation more than he needs warm blankets."

After further discussion, the team agreed that it was time to transfer John Doe to the ICU. On the way, Dr. Bass asked the constable walking with the team, "How long do you think he must have been out, to get this cold?"

"Well, it took almost ninety minutes from the first call until we had him in the ambulance. With the wind chill out there, I think an hour before that is a safe bet. How long will it take to get him warmed up?"

"We will go slowly after we get him up to about 31. Two, three, maybe four days."

Once in the ICU, Dr. Bass, noting that the man's pupils were dilated and not constricting to light, and that his eyes looked yellowish, asked the resident, Dr. Winki Pham, to come up with a comprehensive plan of treatment and to discuss it with her as soon as possible. She knew that this exercise would be a good learning experience, and even if there were some problems with the plan, no one was likely to complain about the care of a John Doe. It seemed clear to her—the booze on his breath, the jaundice, and the fixed, dilated pupils—that John Doe was a hopeless brain-dead alcoholic with cirrhosis; and probably no known relatives. She thought that the best possible outcome of this exercise would be if John Doe were to be declared brain dead the next day, that someone would then identify him, and that they would somehow get consent for organ donation. *At least his kidneys and corneas might be suitable for recycling*, she thought.

The plan that Winki came up with was to first do a CAT scan of John Doe's head and neck to check for fractures; if there was no neck fracture, they would then do an emergency tracheostomy to better control the breathing to deliver warm, moist oxygen to the lungs for re-warming of the core tissues and the blood. And she would consult the nephrology service to consider inserting lines for emergency dialysis for re-warming. And she wanted to splint the obvious left leg fracture, pending more definitive treatment.

"Well, that is hardly a priority right now," Dr. Bass asserted. "Don't waste your time on that." She thought the plan was otherwise reasonable, but added that they should also start an intravenous pump to deliver noradrenaline to raise John Doe's blood pressure.

Winki accompanied John Doe with a nurse as he was transported to the nearby Imaging Department for the CAT scan. By the time they arrived back in the Intensive Care Unit, it was midnight.

Winki learned a lot by caring for John Doe over the weekend. The lab work started to show up on the computer monitor screen just after midnight and the CAT scan images of his head and neck also appeared. In review of the images with Dr. Bass, she noted that there was a severe facial fracture, and the nasal bones were severely shattered, as was the right mandible; but there was no apparent spinal injury. They agreed to undertake an urgent tracheostomy. Dr. Pham held John Doe's head back while Dr. Bass injected some local anaesthetic over the trachea, to ensure there would be no stimulation with the procedure, then made an incision and inserted progressively larger tubes into the trachea. Once the opening was large enough, an appropriately-sized tracheostomy tube was inserted and attached to the ventilator, which began delivering warmed 100 percent oxygen. With adjustment of the ventilator settings, the blood oxygen saturation improved to a satisfactory 92 percent.

A blood ethanol level of 20 mmol per litre showed up on the computer screen. Dr. Winki Pham thought that was insignificant, but Glenna Bass pointed out that the level was reported in mmol/litre, and that "20" in those units actually was a level of 92 mg/

litre. John Doe was legally impaired, but not drunk enough to explain his coma. Other lab tests showed a very low haemoglobin level of 57 g/litre. He had obviously lost a lot of blood, and Winki ordered a transfusion of three units of packed red blood cells, to be infused over six hours. The sodium level in the blood was also dangerously low at 117 mmol/litre, with a reference range of 135–145, and the intravenous fluid was changed to slowly correct that. The kidney function was surprisingly close to normal, and by 2:00 a.m., John Doe was producing about 20 ml of urine per hour, an acceptable amount. The liver tests were abnormal as expected, and Winki, too, concluded that her patient must have alcoholic cirrhosis.

By 3:00 a.m., she decided that her patient was stable enough that she could catch some sleep. She would be available in any case in the on-call room, and would return to review the situation before staff turnover at 7:30 a.m. And she would stick around all weekend to see what more she could learn from her interesting anonymous patient, even though she was not on call on Sunday. Her patient would be in the news for days to come.

At the 7:30 bedside rounds, Winki presented the case of John Doe to the new staff coming on duty. He now had a blood pressure of 70/32 and a heart rate of 34 with a normal rhythm; his rectal temperature was up to 30.1°C. The nurse who had monitored him all night reported that his pupils were now constricting when she shone a light into his eyes. Dr. Bass doubted this observation and had to check for herself. She reflected on her past erroneous conclusion that he was brain dead. *He might actually survive to drink another day,* she thought.

"Let's cancel that kidney consult. His kidneys are almost normal and his temperature is coming up beautifully. But we need to get after that mess of a face; let's get a call in to Plastics." Dr. Bass then launched into a lecture about the classification of facial fractures that none of the team could or wanted to understand.

The urine in the bag turned almost tea-coloured when they stopped the bladder irrigation temporarily to get a sample for analysis. The lab report showed that the undiluted urine contained a moderate amount of bilirubin. *All the data is consistent with a diagnosis of alcoholic cirrhosis,* Glenna Bass concluded.

Dr. Winki Pham then noticed another very abnormal lab result on the bedside computer screen. John Doe's thyroid stimulating hormone, TSH, level was greater than 90 IU/ml, with the lab reporting the normal range as being 3–5. When she related this surprise finding to the team, a lengthy discussion ensued.

Glenna Bass weighed in. "If he is suffering from hypothyroidism, it may help him! It might contribute to his hypothermia and low heart rate, but it would also help his brain to withstand the effects of low temperatures and low oxygen levels. Thyroxin is the regulator of the rate of all metabolic functions, so a low level would decrease the brain's need for oxygen and nutrients."

After a lengthy discussion about this, the team decided to delay any treatment of the hypothyroidism for 24 hours or more. "Intravenous thyroid hormone replacement is very expensive," the on-call pharmacist attending the bedside rounds noted, "and in a few days, he may be able to tolerate the cheap oral formulation."

The on-call dietitian with the team raised the issue of the need for nutritional support for John Doe. Winki commented that he had no bowel sounds and would not tolerate oral feeds, and they would certainly be unable to place a feeding tube into his esophagus and stomach—he really had no recognizable nose to put a tube into. Cost issues again arose when the dietitian suggested feeding him by vein, and the decision on this was delayed for 24 hours. Dr. Bass, squeezing his upper arm, noted that he appeared to be a muscular fellow with some reasonable reserves of subcutaneous fat.

"He is going to need to be fed, but for now, let's just switch to 10% dextrose IV and add some thiamine. He is probably an alcoholic, and if we give him sugars without thiamine, we will damage whatever few brain cells he has left."

Dr. Bass noted that Winki or someone had splinted the tibial fracture; now that John Doe was clearly not brain dead, she said nothing about that.

After the rounds, Winki completed the consultation request form and paged the plastic surgeon on call. When Dr. Ben Speckle returned her call, she discussed the case with him. He was not pleased to be asked to come in on a snowy weekend to see a John Doe with a dismal prognosis, and knew that he might never be paid for doing so. After some discussion, he agreed to come and review John Doe on Monday morning.

Dr. Pham waited and watched over the next 24 hours as John Doe gradually improved. By Sunday morning, his temperature was 33.9°C and his blood pressure was 78/32 with a pulse of 35. His pupils were clearly reacting to light, but he did not show any response to even deep knuckle pressure on his sternum. The lab reported that the level of the thyroid hormone T4 was 1.2 mcg/dl, with the reference range being 4.5–12.5. The lab also made the interpretation of this value easy, even for a surgeon, by adding the note, "Indicative of severe hypothyroidism." Winki changed the intravenous fluid orders to correct a persistently low serum sodium level.

At Sunday morning team rounds, the team again discussed the surprise finding of severe hypothyroidism. Winki tried to make a case for starting John Doe on intravenous thyroid hormone, arguing that his continuing deep coma might be because of the thyroid problem called myxedema coma. The pharmacist argued that this would break his budget for the year.

"There is no intravenous thyroxin left in the central pharmacy this weekend. We would have to call around to other hospital pharmacies to find some and have it couriered to us."

Dr. Bass interrupted the discussion to broaden it. She was keen to observe Winki under pressure, as she knew she would have to soon fill in an evaluation of Winki at the end of her rotation for the Department of Surgery Training Program at McMaster University.

"Where is Dr. Turle when we need him?" she asked. "Sorry. For those of you who never worked with him, he was known around here as The List Man. In this situation, he would have come up with his memorized long list of causes of coma and determined which one was most likely. So, what is on your list of causes of coma, Dr. Pham?"

Winki thought this was a more appropriate question for a neurology trainee than a surgical one, but did her best to answer. "Well, we can start by ruling out structural brain diseases like a stroke, tumour, or hemorrhage, since his brain looks normal on the scan. And a drug overdose seems unlikely, since the toxicology was negative except for the alcohol. That leaves metabolic causes, and we can exclude a low blood sugar or high calcium, based on the blood work. And it can't be because of kidney failure. Although his sodium level is still low, it is not low enough to cause coma now. I guess that leaves hepatic coma from liver cirrhosis, the hypothyroidism, or just the effects of the hypothermia—maybe with a brain deprived of oxygen for too long."

"Are those all the possibilities?" Glenna Bass asked. "I can think of at least two more whole categories."

The group looked on awkwardly to see if Dr. Pham was going to come up with whatever possibilities Dr. Bass was thinking about. Failing to do so, Winki said, "I give up."

"Well, think of the International Classification of Diseases. Have you ever heard of infections?" Dr. Bass responded in a condescending tone. "Okay, it is unlikely that he has encephalitis or meningitis, but we can't exclude those possibilities from the list."

"But there was no evidence of either of those on the CT scan," Dr. Pham argued defensively. "And his white count is not elevated."

"Fair enough. But then there are psychiatric causes. Have you ever heard of hysteria or malingering? I doubt that this poor fellow is having us on and feigning coma, but that should be considered, if only to be dismissed." She had a smirk on her face and was being deliberately provocative. Everyone around her thought that the possibility of feigned coma in John Doe was ridiculous,

After further discussion, Dr. Bass suggested that they should give John Doe a lactulose enema as specific therapy for liver coma, to see if he would rouse with this. The bedside nurse winced. She hated giving enemas, especially those containing lactulose, as she knew that she would be the one left to clean up the showers of liquid stool that would result. The discussion went around in circles with no final decisions, and the team moved on to the next patient. Winki Pham returned to order the lactulose enema.

From the social aspect, the constable at the bedside reported that no one from the GTA had reported any missing loved one or relative. Was John Doe one of the city's nameless, homeless people?

6

out of control

It was too late to change his plan. About 7:00 p.m. on Friday the 13th, Dr. Leslie Turle completed his to-do list made up two days before, leaving lots of time left to reminisce about his botched life. He checked the Weather Channel forecast once again and decided that nine p.m. would be the time of his departure.

He checked his list.

1. Sudoku, Crossword.✓ He had done his daily brain exercises and left them on the kitchen table.
2. Goodwill. ✓ He had delivered some of his clothes that were too tight, his guitar, skis, old tennis racket, and miscellaneous personal items to the Goodwill store. He reasoned that getting rid of these items would make it easier for his wife to clear up his estate once he was no longer around.
3. Hospital Visit.✓ He had visited at the Beaverbrook Hospital where he had previously worked. He told former colleagues and nurses that he was visiting a neighbour who was an in-patient, although his real purpose was to chat with as many people as he could find and show them that he was still the healthy, cheery, joke-telling fellow they had known for years before his retirement.
4. Appointments.✓ He had stopped in to Dr. Ben Speckle's plastic surgery office and made an appointment to see Dr. Speckle about the growth on his neck. The appointment was for February 24. He had then called

the dealership and made an appointment to have his Ford Escape serviced the following Tuesday, and marked the appointment in his iPad calendar and on the paper calendar that Velma used.

5. Birthday gift.✓ He had bought a card and a small silver bracelet for his wife's upcoming sixtieth birthday, wrapped it, and left it on the computer desk with the note "Happy 60th!"

6. Bank. No. He had considered stopping at the bank and closing out his personal account with only $200 in it, transferring that amount to the joint account he shared with his wife, but then decided that it would give away his intentions.

7. Facebook.✓ Upon returning home, he had posted on Facebook a comical comment about his favourite political scoundrel, the mayor of a nearby city.

8. Jokes.✓ He had forwarded to his list of "joke friends" a couple of the carefully saved emails of off-colour jokes that he had received from another friend, being careful to ensure that they went to none of his other friends on other email lists.

9. Beard.✓ He trimmed down and then shaved off the long, scraggly graying beard that he had had for the past 40 years, nicking his face in several places in the process. He realized that a mug shot of him would likely show up in various media sometime after Velma came home and reported that he was missing.

10. Garbage.✓ He had gathered up the garbage and delivered the pail to the curb for pickup. The pickup would be about noon on the following Monday, but ensuring that it happened would convince Velma that he had taken it out on Monday morning. He always got it to the curb just as the truck was coming down the street.

11. Food.✓ He had dumped three of the frozen leftover dinners Velma had left for him into the garberator and turned it on to make it look as though he had eaten them.

12. Wallet.✓ He considered shredding his driver's licence and all of the credit cards and membership cards in his wallet,

but decided that doing so would make it obvious that he was planning to never use them again. He would simply leave his wallet intact on the bedside table when he left the house.

13. Call Velma.✓ He had called Velma, even though she had called him earlier when she arrived and had left a message. Even in this relationship, he felt that he had lost influence and affection. According to Velma, Isaac and Adam had requested that she visit without him. He wondered what he had done to alienate his son and darling grandson.

"How cold is it in Kingston?" he had asked.

Her reply was typically curt; she said she didn't know, as she had not been out of the house since she had arrived. They talked for a few minutes, but there seemed to be little that they had in common to discuss. She felt obliged to warn him to be careful, as there was a snowstorm warning on the weather channel for the whole of Southern Ontario. She told him that he should stay indoors that night, and he promised to do so. Her constant advice about such matters was a frequent annoyance to him, particularly since if he tried to give her any advice about anything at all he would receive a tirade about how little he respected her opinion or way of doing things. He grudgingly acknowledged to himself that her advice was reasonable in this instance, as she and most of their friends knew that he was a thrill-seeking risk-taker. He had persuaded Velma to not call again, as she planned to return home the following Monday, and they really had nothing of importance to discuss.

He reflected on Velma's constant advice about being cautious, and grudgingly realized that he would probably not have survived to this point if he had had no one to restrain his wild risk-taking nature. In the two years between his marriages, his unrestrained adventurous nature had led him to climb Mt. Kilimanjaro with a friend from his motorcycle club, choosing the Machame Route with Ultimate Kilimanjaro Tours. He had rappelled up the sheer ice of the frozen waterfall at the west end of Lake Louise after attending a medical conference at Chateau Lake Louise. He had driven his Kawasaki KZ 900 LTD motorcycle the 3,510 kilometres from

Redfern to the north rim of the Grand Canyon. From there, he did the R2R (rim-to-rim) hike on the Kaibab Trail in one day, in spite of the warnings along the trail to not attempt that. After staying at the El Tovar on the south rim and exploring the village the next day, he decided to return to the North Rim via the Bright Angel Trail on the third day. When recounting this adventure, he usually omitted the small detail about needing to be rescued by the National Parks Service 1000 feet below the North Rim on the return hike and being given a warning by the National Parks rangers about his carelessness. He had collapsed from exhaustion, in a confused state. The rescue team thought he was dehydrated but he insisted that he had been drinking lots of water and that he just needed salt. He seemed to recover quickly after being given salt tablets.

He now carefully measured two shot glasses of his favourite tipple, 15-year-old Islay single malt, into his whisky glass and added precisely six drops of tap water and four frozen whisky stones, then sat down in his recliner to reflect on his life. The three bottles of peaty Lagavulin had been a gift from a grateful Scottish patient whom he had successfully resuscitated from a cardiac arrest; the cache was almost gone three years later. *But that arrest might never have happened if I had been more careful with the man's medication,* he reflected in morbid self-deprecation. He usually restricted himself to one shot about once a week, but this was a special occasion, and Velma would not drink any that was left over anyway, he noted wryly. He was not particular about any food or drink and usually ate or drank whatever was on offer, often without realizing what it was. But the scotch was different—meant for sipping slowly while doing some serious reflection in an almost-sober state, and had to be perfect. He had over an hour left. *Time for some serious reflection on how I managed to screw up my life,* he thought.

In the past, he had been held in high esteem as a compassionate, devoted anaesthesiologist and intensivist who always put the interests of his patients first. The visit to the hospital earlier that day reminded him that he was still seemingly fondly regarded there, although he had lost any influence in the workings of the institution. His ego-driven devotion to medicine had cost him dearly. His first wife had taken off with a funeral director after 12 years of marriage when she realized that he did not intend to do much to help her care for their 5-year-old daughter and 7-year-old son. Then she had sought and obtained custody of them. They had moved to Shacletown, so he still had visits with them every other weekend, hardly enough time to exert a major influence on their lives; and he now reflected that he had done less than he should have to try to guide them.

Had he not been in a hurry to remarry after the divorce, he might have made a wiser choice the second time, but when Velma, the childless-by-choice dietitian he had worked with for years got divorced, she had seemed like a good mate at the time. A scandal had erupted even before they were married, as he was accused of a conflict of interest. While dating Velma, he had vigorously supported her application for a promotion; he honestly had felt that she deserved the promotion. When the rumours got too nasty, she had left the hospital altogether and set up her own weight-loss clinic in a nearby medical office building.

Within eight years after their wedding, there had developed a steadily worsening feud between his daughter, Barb, and his new wife that went on for several years. This related mainly to Barb's wishes to become a professor of moral philosophy and eventually led to complete estrangement from his daughter, who refused to visit and had spurned all contact with her father since her mid-teens. Barb had also deeply resented sharing whatever little time Leslie had for her with his bossy wife; and the resentment over sharing his sparse free time was mutual. Barb had impulsively decided in her teens that her father had no understanding or love for her at all and felt abandoned. He seemed to never be able to display much emotional attachment to anyone, partly because of the need to be detached from emotions at his work.

Barb had succeeded in her dream, getting three degrees from three different universities, thanks in part to his generous child support payments; he got no hint from other family members that she missed him at all. The only contact that he had with her was through his son, and Isaac was very circumspect about what he told his father about Barb. Leslie knew that she was in Maryland somewhere, and was married, but he had no address, and she never answered the calls he made after secretly getting her phone number from Isaac's directory.

Velma acknowledged no responsibility for this state of affairs, blaming him for spending too much time at work and too little time with the children as they were growing up, and not supporting her persistent pleas to Barb to find a more practical and lucrative career than teaching philosophy. So he had not only lost influence in the world of medicine, with his daughter, his son and dear grandson, and with his parents, both of whom were now dead, but even with his wife.

As he looked around the library with his extensive collection of medical, science, and philosophy books, Leslie questioned his decision two years earlier to retire. *Maybe I should have kept working. But am I becoming demented? Sure have become a useless old fart.* He had quite reasonably been fearful about the possibility that he might make some critical error if he worked past his prime; in the high-risk environment of the ICU, such an error might well lead to a needless death. He would feel terrible, a malpractice lawsuit might well be launched, and his reputation would be tarnished. Retirement before he lost any of his clinical skills seemed preferable to him at that time.

He had selfishly enjoyed every day of work, and it had stroked his ego. He had been able to convince himself that what he was doing at work was important. However, since retirement, he felt that he had gone from being the ace at the top to the joker at the bottom of life's deck of cards. To keep busy, he took beginner bridge lessons but friends seldom asked him to play in their social games, and he did not enjoy it. His bidding and play of the hands was slow and erratic and he could not remember the nuances of the many conventions. Duplicate bridge was impossibly complex for him.

He now realized that his ambitious bucket list on the computer would remain uncompleted and his task list for that day was his *de facto* bucket list. But he would leave the bucket list on the computer to show that he planned many more adventures. It included hopes that he had had before fate erased them—to someday learn to pilot a glider plane, to learn to walk on tall stilts and to ride a unicycle to improve his balance, and to raft down the Colorado River all the way though the Grand Canyon. These were adventures that he dreamed of, but that Velma would not allow him to actually experience. He had threatened to leave her because of the restrictions she imposed on his adventures, but felt trapped and knew that he would never do so. In some vague way, he realized that he needed her restraining influence on his reckless nature. And he certainly needed a woman's guidance on his inept social behaviours, such as his bizarre eating and dressing habits.

He had tried to learn to play a musical instrument, choosing guitar, and had bought a cheap Daisy Rock Butterfly Jumbo acoustic, and enrolled for lessons. The instructor had dismissed him after the third lesson, after testing him and finding that he could not detect the difference between two notes of very different pitch; his sense of rhythm was poor, and he was too slow in the fingering. *I guess being left-handed didn't help, either,* he thought. He would certainly never make any contribution in the world of music.

His health was also failing, both physically and mentally. Velma had convinced him that he had early signs of dementia, the ailment that he had most dreaded developing when he was a practicing physician. When playing bridge one night at a friend's home—after getting lost while driving there—he was dealt mostly poor hands, and on the one good hand he held, he opened one spade with 14 high-card points. His partner bid a game-forcing Jacoby two no-trump in support of spades, but Leslie passed, much to the shock of his partner and opponents. He confessed he never understood any cue bid and was not surprised or disappointed when he was never asked to play thereafter.

He realized that he was prone to forgetting items on the shopping list or getting the wrong brand; and forgetting the names of former colleagues, friends, and acquaintances. He often asked Velma what he could do to help her, and then promptly forgot half of her requests. As a consequence, he stopped asking questions altogether and tried, often unsuccessfully, to simply follow her directives.

His physical health also was failing. He noted that most of his clothes were too tight and his abdomen and legs seemed a bit swollen. Velma would frequently order him to "straighten up," as his posture had deteriorated. His top speed was about three miles per hour, yet he still enjoyed long solo walks along the nearby Beaver Trail along the Beaver River. Like most physicians, he neglected his own health, took no pills, and had not had a check-up with his family doctor for at least five years. He ignored Velma's pleas to have the thick pencil-like skin growth on a thin stalk with a black ulcerated tip located above his left clavicle checked out. *It's either a fibroma, in which case it is only of cosmetic concern, or a keratoacanthoma, in which case it would likely just drop off some day,* he mused.

He was fond of making lists—lists of birthdays, names, the Saturday Home Improvement Task list (acronym, SHIT list), lists of medications and their side effects, and lists of differential diagnoses to explain symptoms and signs, and even his bucket list. But he could not think of any of differential diagnosis list for the symptoms and signs he had observed recently in himself as he reviewed them now.

1. Low level of serum sodium. A classmate who tested his blood for a research project three years earlier had found this. Since then, he had privately and morbidly been expecting that some untreatable fatal cancer would sooner or later show up to explain it. He knew that this was commonly due to the syndrome of inappropriate antidiuretic hormone (SIADH) secretion, and, in turn, a cancer of the lung, brain, or pancreas usually caused that. In a morbid way, he was almost pleased to now realize that his diagnostic acumen was still intact.
2. Weight gain, swollen legs, and abdomen.
3. Worsening anorexia.
4. Jaundice. He had noticed that the whites of his eyes had been turning yellow in the past few days.
5. Diffuse itching. He had worried about this for three weeks and it was getting worse.
6. Pale stools and constipation, tea-coloured urine. Two weeks.

The cancer that I have been expecting to show up must be in the head of my pancreas and obstructing the bile duct there to explain the pain and itch. He recalled the old medical adage that painless jaundice and itch in the elderly is due to cancer of the pancreas until proven otherwise. He knew from experience that the cure rate for this was under five percent, even with the heroic Whipple operation that desperate patients and surgeons alike were fond of trying. But two days before, he had experienced a bout of abdominal pain that lasted for two hours; he knew that once patients with pancreatic cancer have experienced pain, it is an indication that the cancer has spread beyond the pancreas and was invariably fatal. He had treated the pain of far too many patients dying of cancer of the pancreas, and was determined never to be reduced to whining for more and more narcotics.

He reflected on his love life. *Messed that up, too,* he thought. He had fallen for Rachael while still in his final year of medical school at Queens University in Kingston, and she seemed to admire his dedication to medicine and to his patients. Later, as his training dragged on and on, however, Rachael frequently reminded him of the sacrifices she had made for his education, and was vocal in her unhappiness with his chosen subspecialty of critical care, one of the lowest-earning specialties at that time. They had moved to Redfern when he got a full-time appointment at Beaverbrook Hospital. Later, he gave up the operating room work and became the only fulltime intensivist, working exclusively in the Intensive Care Unit, accepting the need to be on call 24/7 whenever he was in town.

Rachael found frequent excuses to go to the gym for long workouts, often arriving home quite late. One evening when Isaac was seven and Barb was five, Leslie came home from the hospital late in the evening to find Rachael and the children gone, and a note from Rachael saying that they would not be back. They moved to the Shacletown home of Edgar Jacks and she applied for and got custody of their children with visitation rights to Leslie every second weekend. She then filed for divorce. Thereafter, he often joked at work that he would try anything to avoid sending any business to Edgar Jaccs's funeral home.

Life with his second wife, Velma, started out much better. They seemed to share a quirky sense of humour, and neither of them was concerned very much about material wealth, which was just as well, given the size of his monthly alimony and child support payments. Their sexual exploits in the bedroom and in the darkened backyard hot tub late at night were better than he had ever experienced before, and she seemed to understand his ego need to feel needed and respected in his practice of medicine. *She really was a beautiful, loving wife and partner at one time, but she never understood me. Or did I never understand her?*

Her business was stressful and not very profitable. She had no experience in running a business and the competition in the field

became fierce. She also lacked experience and interest in dealing
with rebellious teens, and thought that Leslie was uninterested
and inadequate in disciplining them. She had caught Barb smoking (Leslie had only lectured her and didn't even ground her for
the weekend for this) and Isaac had been caught hacking into the
supposedly secure high school computer system and changing
the marks of some of his classmates. Isaac was too smart to alter
his own average grades, but had raised those of four friends and
significantly lowered those of the class bully. He had only been
caught because the bully's lawyer mother had complained to the
teacher about the sudden drop in her darling's grades. Leslie had
just laughed at this caper.

Velma had slowly developed a significant depression. *Sure
missed the obvious signs of that. So much for my clinical acumen,* Leslie reflected. He had finally clued in only after she had taken a
mild overdose of the sedative that he had foolishly prescribed for
what he thought was her simple insomnia induced by anxiety.
Faisal Al Taqi had treated that overdose in the emergency department and referred her to Dr. Roy Coachman in Hamilton, recording the episode as being an accidental overdose. After reviewing
her history, Dr. Coachman explained that her depression was better described as *brain serotonin deficit disorder* and serially tried a
number of agents to boost her brain levels of serotonin, finally set-
tling on paroxetine. This had the unfortunate effect of completely
destroying her libido—she no longer needed nor could she experience the high of orgasms to be happy—much to Leslie's annoyance. He felt he had no choice and resigned himself to a life of
celibacy when she shunned his advances. But he was grateful to
Faisal for his kindness and help. *Maybe Faisal at least will miss me
even if no one else does—he has been a great friend; should have done
more to show that I appreciated his kindness.*

He was aware of multiple reasons why his risk-taking nature
did not include seeking sexual thrills outside of the marriage, none
of them relating directly to the morality of casual sex. Partly it was
because he was petrified of ruining his reputation as a happily
married, faithful husband if he had an affair and it was discovered; and it would be even more dangerous to be seen in a sleazy
motel where rooms can be rented by the hour. And if he ever got a

sexually transmitted disease, he would have to attend the "special clinic," and the gossip would be devastating for his reputation. The false image of a happily married, monogamous man was also very important to him, even though the happily married part had become a lie. Mostly, although he knew he was a rarity among men in this respect, he doubted that his equipment would even rise to the occasion for sex unless there was some emotional attachment to his partner—respect and fondness, if not love. Even in his young, single days, his solo performances on his upright organ, Arnold, had been satisfying and sedating only if he was fantasizing about some girl he liked and respected.

He now recalled a witty quote from Billy Crystal: "Women need a reason for sex; men just need a place." *I guess I was always more like a woman than a man in this respect, but only in this respect,* he reflected. He had convinced himself that this was a unique moral virtue, but when he was being honest, realized that it was really nothing more than a physiological fact about the way his brain and his gonads worked together. In his morose state of mind, he now concluded that this trait was actually a physical defect in his ailing body's wiring. Besides, he had long ago forgotten any art he may have once had for picking up women. *Never was much good at understanding women's signals,* he realized. Velma had told him on several occasions, on returning from some social gathering, that some woman had been flagrantly flirting with him, but he had completely failed to notice. He had only ever dated and had intercourse with two, and they had both picked him.

As the scotch started to take effect, he pondered about what might have been. He had long had a secret deep admiration and even love for Inge Glacier. He was not sure when his infatuation with her had begun, but he thought about her daily. They had known each other for many years, and the mutual respect was obvious. She was, as far as he knew, happily married.

He had, at her request, sent a glowing recommendation to the hospital HR department a year before he retired, when she had applied for the Team Leader position, describing her as a natural leader with superb interpersonal skills. He had to restrain himself from mentioning her more often, lest his true feelings were revealed. They shared some personal stories, but more frequently, their conversations were work-related, and they often discussed the urine output, bowel functions, settings for the ventilator, or prognosis of a patient. She was about ten years his junior, and as far as he knew, she was happily married. He had met her husband Joe at a hospital function and knew that he managed a Liquor Control Board of Ontario store in nearby Elmsvale. Joe had seemed like a decent fellow, and he noticed that he never left Inge's side all evening. Leslie did not even know where they lived.

She was always so stylishly but modestly dressed that he never saw cleavage, bra lines, or panty lines. She stood straight and seemed to glide around the ICU rather than to walk on the Crocs she always wore at work. When she fixed her deep blue high beam eyes on him and gave him her very open welcoming smile, he had to look away lest she see the deep affection that he had for her. Elegant and beautiful seemed to sum her up. He had never seen her excited, upset, tearful, or worried, even while attending a cardiac arrest. Her emotional range seemed to be limited from about L to P on an alphabetic scale where A represents severe mania and Z severe despondency. She didn't seem to mind his lack of social graces and his often-inappropriate comments, and unlike other co-workers, never made any comments about his often-outrageous wardrobe combinations.

At one point, while driving to Interhospital Critical Care Grand Rounds at Toronto Western Hospital shortly before retirement, Leslie and Faisal Al Taqi had discussed the new hospital policy of requiring all staff to display unique identification tags of their choice. They agreed that Ben Speckle should be 'Vanity Doctor' and Glenna Bass should be 'Bass Pro.' Leslie suggested that Faisal should be 'Sheik Faisal' and Faisal suggested 'The List Man' for Leslie's moniker. When Leslie mentioned Inge's promotion, Dr. Al Taqi had commented "Now there is one classy lady; and not hard to look at."

"I agree. That smile and those blue eyes could make any man's heart flutter. But everything about her—her clothes, her walk, her talk, her mannerisms, her unflappable composure—says that she is out of bounds. I guess her tag should be 'Trophy wife' or maybe 'Out Of Bounds'. Wait. 'Trophy Wife' should be that gay nurse Roberto's tag," Leslie suggested.

"Oh, you are so—so not politically correct, but I love it."

"Well, no one has accused me of being politically correct. Back to Inge. I think she should wear a 'No Trespassing' sign over her backside, and maybe 'Private Property' on the front of her dress."

"Oh, you are just plain bad, but it does suit her. She is so private and self-controlled. Her husband is one lucky man."

"Well, yes and no. I can't imagine him having much fun with her in bed.

"Why not?"

"Well she is so composed, unemotional, and unexcitable that I can't imagine her giving up that self-control to enjoy great sex. I can see her insisting on the missionary position, with the lights out, under the sheets, having a quick, silent, motionless, and probably fake orgasm, and then politely asking him to roll over so she could go to sleep."

"Now I think you are describing my wife," Faisal joked.

"Well, my fantasy partner would be much more athletic, vocal, and adventurous than Inge. But that individual is just a fantasy now. Since that psychiatrist you sent Velma to after you treated the overdose started her on paroxetine, my sex life has really dwindled to nothing, so I guess you are doing better than I am. And I can't get her to reduce the dose or stop it. By the way, thank you for being so discreet about that overdose. I just wish there were something else for her to try. I guess there is nothing wrong with admitting that one has a mental illness, but I still have a hard time with that, and so does Velma."

* * *

If Inge had detected any signs of his distress earlier that day when they met in the cafeteria, she had not revealed them. He had wandered around the hospital apparently at random, but in fact was not content to leave until he had found her. When he visited the ICU and did not find her, he had guessed that she would be at lunch. As he bought a coffee, he looked for her.

On this occasion, Leslie saw Inge sitting with Brook Falone the hospital CEO. But it was Falone who motioned him to come and join them. Inge stood as he approached, matching his height of five-foot-ten, and gave him a warm hug, and he shook hands with the CEO.

"Why does he get a hug and I don't?" Falone inquired.

Emboldened by the arrival of her idol, Inge retorted. "The difference is that he is a gentleman."

"Ouch! What did you do to deserve that?" Leslie inquired.

"I'll never tell. Probably something I said, not something I did," Brook replied. "But then I'm used to getting no respect around here. Nothing changes."

After catching up on some hospital news, Brook Falone told Leslie that he had been meaning to call him, as someone had suggested Leslie as the replacement for a recently deceased member of the hospital board.

"We always appreciated having you on committees here, and I think you could do a great job on the board, and you'd shake up the old boys' club with great insights."

Leslie replied that he was flattered but didn't think that he was really qualified for the job, and besides he was out of town quite a lot. When Brook Falone insisted that he consider the offer and Inge also suggested that he would be a great addition to the hospital board, Leslie promised that he would think about it and get back to Brook.

After Brook left, Leslie asked Inge why she had insulted the CEO, whom he admired as a capable administrator. Inge then confided in him that Brook Falone had just propositioned her for sex in his office.

"I think I know you better than to try that. I'm surprised that you didn't slap him across the face. Are you going to file a complaint?" Leslie asked.

"Well, I have to tolerate him because of his power around here. And I'm not prepared to endure the character assassination that would come with a complaint. Remember what happened to Anita Hill when she complained about that Supreme Court Justice what's-his-name? The first response from most men to a charge of sexual harassment is to band together and blame the woman who complained. And he has never touched me and could always say he was just joking. But if I were ever going to cheat on my tired old hubby, it would certainly not be with that creep."

Something in the way she said that, as she looked directly into Leslie's eyes, made him uncomfortable, and he looked away and quickly changed the subject. But a pang of jealousy overtook him as he wondered about whom she had in mind. As usual, she was very friendly but he recognized no clue as to her true feelings for him, although she twice mentioned how much she missed him around the ICU. She asked if he had ever considered coming back to work even part time, and he replied that he had enough things on his bucket list to keep him busy for the rest of his life without working.

When she had asked him about his reason for coming to the hospital, he had lied, and pulling down his turtleneck, pointed to the distinctive stubby half-inch-long growth above his left collarbone. He said that he had been to an appointment with Dr. Ben Speckle in Plastics and that he was scheduled for surgical removal of the growth that might be cancerous, saying that the surgery would involve taking a big divot out of the side of his neck, and possibly a skin graft.

"But who cares what this old carcass looks like?" he had asked rhetorically. He wasn't at all sure why he had fed her a different lie than the one he had given everyone else at the hospital that day. Perhaps he unconsciously wanted her to express some concern about him, but if so he was disappointed. She had merely said, "You'll do fine."

As she left to return to the ICU, he watched her in awe of her beauty, elegance, and composure. *Perhaps she will recall that apparently chance meeting and be a least a little sad when the news breaks about the fate awaiting me later today*, he thought.

He had heard someone use the word *limerence* to describe his feelings in a romance, and Leslie had looked it up. *Wikipedia* defined it as "An involuntary state of mind resulting from a romantic attraction to another person combined with an overwhelming obsessive need to have one's feelings reciprocated." It seemed to define his feelings for Inge perfectly, but it was described as involuntary., so he realized that he had no control over it.

So, he had not only lost any influence or control over his work environment, his wife, his son and grandson, his daughter, and his health, but even over his own state of mind. Perhaps his father had been right about the doctrine of predestination after all. He really had no control over his life or actions.

He began to mentally list his losses.

1. Influence and usefulness at work.
2. Family affection, influence. Barb. Isaac, Adam, even Velma. Both parents, sister.
3. Talent. *Not much good at anything anymore.*
4. Health. *Dementia, cancer of the pancreas.*
5. Affection from anyone.

Even though he had been fondly greeted at the hospital earlier that day, he knew how good his colleagues were at hiding their true feelings. Even his dream angel, Inge, did not seem to care what happened to him.

His mother had died a slow and painful death from breast cancer years before, and he had lost his brother-in law five years ago—no great loss there—and his father the year before.

His father had maintained his faith even after developing dementia and reminded Leslie of God's justice in striking down Leslie's brother-in-law. (Leslie had regarded it as a fortuitous coincidence.) When his father was moved into a retirement home, the household belongings that could not go with him were to be divided between Leslie and his somewhat dimwitted sister. Leslie did not want anything from the home, but reminded his father that if any went to his sister, her useless, arrogant, obnoxious, obese, unemployed husband would sell it all to buy booze and cigarettes. After the move, his sister had hired a truck to move all the furniture to their Ottawa home. As his brother-in-law was unloading the truckload of possessions that were not to go to him, he had a heart attack and died suddenly. Leslie, paraphrasing Christopher Hitchens, told Velma at the funeral that if they had just given him an enema, they could have buried him in an infant child's coffin. His crude comment had somehow gotten back to his sister, who had not spoken to him in the intervening five years. So he had lost any affection or influence with everyone everywhere, it seemed. *All because of my big mouth*, he concluded. *Probably pissed a lot of people off with my rants about religion, too. And some of them will be secretly glad to conclude that I have moved on to take up residence in Hell.*

But there was one thing he could control: his future. And he intended to do so.

7

just do it

The Beaver Trail running along the Beaver River was only about 500 metres from their house. He had walked along it many times and had travelled it on skis and snowshoes in the winters. He knew the exact spot in Beaver Park where the short Little Beaver Trail narrowed to a set of large, slippery stones between the lightly forested park and an almost vertical 20-foot drop-off into the Beaver River. He was determined to ensure that the chief coroner, whom he knew well from his working days, would rule that his death was accidental, thus sparing his family the humiliation and embarrassment of explaining a suicide, while they would still collect the quadrupled amount of his $400,000 life insurance policy that would be awarded once it was determined to be an accident. That, combined with his net worth of just over $1.6 million, would ensure that his wife, son, and daughter could live in relative luxury, at least relative to the amount that he had ever spent on his own pleasures and hobbies. His will still listed his daughter as an equal beneficiary of his estate, but it was far too late to cut her out of it now, even though he was angry with her for abandoning him. *But I don't want to be vengeful.* Velma had reminded him on many occasions since his retirement that he was worth more dead than alive, and he had the distinct feeling that she was not entirely joking.

He double-checked the list of things that he had to do that last day of his life, and checked them off. The task list was completed. *Was there anything he had forgotten?*

There was no way anyone would ever suspect suicide, except perhaps his wife, and she had too much to gain to ever admit to her doubts. The thought of death by drowning in frigid water or by hypothermia was so horrible that no one would ever think that it could be planned, particularly by an apparently healthy, happy, retired doctor. But he knew better; he would fool them all. He had experienced hypothermia before on one of his winter bicycle trips, trying to duplicate the 100-mile Born-to-Ride cycling tour on the back roads of Simcoe County, and his recollection of it was that once the delusions of grandeur and the hallucinations had started, it was not at all unpleasant. He had resisted rescue on that occasion until a police officer responded to a 911 call about a man riding a bicycle erratically on the wrong side of the road. The officer found him trying to ride across a snow-covered pasture and singing an off-key version of "Bridge over Troubled Waters." He had force-fully placed Leslie in the back of the cruiser and taken him to Bar-rie's Soldier's Memorial Hospital. They had called Velma and she had picked him up when he was released three days later, but she never let him forget how foolish his winter bicycling was.

He could only clearly envision one future event—his own funeral or memorial service. His atheism made him believe that there was nothing but nothingness for him after death, and he had told Velma that he did not want any religious elements, nor any mention of a possible afterlife. That thought raised an existential dilemma—why should he be concerned at all about leaving his family with a good legacy and good memories of him? But he real-ized that he was not alone among atheists who continued to care about leaving the world better off after death, and the example of Christopher Hitchens came to mind. He hoped that Velma would remember the songs he wanted played at his funeral, although he could not quite understand why it should matter. His choices in music were based on meaningful lyrics, as he had no appreciation for the scores or rhythm. Never one to be traditional, he chose Paul Robson's best rendition of *Old Man River* to emphasize the insig-nificance of any one mere mortal human life in the grand flow of time and nature, Terry Jack's *Seasons in the Sun* to acknowledge the universality of regrets and fear as mere mortals face death, and Susan Boyle singing *I Dreamed a Dream* to point out the universal experience of unfulfilled dreams of mere mortals. *Perhaps one of these songs will bring tears to a few eyes,* he thought. Maybe even Inge would show some emotion.

He left his scotch glass on the kitchen counter. Whoever searched the house would conclude that he had been drinking before he disappeared, and that could not hurt his deception. *Obviously, alcohol had impaired the judgment of the old adventurer when he decided to go snowshoeing in a blizzard,* someone would conclude. He put on his old leather jacket, toque, and light gloves. He laid his wallet out on the bedside table, put on the only pair of light hiking boots he had not taken to Goodwill, and retrieved his old snowshoes from the garage. At the last minute before opening the back door, he panicked—the list! He quickly ran back into the kitchen and took the list to the computer room and shredded it.

The weather was perfect for his mission—snowing heavily with a howling northwest wind, -15°C, and a thick base of snow. His tracks would be invisible within an hour, and no one was likely to search for him for a couple of days in any case. When they did try to locate him, there would be few clues as to where to start the search. Even if Velma reported that his skis and snowshoes were missing and surmised that he had gone out in the blizzard, the chances of finding his body were slim.

He planned to get as far as that point on the Little Beaver Trail where it comes dangerously close to the vertical drop-off to the Beaver River, remove one snowshoe, then "accidentally" fall over the edge of the stone trail into the fast-running, frigid water. He was sure the river would not be frozen over this early in the winter. The snowshoe would tell searchers that he had been there, and they would surmise that he had fallen into the river, but it is doubtful that they would find his body before spring breakup, three months hence. *It might well drift all the way down the river and out into Lake Ontario and never be found,* he thought. By the time he got to his destination, he might well be hallucinating from hypothermia and he might not get that far, but he much preferred to die by drowning than by hypothermia along the trail.

He had researched on the Internet about the process for a declaration of death when no body was found and had determined that in Canada it took seven years if someone just went missing. But there was an exception. A Declaration of Death could be obtained within a couple months if the police and an attorney could convince a judge that he had disappeared "in perilous circumstances" and as a consequence that he really was dead "beyond reasonable doubt." He would leave the snowshoe as sufficient evidence of a perilous circumstance so there should be no difficulty in fulfilling that criterion.

He set out across the backyard and slogged along the Beaver Trail. As he approached the designated spot an hour later, he was shivering uncontrollably. He looked at his watch and noted that he had ten minutes left to live, then took his watch off and hurled it into the fast-flowing river and followed that with the house and car keys. As he peered through the trees, he was startled to see flashing yellow and blue lights in the distance. Then he suddenly felt a tingling sensation all over his body, felt very hot, and thinking that his clothes were on fire, began to furiously tear them off. He undid his belt, lowered his zipper and then forcefully tore his pants and long johns off to cool off from what he perceived to be unbearably intense heat. He then walked on to the Little Beaver Trail and suddenly felt strangely calm and at peace. He vaguely realized that the hallucinations must have started. It was time to get the job done while he could. He sat down, took off his right snowshoe and hung it on a low tree branch, took a deep breath, leaned over, and plunged into the darkness.

8

identities

Inge Glacier arrived at work before 7:00 a.m. that Monday and immediately checked on John Doe. The night nurse reported that he was still unidentified, and that he and the officer assigned to guard him had both had an uninterrupted good night's sleep. He was now breathing mostly on his own at about six breaths per minute and needed the ventilator only intermittently, but showed no signs of re-joining the real world. Inge assigned a very quiet experienced nurse to care for him on the day shift. Then, as she reviewed the assignments and patients, a man flashing a Redfern Regional Police Services badge approached the desk, and asked, "Who is in charge here?"

"Well, I guess I am," she replied. "I am the team leader."

"Can you direct me to John Doe who was admitted on Friday night?"

"I could, but I won't until you tell me why you need to see him."

"I need to get some fingerprints from him to help us identify him."

"Do you have a warrant?"

"Look, ma'am, this is a criminal investigation, and all I need is a fingerprint." This process was proving to be more difficult than he had anticipated.

"I'm sorry to be so difficult, but you can't just walk in here and fingerprint a patient because you want to. But let me check with the higher-ups about this." She called the hospital administration office. When the secretary heard that the call was from Brook Falone's favourite nurse and was about John Doe, she immediately forwarded it to the CEO, already at a breakfast meeting.

"I have a police officer here requesting permission to finger-print John Doe," Inge explained. "I am not sure if this is acceptable or not. He doesn't have a warrant."

"Well, isn't that interesting, my dear. We have just been dis-cussing the request from someone there in the ICU to get a Public Guardian and Trustee appointed to make decisions for John Doe, since I gather he can't make any for himself, but that process will take time. And he has already rung up a big tab here and we have no one to send the bill to. So I guess anything the police can do that will help to identify him should be okay from my viewpoint. If all they need is fingerprints, I will okay that."

Inge hung up and again apologized to Sergeant Atherton for being so difficult, then led him to John Doe's room, and watched closely as he pressed John Doe's fingertips on the pad. Then, look-ing at the further bag of blood being dripped into John Doe's arm, he recorded that he was blood group AB, a relatively rare type. She noted that Atherton also looked closely at the computer screen at the bedside, with some results of the lab work on John Doe open on it. On returning to the desk, still uneasy about this process, Inge asked Atherton to write down his name and badge number. She intended to document the encounter and the permission from the hospital administrator with a note in John Doe's chart.

After completing her paperwork, Inge joined the change-over nursing staff in the conference room reviewing the patients. The ICU nurses took changeover reports at the bedside but were encouraged and expected to attend the sit-down team rounds when the patients they were caring for were being discussed. When the discussion came to John Doe, the update was encourag-ing, but there was a comment about the futility of what they were doing for him from one of the nurses who had come in early to discuss the next patient. Inge made a mental note to discuss ICU burnout with this nurse who seemed to have become quite cyni-cal about several patients. Team bedside rounds with the on-duty intensivist followed the sit-down rounds, but Inge was too busy arranging transfers in and out of the ICU to attend.

Later in the morning, the nurse caring for John Doe asked Inge to help her to turn him on his side to change the bed sheets, which were completely soiled with liquid stool, which was the residual effect of the lactulose enema. As they did this, she suddenly froze, stared, and then screamed. She went running from the room, shouting "No! No! No!" When she reached the staff lounge, she ran to the washroom and vomited, then sat down in the lounge with her head in her hands and sobbed uncontrollably. Two staff followed her and asked what was wrong with her, but she kept crying without saying a word. Twenty minutes later, she looked up, and almost in a whisper, said, "I know who he is."

"Well, tell us. Everyone wants to know," one of the nurses said. "And how can you be so sure?"

"That spot on his neck," she sobbed.

"Well, who is he?" they responded in unison.

"Dr. Turle," she replied, again breaking down in tears.

"No, that can't be! Dr. Turle has a beard, and John Doe doesn't," one of the nurses replied in alarm, wondering if Inge had become delusional.

Dr. Martin Midges, the new ICU attending physician taking over from Dr. Bass, was asked to go to the staff lounge to deal with the distraught Inge Glacier. After reiterating to him that she knew that John Doe was Dr. Leslie Turle, the intensivist that he had replaced on the ICU staff, he persuaded her to return to the bedside and show him how she could be so sure. Introducing her to the constable at the bedside, he said, "This nurse says she knows who he is."

Inge gently pulled down the sheet and the hospital gown and pointed to the skin growth on John Doe's neck. "I saw that growth on Dr. Turle's neck last Friday and I have never seen anything like it before. And Dr. Speckle from Plastics saw it too—Dr. Turle was in on Friday to have it assessed by Dr. Speckle, and he showed it to me when we met in the cafeteria." Then she leaned over and shouted in John Doe's ear.

"Dr. Turle, can you open your eyes for me?" There was a slight twitch of John Doe's upper lip, and his eyes opened very distinctly, then closed again.

Inge returned to the staff lounge and immediately called her best friend, Carol Creek. Carol was off duty, but agreed to come to pick her up; she was alarmed by how distraught Inge sounded on the phone. Dr. Midges agreed that Inge needed time off to deal with her distressing revelation, and Carol assured him that she would not leave her alone. In the car, Inge, still sobbing, repeated for the third time the story of how she had identified John Doe as Dr. Leslie Turle. She confessed to Carol her longstanding infatuation with Dr. Turle, and Carol replied, "Well, what is not to like about him? I think every nurse in the ICU has been in love with him, even Roberto."

At the home of Carol and Ken Creek, they both tried to console Inge. Ken, who had been working from home, gave her a most welcome genuine hug. As Carol prepared a simple chicken soup lunch, Ken noticed the greenish-black bruise on Inge's cheek, exposed as her tears had washed away the makeup. After lunch, of which Inge only took a few sips, they sat down together to talk about her situation. Inge was already quite sure that she could not ever return to work in the ICU; the image of Dr. Turle as John Doe would haunt her there forever. She admitted, when Ken pressed her, that the bruise was because Joe had slapped her roughly on the previous Friday evening.

"What did you do to provoke *that*?" Carol asked.

"It's quite ironic, you know. All I did was mention talking with Dr. Turle at the hospital. You know that Joe is a bit paranoid and jealous, and he accused me of having an affair with Dr. Turle."

"Well, then, you can't go back and tell him about today, can you," Ken interjected. "Are you ready to follow the advice we've been giving you for months to get out of your rotten marriage?"

"I don't want to make any hasty decisions about that. I have had enough stress already today."

"I know that. But how are you going to avoid getting beaten up again when he finds out that you were the one who identified John Doe as Dr. Turle?" Ken asked.

"Well, there is no official identification yet. I can deny that he has been identified, at least for tonight, and see how Joe is taking it when he finds out. And he may never know what I had to do with the identification."

"Inge, I love you dearly, but I think you are being naive," Carol stated. "Joe will find out sooner or later, and then you will pay dearly for deceiving him. And you need to be realistic. I worry that you may pay with your life. Domestic abuse can be fatal."

"Let me think about it. I would like to go home at my usual time today and see how things go, at least for tonight," Inge replied emphatically.

"If you insist," Ken said, "but you know where we are and you are most welcome to stay here for as long as you want. And if you get into any trouble tonight, just call me and I will come and get you."

Carol drove Inge back to the hospital and Inge then drove home on her own. Carol followed her, parking down the street, and insisted on staying with her until Joe got home, leaving by the front door as Joe came in from the garage.

Carol and Ken worried about Inge all evening and called her at about 9:30.

Inge confided that Joe had quizzed her about John Doe, but she had revealed nothing. She said that Joe had already downed six rum and cokes and had fallen asleep watching the Monday night football. She promised to visit Carol again the next morning.

* * *

The officer at the bedside reported Inge's identification of John Doe to the division sergeant, and he decided to dispatch three officers to Dr. Turle's home to check it out. There was only one "Turle, Redfern" in the Canada 411 directory. Best to send Sergeant Bimini and Constable Paula Kaufman, he thought, as they are very familiar with the case and are still on duty together. Then Dr. Ben Speckle stopped by the bedside, as he had promised, and reviewed the X-rays of the facial fractures. He agreed with Dr. Midges to book an urgent O.R. time to get John Doe's facial features back to as close to normal as possible. Dr. Midges asked him to consider guiding a feeding tube through the reconstructed nose into the stomach while he was in the operating room and he agreed to do so. Then Martin Midges asked Ben Speckle if he recognized Dr. Leslie Turle and the skin growth that he believed Speckle had assessed on him the previous Friday.

"I never knew Leslie well, but this guy doesn't look like the Leslie I knew. And I most assuredly did not assess Dr. Turle or this guy last week. That looks like a benign keratoacanthoma. I'll snip it off in the OR if we find someone to give consent for that. The facial repair consent is not a problem—I'll sign an emergency consent form for that."

He promptly left to call Operating Room Bookings and request an urgent time to repair the face of John Doe, a.k.a. Dr. Leslie Turle, but he would have to coordinate this with someone from the dental department. When he checked with his secretary, she related that Dr. Turle had indeed dropped into her office the previous Friday, and she had set up an outpatient appointment for him for February 24.

Dr. Midges was confused. Had Inge Glacier not told him just an hour before that Dr. Speckle had assessed that spot on Dr. Turle's neck just the previous Friday? *Who is lying?* he wondered.

9

revelations

Velma Turle was pleased with herself as she drove home. She felt she had made great progress in enlisting the help of Nancy and Isaac to deal with Leslie's deterioration. Then she noticed the empty garbage can at the end of the driveway. At least Leslie got up in time to take it out for the early pickup, she thought. But he always retrieved it as soon as it was emptied. She drove her old Smart car into the garage and retrieved the empty can. As she was unpacking, the doorbell rang. Thinking that it must be Leslie, who was apparently not in the house and had probably gone for a walk without his keys yet again, Velma answered it. Introducing herself, Constable Paula Kaufman asked if they could come in as they had important information to discuss with her. Sergeant Bimini and another officer from a second cruiser followed her in and sat down, the third officer taking notes.

"Is this the home of Dr. Turle?"

"Yes."

"Is he here?"

"LESLIE!" Velma shouted. "I think he must have gone out for a walk. I just got home."

Paula then explained that she was investigating the possibility that Dr. Turle had gone missing and was possibly in hospital in critical condition. The officers explained the situation in more detail and asked for permission to search the house. A distraught and tearful Velma gave them permission and began the search with them. Paula Kaufman quickly found the empty scotch glass on the kitchen counter and the appointment card for Dr. Ben Speckle and put them in an evidence bag. Velma found Leslie's wallet on the bedside table and checked the contents. It contained about $25 and all of his credit cards, his driver's licence, and his health card. The officer watching her asked her to give him the health card so that he could take it to the hospital, then reflected and said that she could keep it, as she would be going to the hospital anyway. She found the birthday present that Leslie had left, and wryly noted to Paula that at least he had remembered her upcoming birthday, unlike the year before.

Sergeant Bimini explained as delicately as he was capable that they believed that Dr. Turle had been lured to Beaver Park by a gay man on Friday night, and had been robbed, stripped, and thrown over the bank of the Beaver River.

"You mean that the John Doe in the news is Leslie? No way!"

Velma vehemently denied that Leslie had any gay tendencies, and when asked, also denied that he ever used any street drugs. Bimini indicated that they would have to seize the home computer and Leslie's iPad to search for evidence and that they would also be reviewing their phone records maintained by Bell Canada.

After Velma stopped sobbing, with Paula Kaufaman emphasizing to her that she was under no suspicion and that Leslie was alive and might recover, the third officer returned to his cruiser and filed a report to the detectives at Headquarters, while Sergeant Bimini searched the email files for evidence, finding nothing incriminating. But he noted that Dr. Turle had not opened or sent any emails since 6:00 p.m. on Friday the 13th. Finding the interesting computer file called "Leslie's Bucket List," he commented to Velma about the adventures that seemed unrealistically ambitious. He then asked Velma to come to the hospital with him to confirm the identity of the critically ill patient they now were sure was Dr. Leslie Turle. He asked Paula to continue the search of the home, take some photographs, and talk to the neighbours as well. When she called on the neighbours, only one was at home, and she indicated that the only unusual thing she had noticed was that Leslie had put the garbage pail out for pickup the previous Friday. He usually did so just minutes before the pickup. And she had not seen him out on his daily walks since the previous Thursday.

Detective Sergeant Joe Pickett at headquarters discussed the situation with the officer filing the report from the Turle house, and they agreed that he should meet Mrs. Turle at the hospital. It would be less stressful for her if a plainclothes detective, rather than a uniformed officer, accompanied her through the familiar hospital corridors to the ICU; and he could quickly close the Forensic ID file on John Doe if Velma Turle gave them positive identification.

Bimini introduced Pickett to Velma in the hospital lobby and returned to help with the search of the Turle house, determined to find something that would support his belief that Eric Clouser was responsible for Dr. Turle's fate. When Velma and Joe Pickett reached the ICU, startled and sympathetic staff greeted her and led her to John Doe's bedside.

"That is not my husband. He has a beard, and this fellow is far too old to be Leslie."

A nurse then pulled down the warming blanket and exposed the growth on John Doe's neck. Velma suddenly began to sob uncontrollably to the point that everyone present knew immediately that John Doe was Dr. Leslie Turle, without her needing to say a word.

Dr. Martin Midges asked the team leader filling in for Inge Glacier to notify the hospital business office and the CEO. Velma handed the nurse Leslie's all-important health card. Velma wished she had her best friend with her at that point, but knew that she had just left for Florida; the ICU social worker would have to provide the only support she could expect over the next few hours.

Brook Falone, on receiving the news on a note handed to him by his secretary, immediately went to the ICU. He expressed his sympathies to Velma and invited her and Sergeant Pickett to come with him to his office. There, between tears, she requested that they not notify anyone until she had contacted the rest of the family. She was handed the phone and called Isaac's home number, then his cell phone, but there was no answer at either. *Likely both Isaac and Nancy are still at work,* she thought. She knew that she could reach Isaac at work through the Kingston office of ADT, but did not mention that. When Joe Pickett, asking where Isaac worked, offered to ask the Kingston police to contact Isaac through ADT, she declined, saying that she wanted the news to come directly from her, so as not to alarm Isaac by having the police contact him.

Joe Pickett promised to release no information from the police department.

"This is going to be hard for you. We will not say a word until you okay it. The media are going to go wild."

Brook Falone called the one-person public relations department, and the spokeswoman from there joined them in his office. They drafted a statement to be read as a later press release, and the spokeswoman notified the usual media contacts to expect breaking news about John Doe later in the evening.

Velma returned to the ICU and sat at her comatose husband's bedside. The only response she could get from him was a single brief eye opening when she yelled his name. Dr. Midges and Winki came by and asked her to join them in the quiet room outside of the ICU to get an update. The ICU social worker and the acting Team Leader also came along. As they walked to the room, Dr. Midges asked Dr. Pham if she wanted to lead the discussion, but she declined, saying that she really didn't feel comfortable explaining such a complicated problem, especially when the patient was a fellow physician. After carefully explaining that Dr. Turle was critically ill, but with nothing that was inevitably fatal, Dr. Midges asked Velma to fill them in on the medical history of John Doe, a.k.a. Dr. Leslie Turle.

"Well, since he retired, his health has deteriorated dramatically." she stated. "But prior to that, he was always healthy."

"In what way has he deteriorated? Can you be more specific?" Dr. Midges inquired.

Velma related all of the concerns she had expressed to Nancy and Isaac that weekend, emphasizing the conclusion that Leslie had Alzheimer's disease.

"Was he taking any medication?" Dr. Midges asked.

"None. He wouldn't even take an aspirin."

"Allergies?"

"None."

"Alcohol problems?"

"None. He only drank at most about two or three drinks a week."

"Did you know that he is profoundly hypothyroid?"

"No. He never said anything about that."

"Well, he probably didn't know it, but he is."

"What symptoms would that cause?" Velma asked. "I should probably explain that I worked here many years ago as a dietitian, but my knowledge about medical things is pretty rusty now, outside of the world of nutrition."

Dr. Midges, sensing a good teaching opportunity, asked Dr. Pham to answer her question. Dr. Pham hesitated, composing an explanation of the role of the thyroid that would be understandable to a layperson, in her head.

"Well, the thyroid gland is like the throttle for the whole body. When it fails to produce enough hormones, everything slows down, physical activity, mental functions, metabolism, everything. Typically, people slowly get lethargic, develop a hoarse voice, and gain weight. They sleep excessively and become intolerant of the cold. In cases as severe as his, they may get confused and even go in to a coma. And they often get depressed."

"That certainly explains a lot. He was very intolerant of the cold in the last six months. He always wore long johns and three layers of clothes around the house, even though we keep it at 20 Celsius in the winter."

"Have you observed any other changes in his behaviour recently?" Dr. Midges asked.

"Last week he was complaining all week about being itchy from head to toe."

"That is interesting" Martin Midges noted. "He is jaundiced. Has he ever had jaundice before?"

"Not as far as I know."

The social worker spoke up to ask what he could do to help Velma cope with the new reality, and offered to arrange for her to stay overnight in the hospital guest suite used for relatives of critically ill patients. She graciously accepted and said that she would return home by taxi to get some belongings and come back. He also asked if she wanted to have a member of the clergy come to talk to her, and she declined. She would call Isaac and Nancy while she was at home.

On their way back to the ICU together, Martin Midges congratulated Winki for her layman's explanation of the function of the thyroid gland and said that he could use the throttle analogy in the future.

"And I'm glad that you didn't mention that when we find hypothyroidism in the investigation of dementia, the dementia usually persists even after the thyroid problem is corrected. She didn't need to hear that now."

"Well, that was because I did not know that," Winki confessed.

"Well, the dementia often persists, but at times it just goes away, and it is certainly worthwhile to check thyroid function when dealing with new-onset dementia, because it is one of the easiest, simplest, and cheapest treatments you can ever prescribe." Dr. Midges said. "And at times the results are remarkable."

"One other problem," Winki Pham noted. "If he isn't an alcoholic with cirrhosis, why is he jaundiced?"

"Well, the itch doesn't fit with alcoholic liver disease either. It is much more common with bile duct obstruction, and the liver enzyme pattern is more in keeping with biliary obstruction." Martin commented.

"Maybe he has a cancer of the pancreas or of the bile duct. His pancreatic enzyme levels are a bit high."

"Or?"

"Well, I don't know. He could have something as simple as a gallstone in his bile duct. I guess the pancreatic enzyme elevation could be due to gallstone pancreatitis and not alcoholic pancreatitis."

"Exactly. You should always hope to find something you can do something about. No one is ever going to be too upset if you miss something that you can't treat anyway, but a gallstone in the bile duct—now, that is easily treated."

"Let's do an ultrasound of his liver and bile ducts, then."

The news about the identity of John Doe ran through the hospital gossip lines faster than a cheetah on steroids. Many of the staff that knew him well expressed no surprise that he had apparently gone out snowshoeing in a snowstorm. Those who were not aware of his adventurous nature, expressed amazement that he had been lured out in to a snowstorm for sex or drugs, as some media reports over the weekend had suggested. Few staff that knew him paid any heed to the request for privacy, which the Turle family had made at the end of the hospital news release and went to the ICU to see him, and to express concern and wish Velma well. There were so many that, at the request of Dr. Glenna Bass, a hospital security guard was assigned to the doors to the ICU to turn away everyone except immediate family.

* * *

On Tuesday morning, Inge left at the usual early hour as though she were going to work, but drove to Ken and Carol's home instead. She picked up the Toronto Star from their front porch, and Carol welcomed her in. As they sat at the kitchen table, Carol searched through the newspaper for any news about John Doe. The story, again on the front page of the GTA Section read:

John Doe Identified as Prominent Local Physician
— *Garth Rowley, Staff Reporter*

The Beaverbrook Hospital and the Redfern Regional Police Services have announced that the man known only as John Doe has been identified as Dr. Leslie Turle, a retired prominent local physician. A senior nurse at the hospital, who recognized him from her previous work with him, first made the identification; his family has confirmed it. The identification was not made earlier because his severe facial injuries made him almost unrecognizable. Police are not speculating on why he was wandering in Beaver Park in the midst of a snowstorm last Friday evening. He is still listed as in critical condition and ironically is being treated in the hospital's intensive care unit where he was formerly the medical director. The police have charged 31-year-old Eric Clouser of Shacletown with the attempted murder of Dr.Turle, and with possession of marijuana for the purpose of trafficking. Clouser was arrested as he tried to flee from the park shortly after a 911 caller reported the discovery of the critically injured nude victim on the banks of the Beaver River. The family of Dr. Turle request that the media and the public respect their need for privacy in this situation.

It struck Inge that someone at the hospital had given the
reporter information about her identification of John Doe, *but
who would that be?* she wondered. In a way, it didn't matter;
the news was out there, and she knew that Joe would have read
it. Ken Creek joined them at the breakfast table and Carol reread
the report to him. He noticed a new bruise on Inge's wrist, and
concluded that Joe had assaulted her again the night before, but
thought that it was not necessary or even kind to point that observation out to her.

"Inge," he said softly, "you can't go back home. When Joe finds
out that you were that senior nurse, he will show no mercy. You
may need a restraining order against him. You are going to stay
here for the next while."

"I guess you are right; I expect Joe will read the *Star*—he always
does—and quiz me about John Doe if I go back home tonight. I
really don't have much choice, do I?"

"Not if you value your life," Carol inserted.

They planned their strategy together. Carol called a co-worker
to switch with her for a half shift she was due to work later that
day, and she, Ken, and Inge all drove to Inge's home, on the west
side of the Beaver River, well north of Beaver Park. Ken suggested
that they should change the locks on the house and stay with Inge
to protect her when Joe came home.

Inge thought about this but then said the house held bad memories for her and she would prefer to be the one to move out. They
loaded up tote boxes of her clothes, jewellery, and personal papers,
including her passport and her will. She retrieved her MacBook
laptop. Inge left a note on the kitchen counter: "I will not be back. I
think you know why. Please do not come looking for me. I will be
seeking a divorce. Inge."

They took three carloads of her belongings back to the Creek
house. They parked Inge's car in the garage and closed the door in
case Joe decided to cruise the neighbourhood looking for her when
he got home and found the note.

Later in the evening, Inge decided to call Kevin and fill him
in on the developments. It would not be easy, with Kevin's pious
belief in the sanctity of marriage, but she hoped that he would
understand her plight. She need not have worried. Kevin related

that he had already had a call from an irate Joe Glacier, and had said truthfully that he knew nothing about his mother's where-abouts. Kevin said that Joe was slurring his words and uttered a string of unrepeatable expletives to the priest when Kevin had suggested that he could help Joe with his drinking problem and perhaps persuade Inge to give him another chance. Kevin was obviously relieved to know that she was safe, and asked what he could do to help her, saying that he understood perfectly why she felt she had no choice but to leave Joe.

"I knew you and Joe were not a fit, and until he stops drinking, you should stay clear of him. I am trying to be charitable to him, but there is a limit." He promised to give Joe no information about her, and said he could come to discuss her new reality in person after conducting a funeral service the next morning. They agreed to meet at an Italian eatery in Shacletown at 5:30 p.m. He would make the reservation.

Later that night, Inge lay awake, reviewing her options. She would certainly never return to live with Joe. She could find an apartment in St. Catharines to be closer to Kevin, but she feared that he might be moved at the whim of the bishop any time. He was a diocesan priest unattached to any order of priests, so the bishop was free to move him as the need arose. She had many friends and acquaintances in Redfern and would miss them if she moved far away. About midnight, she fell into a sound sleep, somehow more relaxed than she had been in many months, and did not awaken until 7:30 the next morning.

Carol called from the ICU at about 9:30 that Wednesday morn-ing. She recounted how Velma Turle had confirmed that John Doe was indeed Dr. Leslie Turle, and the news was all over the hospi-tal. Carol also related that Dr. Ben Speckle had denied having seen Dr. Turle the previous Friday. *Why had Dr. Turle lied to her about that? Or was it Dr. Speckle who was lying? But there was no earthly reason for him to lie so it must have been Leslie.* Dr. Turle's condition had not changed much, and his name, now Dr. Leslie Turle and not John Doe, was still "on the board" in the OR bookings for urgent repair of his facial injuries. Carol had asked to not be assigned to care for him as she felt it would be too emotionally draining to do so. Early that Wednesday morning, the clerk at the ICU desk had received a

call from Joe Glacier asking to speak to Inge. She put her hand over
the mouthpiece and paged Carol Creek.

"What should I tell him?" she inquired. "He seems very upset."

"Just tell him that she can't come to the phone right now,"
Carol instructed.

The hospital news release confirming the identity of John Doe
had been delayed until late Monday evening after Velma Turle's
consent and approval of its wording.

Inge, alone in the home of Carol and Ken Creek, again reviewed
her options for the future. There was a call from Joe later in the day,
but she recognized the number and refused to answer it, and he
left no message. She made a firm decision to proceed with seeking a divorce, and late in the afternoon called a recently divorced
acquaintance to get the name of a law firm to represent her. She got
the names of two, and called the first. She had mixed feelings when
the clerk related that they would be unable to represent her, as they
had just agreed to represent her husband. At least Joe was preparing to get on with a divorce and was not going to beg her to come
back. The next law firm agreed to take her case and Anita Wade
called her back to set up an appointment for Thursday morning.
Inge was most impressed with the understanding and empathy
that the lawyer expressed on the phone.

She next turned her thoughts to her job. She knew that she
would find it difficult, if not impossible, to return to the nursing
team leader role in the ICU of the Beaverbrook Hospital. She called
the HR department and got an update on her pension, outstand-
ing sick days, and their policies with respect to compassionate or
stress leave. She then explained the considerable stress she was
experiencing with her identification of John Doe and her sudden
recent decision to seek a divorce.

"I know all about the situation with Dr. Turle—you were the
one who identified him. I will grant you two weeks paid compassionate leave, and then we can discuss where we go from there.
This must a terrible stress for you. You have my sympathy." Inge
thanked her and hung up.

Her next considerations were about her living arrangements.
She hated taking advantage of Carol and Ken's generous hospi-
tality, and decided that she would find an apartment of her own

as soon as possible. Online, she found three such apartments that were immediately available and made appointments to view all of them on Friday. *Wednesday is for Kevin, Thursday is for the lawyer, and Friday is for apartment hunting,* she thought. By Christmas, she hoped to have her own place, her process for divorce started, and a final decision about her employment future. She reflected that Christmas would be lonely, but perhaps better than the one the year before when Joe had gotten very drunk and had tried unsuccessfully to have sex with her, pinning her down on the bed and climbing on top of her. He had then promptly passed out, his hiccoughs jarring her and his boozy, smoky breath making her nauseated.

The dinner with Kevin was very pleasant and he showed a surprising amount of understanding of her domestic and emotional difficulties. *Perhaps one does not need to have firsthand experience with marriage and sex to understand the difficulties they inevitably bring with them,* she reflected. On her drive home, she had an distinct sense that she had met Kevin at some point prior to their later reconciliation, but she couldn't recall where or when that might have been. The next morning, trying to sleep, she was neither awake nor asleep when she had a lucid dream. She saw herself sitting on a park bench with a tall, lanky curly-haired boy and an open book. She was reading to him and teaching him the proper pronunciation of the Latin Salve Regina. Suddenly, she sat up, grabbed her cellphone and sent a text message to Kevin. "Were you ever an altar boy in the Church?"

Later that morning Kevin called her. "I was an altar server-that is what we call them now since girls are allowed to serve as well-in my early teens. Why do you ask?"

"Then I think you were at my wedding!"

"Strange thought. I doubt it. I can't remember seeing you, and I never served at any wedding in Redfern."

"We were married in a church in Burlington that is now closed, as our church was undergoing renovations."

"Strange coincidence. I was an altar boy there; that is where I grew up. I thought when you first introduced me to Joe that I had seen him somewhere before. Maybe it was at your wedding. What year?"

"Let's see. That was when I was thirty, so you would be twelve."

"Then I guess I was there. Small world!"

The meeting with Anita Wade on Thursday also went well. The lawyer seemed sympathetic and intrigued as Inge related her reasons for seeking a divorce. She had also heard the story about John Doe on the news. Anita asked if she felt that she needed a restraining order to keep Joe from pursuing her, and Inge declined, saying that Joe was apparently already getting ready for the divorce. She never even mentioned the possibility of reconciliation with Joe, sensing the finality of Inge's decision to proceed with divorce. On the phone, she had requested that Inge bring in a copy of her Last Will and Testament, and when Inge handed that to her, she asked an associate to join them and set up an urgent time to meet with Inge to revise that document.

They reviewed the financial arrangements in the marriage. Joe and Inge had maintained separate bank accounts, pensions, and investment portfolios, and there were no custody issues. But Inge had contributed her share to the mortgage payments and would be entitled to 50 percent of the value of the house and contents.

The lawyer explained the requirements: "A separation agreement with an agreed equalization payment of net family assets comes first. In the absence of a separation agreement, we need to wait a year. Even with a separation agreement, we wait months after that is filed before being granted an absolute decree of divorce, as Canadian law no longer uses decree nisi in divorce cases. But if you are in a rush and can testify to abuse in court, we can speed this up, with or without a separation agreement."

"Let's try for an agreement. You and your husband will need to fill out this financial disclosure form and then I can write a draft agreement with you and send it to his lawyer."

Inge said that she was in no hurry. "I certainly do not want to testify to abuse in court. I'll get this form back to you, probably tomorrow."

The hunt for an apartment was more difficult. The first two that she saw that Friday were dirty, old, and in a neighbourhood that seemed to be mostly populated by new immigrants with little or nothing in common with her. The third, on the ninth floor of an apartment a kilometre from the hospital, was a six-month sublet from a recently widowed woman who had already moved out. It was neat, larger than she needed, expensive, and came with some old furniture, but it was a short-term commitment and it would have to do. She signed the documents and planned to move in before Christmas.

By that Friday, she decided that she did not want to be reminded about Dr. Turle any longer. She could never understand why he had lied to her, and he would never be part of her future. She asked Carol to stop giving her daily reports of his progress. She had managed to deceive almost everyone about her domestic abuse and about her son and took pride in doing so successfully. But she held to a double standard when it came to others trying to deceive her, and considered any such attempts as ad hominem attacks on her integrity and her intelligence. And Dr. Leslie Turle, her idol of all people, had certainly deliberately tried to deceive her and had succeeded in doing so. For lack of a better explanation, she believed the media stories about him being lured out into a snowstorm for drugs or sex. It fit with her knowledge of his thrill-seeking nature, but she was upset with herself because she had never detected any hint of this in her interactions with him, and was angry that she had been deceived so completely by him a week before. She decided that she did not want to be associated with such an individual.

* * *

Velma Turle phoned Isaac from home at 5:05 p.m. on the Monday of her grim discovery. "Are you sitting down?" she asked. "Guess what? Remember that story about John Doe in Beaver Park on the weekend? John Doe is your father! He is in critical condition in the ICU, but the medical team are doing everything they can to save him."

Isaac was stunned, but was somehow not surprised that the old man had apparently gone snowshoeing in a storm. After a lengthy discussion, Isaac agreed to come to the hospital the next morning, and would also call his sister in Baltimore.

"The news will break sometime later tonight," Velma warned Isaac. "Don't expect the media hounds to leave us alone for the next few days."

* * *

Dr. Barbara Turle–Knott, Ph.D., had started to grade the term paper that one of the five students in her Ethics in Modern Society course in the Masters program at St. Andrew's College had turned in. She had asked them to describe five separate scenarios where a modern person would act differently if he/she were an existential-ist, a religious follower of the Golden Rule, or a humanist follow-ing the expanded consequence-based decision-making model of ethics espoused by Dr. Robert Buckman.

"Who can complain that philosophy is not a practical disci-pline?" she had asked her class as she discussed this assignment, emphasizing that all three actions should be different from each other.

Then Isaac called to relate the news about her father. To say that she was shocked to hear that John Doe was her estranged father would be the grossest of understatements. An hour later, she had calmed down enough to discuss the situation with her jet-lagged husband, Lyle Knott.

At 34, she was pregnant, and it was considered to be a high-risk pregnancy, as she had had two previous miscarriages; her due date was February 15. She could use some of her maternity or sick leave at any point, and they agreed that she should fly to Toronto to help if she could. *Could she also learn to tolerate or even like Velma, as Isaac suggested?* she wondered. She would use Tuesday to make the arrangements for time off with the HR department at St. Andrews, and fly on Wednesday. She checked with her obstetrician and the airline on Tuesday and got permission to fly even though she was 31 weeks pregnant. After booking a flight online, she called Isaac back, and he agreed to pick her up at Pearson International Airport on Wednesday morning.

Before noon on Tuesday, Isaac arrived in the ICU. With a new appreciation of Velma's distress and love for Leslie, he greeted her warmly with a big hug; it was the first time that they had ever embraced. Isaac was never comfortable around anyone who was sick or in hospital, and was horrified by the appearance of his comatose, unrecognizable father on the breathing machine in the ICU bed with several beeping machines at his side. He quickly persuaded Velma to go to the ICU waiting room to talk.

"Barb is coming in tomorrow. How do you feel about her getting involved? I think she is feeling very guilty about losing touch with dad and you, and is ready to make up."

Velma indicated that she held no animosity for Barb, and would welcome both Barb and Isaac into her home. "If both of you can stand me," she said.

* * *

Dr. Midges and Winki updated Velma and Isaac in the early afternoon. Leslie was responding to painful stimuli and opening his eyes. Velma even got him to squeeze her hand. His temperature was up to 34.1 and his blood pressure was 80/38 with a pulse of 46. The noradrenalin infusion was going to be tapered and stopped after Dr. Ben Speckle and a dentist finished repairing the facial fracture, and they had a time slot in the operating room to do that at 2:00 p.m. Velma signed the consent form for that operation, including removal of the neck growth. After the surgery, the team planned to start thyroxin treatment through the tube that Dr. Speckle would place through the reconstructed nose into Leslie's stomach. And they would do an abdominal ultrasound later in the week to investigate the jaundice and itch. Hopefully, said Dr. Midges, the orthopaedic service would be able to find a time to repair the tibial fracture as well before the weekend. It would be a busy week for Dr. Leslie Turle, but everyone, including the previously skeptical Dr. Glenna Bass, was now working on the assumption that he might just recover completely.

Glenna Bass reflected on the lesson she learned from this case. *In the future, avoid making any premature value judgements about patients that you do not know well.* She had made erroneous assumptions and a value judgment about the worthiness of John Doe's life, and then erroneous diagnoses of his condition based on those wrong assumptions.

Isaac decided to stay at Velma's overnight. On Wednesday morning when Velma returned to the hospital, she was stunned by the almost magical reconstruction of Leslie's face. He had a new nose covered in white bloodstained dressings that made it look like a ski jump, and a mouth and lips that looked almost normal. His cheeks were covered in dressings, and a nasogastric tube had been inserted in his nose. The old dietician in her made her check the contents of the feedings in the bottle: diluted Boost VHC, a product that she knew well, as she had often recommended it in her years there as a dietician, but without the VHC, an acronym for Very High Calorie. At that time, it had been known as Carnation Instant Breakfast. A nurse disconnected the tube and injected a dose of thyroxin directly into the tube. Velma returned home at noon and met Isaac and Barb. Barb greeted her with a hug and a simple, "I'm sorry."

Velma was startled by the distinct baby bump she noticed as she hugged Barb.

"You're sorry for what?" Velma asked. "I think it is I who should apologize."

"I'm sorry for what Dad is going through and for what I have put you and him through over the years."

"Do you want to see him?" Velma asked. "He looks so much better than he did yesterday."

"Yes. The sooner, the better."

"Isaac, do you want to come along?" Velma asked.

Isaac declined, saying that he would visit his father later in the evening before returning home to Kingston. Velma drove Barb to the hospital and inquired about the obvious bulge in Barb's abdomen, receiving the news of the possible impending arrival of a new step-grandson warmly. She warned Barb as they entered the ICU to not be too shocked by Leslie's appearance, but it did little to prepare Barb for what she saw.

"Oh, my God!" Barb exclaimed as she stared at her father for the first time in almost sixteen years. "I don't think I was prepared for this." There was suddenly a violent kick to her abdominal wall.

"Why don't you see if you can get a response from him?" Velma suggested.

"Dad, it's Barbara," she shouted. "Can you squeeze my hand?" This time there was not only a definite squeeze, but also his eyes flew open, and he stared at her. And a distinct transient smile appeared on his newly reconstructed lips.

"That is more of a response than anyone has gotten so far," Velma exclaimed. "He certainly recognized you."

On Thursday, Dr. Winki Pham reported more good news to Velma and Barb at the bedside. The abdominal ultrasound had been reported to show a normal liver, pancreas, and spleen, and multiple stones in the gallbladder; the common bile duct was dilated to 18 mm, with an opacity seen just above the pancreas within the bile duct.

"Can you translate that into English for me?" Barb asked.

"Sorry. I can do better than that," Dr. Pham responded. She fiddled with the bedside computer until the ultrasound images appeared on the screen and showed them to Velma and Barb. "In English, the reason for his jaundice is that he has a gallstone stuck right here in the bile duct," pointing to the screen. "That is keeping bile from draining from his liver, here, down this tree-like structure in black, here, to his small bowel, down here," again pointing on the screen. "It is like a dam in a river, and the river, in this case the bile duct in black, gets wider and wider, and little or no bile gets though. The bile pigment that leaks back into the blood is yellow and causes the jaundice."

"Well, how do you plan to get rid of the stone?" Velma asked.

"The usual way is to do an ERCP and remove the stone. Sorry—'ERCP' stands for endoscopic retrograde cholaniopancre-atography. In simple terms, that involves using a fibre optic tube through the mouth to the stomach and small bowel, finding the opening where the bile duct drains into the small bowel, and with some instruments pulling the stone out of the duct. It is a fiddly procedure, but usually very successful in relieving the obstruction. It may be a challenge to get the tube in through his mouth, as his tongue is very swollen, but I have been with Dr. Tellico when he does these procedures here and he is pretty slick at that."

"When can you get on with that?" Velma asked.

"We may have trouble getting that scheduled before the endoscopy clinic is closed except for emergencies for the Christmas break, but I am going to call Dr. Tellico right now and see if it can be done on Monday."

On their Friday visit, Barb and Velma found Leslie moving his hands in what appeared to be attempts to scratch his arms. His smile was more obvious and his eyes tracked them as they moved around the room. He was still hooked up to the breathing machine, but the nurse said that he was breathing on his own except at night, and might be weaned from the ventilator completely over the weekend.

On Friday afternoon, Dr. Tony Tellico explained the procedure for removing the gallstone in more detail and said he would fight hard to get a time to do that the following Monday, in spite of the closures for the holidays. He called the endoscopy clinic from the bedside and then called his colleague who was scheduled for procedures there on Monday mornings. The colleague agreed to reschedule an elective ERCP and slot Dr. Tellico in to do his ERCP instead as soon as he heard the patient's name, reminding Dr. Tellico to reciprocate at some point. The orthopaedic surgeon came by and was annoyed that he had been consulted only on Thursday about a fracture that had been sustained the previous Friday. None of the team had completed the online request for consultation to him and Winki, as the most junior member of the team, took the blame for the delay. The repair of the fracture was surgically completed on Saturday, with open reduction and internal fixation with a rod in the tibia, and a cast was applied.

Over the weekend, Leslie's condition continued to improve, but he could not talk, because of the tracheostomy. He refused to write anything on the slate the nurse provided to facilitate communication, but nodded his head when she asked if he was thirsty. Redfern Regional Police Services finally decided that a guard at the bedside was not necessary. They would send a detective back to interview him and get a statement if or when the hospital indicated that he was able to talk and was coherent and rational. But he still spent long periods not responding to anyone.

On Monday, around noon, a beaming Dr. Tony Tellico walked into the ICU waiting room and handed Velma a clear plastic bag containing a 1.7-cm shiny, golden-brown, multifaceted hard stone with smooth sides and sharp angles.

"I fished that out of his bile duct a few minutes ago. His jaundice should be gone in three or four days. But there are more in his gallbladder. He will need to have that out at some point in a few months." There was now nothing in Leslie's situation that looked at all likely to be fatal.

That night, Velma called Isaac and Nancy, inviting them to bring Adam to the Redfern house that Isaac had spent a lot of time in, to celebrate what was to be in many ways a very different Christmas for all of them than what they had planned just a few days earlier. Then Barb called Lyle and asked if he could get a flight to Toronto before Christmas to join them. Lyle Knott's response was immediate. He would pack up and drive to Redfern the next day and stay as long as he was needed. He got the address and planned his route on Google Maps.

* * *

At the preliminary hearing on Monday morning, Paul Albright, following his client's instructions, declined to apply for bail on behalf of Eric Clouser. He decided not to indicate what plea Eric would enter at trial, reckoning that if he did indicate that he would plead guilty to the trafficking charge, Eric might well be sent for an expedited trial and would be sent to a Kingston facility earlier than if they entered no plea, in which case Eric would be held in custody at a much newer and better facility somewhere closer. The justice of the peace felt he had no choice other than to order that Eric be remanded in custody at the local facility until a trial date, which might be set for many months later.

Eric was returned to the district lockup and looked forward to a Merry Christmas there—good, free Christmas dinner, warmth, and free accommodations. *What more could he hope for? Perhaps Tom would pay him a visit on Christmas Day.*

10

forget it

By New Year's Eve, Dr. Turle was completely free of the ventilator and was moved to a general medicine ward. Velma visited
him daily, and the staff members were all very impressed by her
dedication to his recovery, although at times she seemed unrea-
sonable in her requests for them to attend to what she perceived
as his needs. But she, Isaac, and Barbara were the only people
who could get him to communicate and obey commands. He
remained mute. When the nurses asked him questions, he invariably remained mute and sometimes nodded or shook his head,
but at other times didn't even do that. Velma spent hours trying to
get him to swallow the pureed food the kitchen sent on his meal
trays daily, with limited success. Even with the neck opening to the
trachea taped off and healing over, he refused to speak or even to
moan or yell.

In early January, Detective Inspector Jim Hendrickson called to
ask if Dr. Turle was able to give a statement to the police, and the
nursing team leader on the ward indicated that he was not able to
do that, and probably never would be.

By the second week in January, Velma had some hard decisions
to make. Both Barbara and Isaac had returned to their homes, and
she updated them on the progress with daily, lengthy, and unduly
optimistic emails. However, she had neglected her business and
needed to either return to run it, or get rid of it. Her lease of space
in the medical office building would expire at the end of February,
and she announced to her staff that she was not going to renew
it. She was about to give the landlord her notice of non-renewal
as required in the lease agreement when one of the instructors
decided to continue the business and offered to take it over. Velma

had the change of tenant approved by the landlord and signed off. She could now focus all of her energy on the daunting task of getting her beloved Leslie back to his usual self.

A variety of investigations were performed to assess his cognitive functioning. An electroencephalogram was reported to show no focal abnormalities in his brain and only mild diffuse slowing of the brain's electrical activity. An MRI scan was reported to show no brain abnormality at all. His TSH level had fallen to 21, and the dose of thyroxin was gradually increased. By the end of January, thanks in large part to Velma's diligence, he was able to feed himself, and the nasogastric feeding tube was removed.

Dr. Will Turbot, the internal medicine specialist now supervising Leslie's care, met with Velma frequently and was puzzled and frustrated. He strongly hinted that she should accept that her husband needed long-term care in a chronic care hospital or a nursing home. But the doctor was also faced with an unanswerable question. *Why was his patient still refusing to talk or write when the brain imaging showed a normal brain, including the Broca's area, which was mainly responsible for controlling speech and language?* Velma begged him to not even apply to move Leslie for at least a week or two and to do something more to better define the reason for his poor communication; he reluctantly agreed.

The next day, Leslie's best friend, Dr. Faisal Al Taqi, dropped in to visit. The nurse and Velma witnessed a most remarkable response. Leslie opened his eyes widely, gave Faisal a broad smile, and distinctly said "Hi, Faisal," as he reached out and shook his hand. Faisal persuaded him to sit up at the edge of the bed and tried to get a further few words out of him, but to no avail. Velma's response to Leslie's first utterance in a month, and that of the nurse were identical.

"Wow! He can talk!" they exclaimed in unison. "And identify people," Velma added.

Her email update to Barb and Isaac that evening reflected her optimism and enthusiasm. "He is going to recover completely! Today he started to talk!" It was almost like a mother hearing her deaf child utter his first garbled words after a cochlear implant.

When Velma related this episode to Dr. Turbot on his rounds the next morning, he was skeptical, until the nurse confirmed that their patient had clearly spoken two appropriate words. Velma suggested that they should have a speech language pathologist assess Leslie. Dr. Turbot was already considering the possibility that his patient's muteness was not because of a physical ailment at all but due to severe emotional trauma. *Is my patient mute because of a hysterical conversion reaction that he has developed to blank out bad memories?* However, he agreed to consult the speech language pathologist. After three days and detailed assessment by the pathologist, Leslie was talking in short sentences, but not always rationally. The speech language pathologist's report concluded that there was no evidence of a physical defect in his brain control centres for speech or in the muscles used to speak and stated firmly that his limitations appeared to be primarily due to profound amnesia or possibly had a psychological basis. She concluded that he would need to relearn how to talk, starting as a three-year-old.

His mobility and coordination also improved steadily. The ward physiotherapist was very busy but gave Velma instructions in bed exercises and assisted walking for him and she diligently forced him to go through these several times a day. In late January, X-rays of the tibial fracture showed good alignment and satisfactory healing and the rigid cast was replaced with a more flexible plastic walking cast although he was still prohibited from any weight bearing.

His recall and memory were a different matter. He had difficulty keeping track of the date and time, and a calendar was set up for him to tick off the days. He recognized some pictures of their home which Velma brought in and quizzed him about, but could not locate their house on her iPad Google Earth Map. And he claimed that he did not remember anything from his pre-Christmas activities. And when specifically asked, he claimed to have never heard of anyone called Eric Clouser. Even asking that question, Dr. Turbot noted, violated the first rule of assessing a patient's mental status; never ask a question to which you yourself cannot be sure of the correct answer.

A neurologist, asked to assess Leslie's memory deficits and amnesia, concurred with Dr. Turbot's conclusion that the problem lay in his psyche and not in his brain or muscles controlling speech; Velma, with her previous experience with a psychiatrist, agreed with his recommendation to have a psychiatrist assess Leslie.

The Request for Consultation form to the psychiatrist, Dr. Shanks, was terse, simply stating: "Profound amnesia. Hypnotherapy? Amytal interview?" However, when Dr. Shanks came by the next day, Leslie refused to talk to him at all. Dr. Shanks interviewed Velma outside the room and questioned her about why the team wanted or needed to get Leslie to recall the details of his traumatic experience, since his ability to retain new information and his recall of remote events was improving quickly and was close to normal, as Velma acknowledged.

"In my opinion, hypnosis is notorious for dredging up false memories as true events, and often events recalled with hypnosis are a peculiar jumble of events from different times in the past all mixed up together. And besides, there is no one at the hospital who is proficient in hypnotherapy. And the barbiturate Amytal, 'truth serum,' interviewing is passé. The more modern approach to eliciting drug-induced recall is to use a short-acting, newer sedative such as the benzodiazepine midazolam."

Leslie, straining to hear the conversation outside of the room heard Velma explain that the police were anxious to get Leslie's version of the events of Friday the 13th, as they were holding a man in custody in connection with the apparent assault and attempted murder of him. She also wanted to get to the truth about that fateful night, to clear her husband's reputation, as she was sure that he would never have responded to a gay man trying to tempt him out into a snowstorm for drugs or sex.

Dr. Shanks's response was immediate and decisive.

"If the primary reason for requesting an interview under drug-induced removal of inhibitions is for the police, they will need to obtain a warrant and observe and record the structured interview being done by a qualified forensic psychiatrist. If the reason is for your reassurance, you might be better off to live with the uncertainty, rather than with the answers that he might give."

Velma reluctantly agreed.

* * *

When Detective Inspector Jim Hendrickson called the hospital again in mid-February to inquire about the status of his star witness for the prosecution of Eric Clouser, the nursing team leader told him that Dr. Turle's memory was almost normal, but that he professed to have complete amnesia of all events that had occurred between early December and mid-January. She did not mention the possibility of an interview under drug-induced relaxation. Jim Hendrickson decided to pay Dr. Turle a surreptitious visit. Choosing a Saturday morning, he introduced himself to the information clerk as a friend of Dr. Turle's, and was directed to the room.

Hendrickson was lucky to be alone when he introduced himself to Leslie as a friend of Eric Clouser. He asked Leslie how he knew Eric. Leslie admitted to having heard the name, but denied ever meeting Eric. He immediately suspected some subterfuge on the part of his strange visitor. His nurse entered the room and Leslie complained to her about his unwelcome visitor. When Hendrickson explained that he was just a friend of a friend, Leslie told him to "bugger off," and the nurse also more politely asked him to leave her patient alone. With all the bizarre aspects of the case, she also wrote a note in the chart about the strange visit. Hendrickson had no choice but to leave promptly, with a sense that the evidence against Eric Clouser was evaporating quickly. The Crown might refuse to prosecute it at all. It appeared that he would have to rely entirely on the finding of the torn clothes at the scene to even make a case for a charge of assault.

* * *

By Christmas, Inge Glacier had signed the draft separation agreement, officially accepted the buyout package and pension from the hospital, and moved into her new sparsely furnished apartment. After Christmas, which she spent with Kevin in St. Catharines, she spent several days shopping for furniture, groceries, and small appliances that she could take with her when she moved again. She spent New Year's Eve with Kevin attending the Midnight Mass, and they stayed up until 3:00 a.m., chatting and planning for her future. Kevin was pleased to see his mother so happy after her turbulent December and her social upheavals.

On January the 4th, Ken and Carol Creek planned a surprise catered retirement party for Inge in their home, after checking to make sure that she would come for an "intimate dinner" with them that evening. When she walked in, about 25 well-wishers, mostly former co-workers and ICU staff greeted her, including Dr. Martin Midges and Dr. Glenna Bass. Carol had been careful to not invite Velma Turle, even though Inge had worked with her for years, sensing that Inge did not want to be reminded about the Turles at all.

Milling around a sumptuous catered meal and making small talk, Inge found herself beside Dr. Midges, and he pressed her about how she was coping. Without thinking, he gave her an update about Dr. Leslie Turle, saying that he was off the ventilator and had been moved to the Internal Medicine ward but appeared to have lost most of his ability to communicate with anyone. He predicted that Dr. Turle would spend the rest of his life in a nursing home somewhere. Inge remained calm but thought bitterly, *At least he won't be able to lie to me anymore.* But she simply said, "That's too bad. I feel sorry for Velma and the family."

Dr. Midges had already heard through the hospital grapevine about Inge's separation from her husband and asked her again how she was coping with all the recent changes in her life. Carol Creek had been diligent around the hospital in making sure that anyone talking about Inge's separation and retirement was informed that it had to do with Joe's drinking problem and never mentioned the abuse Inge had experienced or her infatuation with Dr. Turle. Inge replied that she was enjoying retirement and her new life as a single woman and joked that she was looking for an older, rich widower—"preferably in poor health."

In mid-January, Anita Brooks reviewed a draft separation agreement she had received from Joe's attorney and, after discussion with Inge, returned a revised counter-proposal, which Joe accepted promptly. In this, he would assume sole ownership of the matrimonial home, but would pay equalization payments totalling $180,000 to Inge, spread out over the next 24 months.

Over the next two months, Inge kept very busy. She began to volunteer as a parish nurse, caring for the homeless and needy in nearby Elmsville once or twice a week, and attended a continuing nursing education seminar on psychiatric nursing. She attended yoga classes once a week. She struck up a friendship with a lady from her apartment building, an avid curler and curling coach, who persuaded her to accept two 2-hour one-on-one lessons on an unused sheet of ice at the local club, and she took advantage of the club's offer of a single free beginner's lesson. She found that she enjoyed both the physical and mental challenges of precisely aiming 20 kilograms of granite on slippery ice at targets more than 45 metres away and getting them to stop at precisely the right spot or hit another rock at precisely the right angle and speed. She also enjoyed the social aspects of curling, meeting new people weekly; and the older male coaches all seemed to be keen to help her. She vowed to join a curling club somewhere for the next season. *Maybe I'll meet that older rich widower at the curling club,* she mused.

For a late February break from an awful winter, Carol Creek persuaded her to accompany her for a week's vacation in Cuba, flying to Varadero and staying at the Melia Peninsula Varadero. She flirted with a man from Markham that she met there, but would not give him her phone number or address and assured Carol that she would never again get into a serious relationship with any man. But she was pleased to see that she could still turn the heads of both younger and older men when walking on the beach.

Inge's supervisor for the street mission work suggested that she should attend an AA meeting to better understand the help they could offer to many of the alcoholic street people she was dealing with. She chose to attend the open noon meeting at the Westfield Community Church. She arrived early and sat in the back corner of the room, hiding behind a newspaper. The leader, before the meeting, asked her why she was there and she replied that she was a professional nurse observer working with the disadvantaged and was there to learn.

Taking few notes during the session, she felt that she had learned little that she didn't already know from living with an alcoholic husband for years. As the members began to file out after the closing prayer, she was startled to see Joe among them, chatting amicably with a younger woman. When he met her gaze, he was equally startled and barely managed a "Hi, how are you?"

"I'm fine, and so are you, it seems." She had a slight smile on her face as she asked, "Do you want to go for a coffee?"

"Sure, why not?" he answered. He excused himself from his companion, explaining that he was going for coffee with his ex. As

they walked up the street to the nearby mall with a food court, Joe
asked her why she had attended the AA meeting. She related that
she had been instructed to attend to learn about what AA had to
offer the homeless alcoholics she was now trying to help as a parish nurse.

"Well, did you learn anything?"

"Not much that I didn't already know. You taught me a lot
about alcoholism."

He responded to her question about why he was at the AA
meeting with the obvious answer.

"I have been a member for 41 days, and have had only one
twenty-hour fall off the wagon in that time." He then related that
he had driven his truck into the guardrail on the Highway 5 bridge
late on December 17th while cruising around trying to find Inge's
car and had been charged with driving under the influence. The
cops had also found an open bottle of Bacardi in the truck. Since
his blood alcohol level had been twice the legal limit for driving,
and it was his third offence, he had had his licence immediately
suspended and his car impounded. He had spent that night in the
Redfern police lockup, and then posted bail. His lawyer had plea-
bargained and got him off with a one-month licence suspension,
50 hours of community service and a commitment to enrol in an
alcohol rehabilitation program. Although not court-approved, he
asked for permission to choose AA and agreed to be monitored by
a sponsor there as an alternative to the approved programs. The
judge, also a member of AA, had agreed to that.

On this occasion, he apologized profusely for his treatment of
her when he was drinking, calling himself a first-class jerk, and noting the terrible controlling grip that alcohol can have on a person.

"I don't know if you keep in touch with anyone at the hospital, but I was there for five days when I tried to stop cold turkey.
I don't want to ever go through that hell again. I think it would
have been easier if I had done it by gradually cutting back, and not
trying to quit smoking at the exact same time. I guess I can either
keep drinking like a fish until it kills me or I keep dry until I die of
something else."

"Who cared for you in the hospital?"

"I don't know who the female doctor was, but I can remember
being wheeled in to the ICU. I guess I almost stopped breathing

from all the sedation they had to give me to keep me from trying to climb out the window. I'm sure glad that you were not there to see me in that state. And I remember that later your friend gave me an injection in my ass. By the way, you were that senior nurse who first identified Dr. Turle there, weren't you?"

"Yes."

"Well, are you still seeing him?"

"I never was 'seeing him' in the way you thought I was," Inge replied, signalling quotation marks with her hands. "He was just a friend and co-worker, and I haven't seen him since the day I identified him. You have to believe me. And if he really was lured out into a snowstorm for a drug deal, I don't ever want to see him again."

"Really? I'm amazed. I was so sure that you were having an affair with him."

There was a long pause in their conversation as though all the actors had forgotten their lines; Inge considered asking if he wanted her to come back, but decided that she would be in a very awkward position if he replied in the affirmative. He seemed to anticipate the question and broke the silence.

"I don't deserve you—never did. You are far too good for me, and I couldn't live with you again, knowing what I have already put you through. Living with your perfection would drive me back to drink. And I do believe you now."

She felt she had dodged a bullet. "Well, can we be friends again? Maybe Kevin and I can be of some help to you in maintaining your sobriety," she replied, trying to conceal her relief.

"Friends, yes, but nothing more," he replied. "FYI, I have retired. The work environment was just too much of a temptation for me with all that cheap booze, and when I lost my licence, it was really difficult to get up to the store. I am spending a lot of time with that younger woman you saw me with at the meeting, she's my sponsor. It is a completely platonic relationship. As you know well, I can't have any other kind of relationship with a woman, but she is probably the only person in the world who has any chance of keeping me sober for the rest of my life, and she has saved my life. I hope you are not jealous."

"Not at all," Inge said truthfully. "Good luck to the both of you. Who was that big authoritative man with the booming voice who was leading the meeting?"

"Can't tell you. You know that the second A in AA is 'Anony-mous.' But he would not mind me telling you that I have known him since my day in court, and he was the one who more or less got me to join. A great guy."

"It's none of my business, but are you seeing anyone?"

"Not yet. But I am on the lookout for some rich older widower in poor health," Inge joked.

"Well, get on with it! I would love to get out of the payments." He recalled the carefully worded standard remarriage-cancella-tion-of-equalization-payments clause that he had insisted on in their separation agreement. "Just kidding. You deserve anything I can give you."

Before they parted, Joe wished her well and asked if there was anything that she needed or wanted from the home that they had shared. She could only think of asking for some of the pictures from their home computer, and he promised to send as many as he could find to her by email attachment. As they parted, Joe said, "Give my best regards to Kevin. He is a nice guy, and I know he tried hard to help me, but I wasn't ready to accept any help then."

"Speaking of Kevin, did you know that he was at our wedding?"

"No. Did anyone ever tell you what a great liar you are?"

"I'm not lying-at least not about that."

"You already knew him away back then and invited him? Which of your lies am I to believe?"

"No. I didn't invite him but he was there." She was enjoying keeping Joe in a state of confusion.

"How did you come to that ridiculous conclusion, then?"

"O.K. He and I just figured it out recently. Time to fill you in. He was the cute, tall curly-haired altar boy. The truth is sometimes stranger than fiction."

"I guess so!"

* * *

By late January, Velma was spending more time at home and began to make some strange observations. Where were Leslie's keys, watch, skis, guitar and some of his shoes and clothes that were missing? Had he let someone in to the house and been robbed? And why had he shaved off his beard? But the police had searched the house and found no evidence of a violent confrontation. Had the police taken some of those items when they searched the house in her absence? She called the number of the Redfern district station and asked for a call back from one of the officers who had searched the house on December 16th. Paula Kaufman was anxious to disprove the theory that Bimini and Hendrickson were convinced was the cause of the incident. She thought it was unlikely that Dr. Leslie Turle had been lured out into a snowstorm for sex or drugs, but could not think of a better explanation. She returned Velma's call before one of the other officers had a chance to do so. When Velma reported her observations and concerns to Paula, she promised to pay Velma a visit the next day, even though she was off duty, and she assured Velma that the police had not taken anything from the house other than the computer and Leslie's iPad, which they had returned. She was hoping that a woman-to-woman chat would be fruitful in solving the mystery.

After Velma gave her an update on Leslie's remarkable progress, she discussed her new observations and concerns. Then it struck Paula like a bolt of lightning.

"What if he staged it all to look like an accident?" she asked. "He may have shaved his beard in preparation for that plastic surgery, or just to disguise his looks. But you said he felt useless and alienated. And those undiagnosed medical issues may have convinced him that he was really ill. Maybe he tried to commit suicide, and Eric Clouser was the only witness and thwarted his attempt and saved his life." Paula vaguely knew she was stepping over the boundaries of police professionalism in discussing the case at all when she was not on duty, but felt she needed to help Velma.

"Oh, my God!" Velma exclaimed, breaking down in tears. "He always liked to be in control and was very independently minded, so in a way that makes sense. But I know my Leslie, and I just can't believe that he would do that."

"Well, covert suicide is not that uncommon among retired, intelligent professionals, especially doctors, and particularly if their health is also failing. And they are prone to making some silly diagnosis on themselves, often picking the worst possible diagnosis. My uncle made a wrong diagnosis of a brain tumour on himself shortly after he retired from practice as a psychiatrist,

just because he had an unusual headache. And they usually try to
cover up their suicide and make it look like an accident or a death
from natural causes. You know. They overdose and the obliging
coroner decides to record it as a heart attack."

"How can we test your theory?" Velma asked.

"We—or at least you—could directly confront him about the
possibility, but that might be unwise. His loss of memory about
the event is likely real, and dredging those memories up would be
emotionally traumatic for him. It might make him plan to do something else equally stupid. You know how fragile the male ego is. It
would likely be best if you simply continue to treat the whole thing
as a mystery and not admit to any suspicions. But think about it."

"I guess I could do that, but what about that poor Eric Clouser?"

"Leave that to me," Paula answered. "I think I can persuade
those jerks on the case to drop the charge of attempted murder,
at least." She immediately regretted calling her superior officers
jerks, realizing how far over the line she had now crossed, but in
a way she didn't care; she felt she was now acting just as a friend
of Velma's, and not as a police officer at all. "But please don't say
anything about me being here today. That would be considered as
a lapse of judgment on my part. I can't even file a report, but I will
find a way of trying to convince them to drop the charges." She left
before she got herself into deeper trouble, but promised to keep in
touch.

Leslie was discharged home on February 28, still walking on
his cast and two canes, but otherwise feeling quite well. Velma
hosted a welcome home party four days later, inviting Isaac, Nancy,
Adam, a few neighbours and Drs. Midges, Bass and Al Taqi. Carol
Creek and Inge were invited through the hospital but it coincided
with their vacation in Cuba and Carol Creek was the only one
who sent her regrets. Everyone remarked on Leslie's amazing fast
recovery and wished him well for the future. And he reiterated to
anyone who asked that he had no recall of the events of that fateful Friday the 13th, or of anything from about the first of December
until well after Christmas. Leslie was not sure if he should even
ask about Inge, but Dr. Bass told him, without being asked, that
she had retired and was separated from her husband.

"My, that is a lot of stress for her in a short period of time. I didn't ever get any clue that she was having any troubles at home," Leslie remarked.

"Neither did I, but according to the gossip from Carol Creek, her husband was overusing products he promoted at work, and I know that for a fact. Probably couldn't satisfy her in bed."

"How's she coping?"

"Remarkably well," Glenna answered. "But I think that seeing you out cold in the ICU added to her stress. When I saw her at her retirement party, she seemed happy and relaxed, and even joked about looking for an older rich widower. She is one classy tough lady."

Leslie was happy to be home after two and a half months in hospital and realized that some good had come out of his near-death experience. He had reconnected with his daughter and would certainly work to re-establish a meaningful relationship with her. After the guests had left, he reviewed his bucket list on the computer and vowed to get back in shape so that he could check at least some of the items off in the years to come. He deleted "Reconnect with Barb," as he had accomplished that goal.

Leslie's face was still far from normal and he had to attend several appointments with different dentists to have a partial plate fitted and a tooth capped to restore his previous ability to chew solid foods. As well, there were two further outpatient appointments with Dr. Ben Speckle for minor repairs of his facial scars, but all of this was done without further hospitalization.

On February 12th, Barb Turle–Knott called and announced the arrival, the day before, of Leslie Knott, a seven-pound healthy baby boy, and sent some pictures of him. Leslie Turle said he was flattered and thrilled that they had decided to name his grandson after him. Barb explained that it seemed very appropriate, as it was almost a miracle that he had arrived alive and healthy after the emotional trauma she had experienced while she was carrying him.

"If you believe in miracles," she added.

* * *

One night in March, when Leslie left the bed to urinate, he realized that Arnold was somehow a bit different. He asked Velma about that, and she laughed.

"Well, Dr. Pham did a partial circumcision on you because part of your foreskin was gangrenous from severe frostbite."

He was initially aghast when told that they had done this without any anaesthetic and without his permission, now feeling the pain that it must have entailed. Velma reassured him that they had done it toward the end of the first week in the ICU when he was minimally responsive, and she had watched the procedure, done right in his ICU bed. She said he had not flinched as they removed only a small amount of dead tissue.

"Don't be so upset," she said. "It is not as though they took anything that you really have any use for."

He had to agree with her and decided that that was the least of his problems at that point, but still worried about what might have happened. He asked what other parts of his anatomy they had rearranged while he was unconscious. She replied that the only other surgeries she had consented to were the facial reconstruction, the fracture reduction, and the ERCP to remove the gallstone.

In mid-March, his cast was removed, and he religiously followed the instructions the home physiotherapist gave him and began to walk with only one cane. He got permission from his orthopaedic surgeon to drive, and planned to drive to Kingston to spend Easter weekend with Isaac, Nancy, and Adam, but Velma insisted that she would do the driving. Barb, nursing one-month-old Leslie Jr., declined to join them but called while he was there to wish him well and to remind him that he should come to meet his namesake soon. He planned an elaborate Easter egg hunt for Adam.

11

liar!

The next week, Dr. Leslie Turle was served a subpoena to appear as a witness for the prosecution at the preliminary hearing before an Ontario Court of Justice judge on the attempted murder charge against Eric Clouser, in a courthouse in Elmsville. He called his lawyer, Jeff Salmon, and explained the situation.

"If you testify under oath that you have never used street drugs or had any gay sex and have never met or heard of Eric Clouser, the Crown may regret having you as a witness. But for God's sake, don't lie." He agreed to attend to ensure that the questions to Dr. Turle were all appropriate and to advise him of his rights.

Paul Albright had briefed Eric about the upcoming preliminary inquiry, saying that it was a somewhat less rigid process than a formal trial, and if they were lucky they might get Judge Joanna Fisher, known to be all business but very fair and no friend of the police or the Crown prosecutor. As handcuffed Eric Clouser in standard "Versace orange" prison issue shuffled into the room escorted by guards from the Corrections Canada Collins Bay medium security institution, he did not acknowledge anyone, except his friend and lover, Tom Stone. The prior conviction was for a federal offence under the *Controlled Substances Act*, and the police detectives had convinced the judge that his tackle shop was near a school, even though it was just a small junior kindergarten. The judge had been obliged because of this and the wording of the *Safe Streets and Communities Act* to sentence him to the mandatory two years dictated by that C-10 crime omnibus bill. Eric had been promptly moved to Collins Bay as soon as he pleaded guilty.

Leslie watched as Eric Clouser was escorted into the courtroom and realized that he had seen the prisoner somewhere before but could not remember where. When Eric turned and nodded to the man sitting two rows behind him in the courtroom, that man in the bright yellow shirt also looked familiar to Dr. Turle. Then he remembered the two fly fishermen in the middle of the Beaver River on a tranquil spring morning. He had taken close-up pictures of them in the river, timing one perfectly to capture the fisherman with the black beard holding his bent rod high and a silvery fish in midair in front of him. And he had added fly-fishing to his bucket list that morning. He remembered the day clearly, as it was the same day that a neighbour walking her dogs in the park had complained to him about the public display of affection of two gay fellows in the park. Now he realized for the first time where he had seen Eric Clouser before. When Detective Inspector Jim Hendrickson arrived, he also looked familiar to Leslie, but he could not recall where he had seen him before.

Before the hearing began, Sergeant Bimini stared at Eric for the first time but realized that he too had seen that distinctive black beard before. Then it struck him.

Velma Turle also thought she had seen that distinctive beard before, but she decided that her mind must be deceiving her and concentrated on the drama unfolding in front of her. She had seen many TV courtroom scenes, had read about them in crime novels, and was anxious to see how they measured up to the real thing. As Madam Justice Joanna Fisher entered the court and the case of *The Crown vs Eric Clouser* was announced, Paul Atherton gave Eric Clouser a thumbs-up.

Crown prosecutor Rod Strike had already submitted the evidence, including almost all of the police records and Eric Clouser's statement, to the court and to the defence attorney, as required. He called on Sergeant Bimini and Detective Hendrickson together. After they reviewed their findings in the park that night and their actions thereafter, Strike asked if they had any further relevant information about the case.

This was Sergeant Bimini's chance to show everyone that he really was detective material.

"Your Honour," he replied "There is a photograph of the accused Eric Clouser on the iPad of the victim, Dr. Leslie Turle."

Velma Turle, seated in the open court, frowned in puzzlement. For the first time in her life, she began to wonder if her Leslie really was a closet gay or a street drug user. Paul Albright was also startled and stared at his client, wondering if Eric was such a convincing con artist that even he had been taken in. He could not at that point think of any questions for the two officers.

Strike next called on Dr. Turle who claimed to have no recollection whatsoever of the events of that Friday and denied having any gay experiences or desires. But on specific questioning, he admitted that he had seen the prisoner on one occasion in Beaver Park the previous spring and had taken a photograph that included him, but that they had never spoken to each other or been introduced.

"Does it not seem odd, Your Honour, that the good doctor recognizes the accused from a single casual encounter in a busy park a year earlier, but claims to have completely forgotten one of the most memorable more recent events in his life?" Strike asked.

Justice Fisher asked Leslie to explain such a discrepancy and Leslie hesitated. After consulting with Jeff Salmon, he replied, "Your Honour, one day almost a year ago, I watched two men fly-fishing in the Beaver River, and it was such a tranquil scene that I studied their casting for a long time and took some pictures. And I put one of those on my iPad as a background. I did not realize until today that that picture was of the accused and his friend sitting behind him there."

"And what about forgetting the more recent events of Friday the 13th?" the judge asked, still sounding skeptical.

"Well, as a physician with a lot of experience with critical injuries, I can tell you that amnesia is almost universal when someone experiences a severe injury causing temporary coma. They typically lose all recall for events from before and after the injury for a period of time at least as long as the duration of the coma, both before and after it, and that is what must have happened to me."

The crown prosecutor then asked Leslie about his use of marijuana. Leslie denied being a current user, but admitted that he had tried it once and only once, in his university days.

"And those two fishermen that you just happened to take a photograph of and that photograph that you just happened to choose for your computer screen background are pictures of the accused and his partner. Is that correct?"

"Yes, but I just realized that today. As I said, I had never seen them before that or since until today."

Jeff Salmon decided to intervene and asked to speak. He pointed out to the judge that both the accused and the victim were frequent visitors to Beaver Park and the apparently unlikely coincidence was not as farfetched as it would seem at first. "Truth is often stranger than fiction," he concluded.

Paul Albright had warned Eric that the Crown prosecutor and the police would try to besmirch his character and describe him to the judge as a drug dealer and sexual predator, and Eric was prepared, but the prosecutor started off in a friendly manner.

"Your name, sir?"

"Eric Clouser."

"Your occupation?"

"Currently I occupy a cell in Collins Bay penitentiary. Previously, I was the owner of the Hook Line and Sinker tackle store in Shacletown."

"This is not a comedy show, and I am not Judge Judy," Justice Fisher snarled. "Please answer the questions without trying to crack lame jokes.

Strike continued. "What else did you do to earn money?"

"I had a part-time job running a municipal snowplough."

"And?"

I did some teaching—fly-fishing."

"And?"

"Okay. I sold some weed."

At that point, Paul Albright objected to the line of questioning, pointing out that his client was already serving time for his drug dealing, but was overruled.

Strike continued. "Would you tell the court why you were in Beaver Park on that Friday the thirteenth?"

Eric reiterated his story about going to Beaver Park to clear some parking spaces for his fishing expedition the next day. Asked what he had found in Beaver Park that night, Eric told the court that he had seen a naked man walking down Beaver Trail, had later found the man on the edge of the Beaver River, and had called 911 to report his grim discovery. The prosecutor then got Eric to admit to being gay, and Albright again objected to this bit of irrelevant information but was again overruled.

When asked why he had fled the scene of the crime, an alert Eric replied. "Well, your Honour, it was not the scene of a crime at all, and I simply panicked."

Paul Albright had only one question for his client. "Would you tell this court about any previous acquaintance with, knowledge of, contact with, or correspondence of any kind with one Dr. Leslie Turle prior to that Friday?"

"None. I had never heard of him."

With no further questions from the prosecutor, and none from Albright, Eric was led back to his seat.

It was Paul Albright's turn to shine. He called Tom Stone, who testified that he and Eric had indeed planned a fishing trip in the Beaver River the next day. "And did you in fact go fishing the next day?"

"Well, I went to the park, but obviously Eric did not show up, so I went back home."

Next, Albright, having regained some composure, called back Sergeant Bimini and Detective Jim Hendrickson for cross-examination, succeeding in getting them both to admit that their evidence on the attempted murder charge rested mainly or solely on the finding of torn clothes at the scene. Sergeant Bimini initially tried to resurrect the fact that the photograph that he had found of Eric Clouser on Dr. Turle's iPad indicated an ongoing relationship between them, but the judge cut him off, saying the photograph had been discussed in enough detail. Albright then suggested that they had not even proved that the clothes belonged to Dr. Turle, "and even if they did belong to him, you are aware that some individuals experiencing severe hypothermia paradoxically, suddenly, and violently remove all their clothes, are you not?" he asked.

"I was not aware of that," Inspector Hendrickson stated.

"Liar!" Paula Kaufman, sitting in the open court, muttered under her breath, recalling that Detective Hendrickson was the one at the scene who had enlightened her on that point. But she had not been summoned as a witness, and in any case was initially grateful that she would not have to contradict a superior officer. But Hendrickson's blatant lie under oath was grating on her.

"And there is no evidence connecting Eric Clouser to the clothes or to the victim—no fingerprints, DNA, nothing," Paul Albright continued. At that point, Detective Hendrickson carelessly asserted that they did have evidence that the clothes belonged to Dr. Leslie Turle. He stated that a receipt found in a pocket had fingerprints that matched those of Dr. Turle.

A startled Jeff Salmon then rose and requested permission to question Detective Hendrickson, pointing out that the discussion now was about his client's fingerprints, and his client was not on trial. He was surprised to hear that the police had fingerprinted his client, as were Leslie and Velma, who was sitting in the open court.

"Just when did you obtain the fingerprints of my client, and who gave you consent for that?" he asked Hendrickson.

"Those fingerprints were obtained at the hospital by the Forensic Identification Unit people at my request. I believe it was on the Monday following his admission," Hendrickson answered.

"Now, my client at that point was in a coma and incapable of giving any consent to have his fingerprints taken. He was being treated as a victim and not as a suspect, so who acted on his behalf to give the consent? Was it his next-of- kin, his designated public guardian, or some other individual? Was a warrant issued to obtain them?" Salmon asked.

Hendrickson began to squirm. "I am not sure who gave the consent," he responded. "I believe it was someone in the hospital administration."

Justice Fisher stared at the crown prosecutor and flipped through the documents in front of her, then turned to Rod Strike. "I always review the documents in the disclosure before hearing a case. Why was the evidence of those fingerprints of the victim not included in your disclosure to this court and to the defence counsel?"

"Your honour, I did not receive that evidence and was unaware of its existence until today."

Turning her attention to Detective Inspector Hendrickson, the judge asked, "Why was that evidence not provided to the Crown, the defence and to me?"

"Your honour, I did not realize until today that that evidence was at all relevant."

"That is not good enough. You are not the judge in this court to decide what is and what is not relevant. I will decide that. You know better. Carry on, Mr. Salmon."

When Jeff Salmon decided to ask no further questions, Paul Albright immediately asked for permission to speak yet again.

"Your Honour, far from being the dangerous drug-dealing sexual predator that the Crown and the police are trying to portray my client as, he is and should be hailed as a hero. He stumbled upon the scene of an accident of a man suffering from hypothermia and did everything in his power to rescue that unfortunate, reckless man." And he commented that the evidence linking the clothes found at the scene to Dr. Leslie Turle rested entirely on fingerprints that may have been obtained by "dubious and perhaps illegal means."

"Would you agree with my interpretation of this?" he asked Hendrickson, almost rhetorically. When the detective reluctantly agreed that differing interpretations of the evidence were possible, Albright suggested that the police might not want to present that fingerprint evidence to a judge at a formal trial. And he moved to have the charge against his client dismissed forthwith, because of lack of evidence. The judge, with no further evidence forthcoming, called for a lunch recess, announcing that they would reconvene at 2:00 p.m., and unless someone had further evidence to present, she would bring down a decision at that time about whether or not to send the case to trial.

At lunch with Jeff Salmon and Velma, Leslie had nothing but a black coffee. He reassured Velma again and again that he was not a closet gay or a drug user, and she finally assured him that she believed him, saying that the tranquil picture on his iPad was just unfortunately of the wrong fishermen but was really worthy of a place in an art gallery. She described the picture to Jeff Salmon.

"There are these two fly fishermen standing knee-deep in the middle of the river, with wisps of mist over the surface. One of them is holding his bent rod high and a very silvery fish is leaping out of the water in front of him reflected in the sunlight. And you can even see the orange fly line straight as an arrow from the rod tip to a few feet in front of the fish. But I think I'll go home and delete all the fisherman pictures from the iPad right now."

"Don't you dare! If the decision is to go to trial, Eric is going to serve major time unless you present that picture to the presiding judge there. In fact," Jeff said, glancing at his watch, "we have lots of time. I would like you to go and fetch that iPad and give it to me. It may come in handy this afternoon. For God's sake, don't delete that photo!"

Before Velma left, they also discussed the startling revelation that the police had fingerprinted Leslie. Velma was livid when Jeff stated that those fingerprints would be kept on file and available to the police anywhere in Canada. Leslie was less upset, saying that he felt he had nothing to hide from any police.

"Well, I may be able to do something about those fingerprints, too," Jeff commented.

* * *

When the court session reconvened, and Madam Justice Fisher first asked again if there was any further evidence to present, Jeff Salmon spoke up, saying that he had one further exhibit to present. He approached the bench with the iPad open and handed it to Justice Fisher. She stared at the photograph for what seemed to be an hour, and was in fact at least two minutes. Then she looked up at Dr. Turle.

"Doctor, this a one-in-a-million piece of photographic art."

Smiles erupted on the faces of Jeff Salmon, Eric Clouser, Paul Albright, and Dr. Leslie Turle, as quickly as the frowns on the faces of the police and the prosecutor.

"But it does not belong on your iPad." The smiles and frowns swapped places except for the proud broad grin that seemed to be permanently implanted on the reconstructed face of Dr. Leslie Turle.

Pause. "It belongs in a good frame on the wall in some art gallery, or in some famous photo contest. With my last name and a 'The' attached."

The smiles and frowns again switched owners and Paul Albright's jaw dropped. He had never known Madame Justice Fisher to ever introduce any element of levity into any court proceedings.

Justice Fisher was prepared to announce her verdict.

"I accept that the seemingly unlikely coincidence surrounding this photograph was just that. I believe that the good doctor, the accused, and his friend have been honest with this court, and do not believe that there is any chance that a jury of his peers could ever be convinced that Mr. Eric Clouser attempted to kill the doctor or committed any other violent crime, based on the evidence that we have heard here today. I therefore am dismissing the charges against him ... but, Mr. Clouser, the next time you have occasion to call 911, don't panic and don't disobey orders."

Jeff Salmon was quick. Before the justice brought down the gavel to end the hearing, he spoke up.

"Your Honour, if I may ... one further small detail ... as we have heard, the fingerprints of my client that we have heard about were obtained by dubious and perhaps illegal means—and from a man who has never been accused of any crime—without his consent or a warrant. In view of this, I request that those prints be expunged from all the police records and databases."

The judge reflected for a long time—so long that her assembled audience began to wonder if she had taken a post-prandial nap. Then she looked up and, turning to Detective Hendrickson, said, "I am granting that request and so order. Whether the obtaining of those fingerprints was illegal or just dubious, it would have been very easy to do the proper thing and obtain a warrant to get them. Perhaps your forensic identification investigators need some education in proper procedures to follow in obtaining evidence. I am aware that obtaining fingerprints is considered a minor procedure, but this is not the first time I have heard of illegal procedures being used in collecting evidence. Do I need to remind the officers of the Redfern Regional Police by bringing up the name of Guy Paul Morin?"

Then she lowered the gavel.

Paula Kaufman was sitting in the public court at a discreet two seats away from Velma Turle. The crown prosecutor had asked her to attend, but she had not been called as a witness. At this point, she passed a scribbled note to Velma.

"I'm sorry I couldn't persuade them to drop the charges before it came to this."

"I'm sure you tried, and thank you for trying. I'm glad that they have cleared Leslie of any suspicion in public, at least sort of," Velma wrote back. Paula tore the note to shreds and smiled to Velma. As Eric Clouser was being led out of the court, he looked around and managed to nod to Tom. Then he glanced at a startled Dr. Leslie Turle, who mouthed a silent *Thank you*.

As the crowd left the court, Paula Kaufman caught up to Detective Inspector Hendrickson. She was trembling but livid and determined, and her heart was pounding. He scowled when she asked: "Do you realize that you committed perjury just now?"

"Just leave me alone."

She couldn't resist making him squirm some more. "Well, if there is an internal inquiry into this, I could get you fired."

"You wouldn't dare."

"Is that a threat? I have witnesses, and I have notes to prove it."

"No. Just leave it alone if you know what is good for you. We can probably still nail that guy with disobeying a police order, giving false information and leaving the scene of an accident."

Sore loser, Paula thought as she hurried away.

* * *

Garth Rowley was stunned. Suddenly a hearing on a charge of attempted murder had taken a sharp turn. In reporting on it for the Star, he would report that the charges had been dismissed for lack of evidence, and he would love to include a copy of the controversial photograph, if he could get his hands on one. Should the focus of the story be on the "on-in-a-million" photograph or on the judge's reprimand of the Crown prosecutor and the police? Why not both? he thought. He caught up to Leslie and Velma as they were crossing the parking lot and, introducing himself, asked if he could get a copy of the photo for a story in the Star.

Leslie said he would be pleased to send him a copy by email attachment, but Velma immediately recognized an opportunity.

"We'll gladly send you a copy of that photo as soon as you give me an advance copy of the story you are going to write about it. And only if that story does not repeat the previous suggestions that Leslie is a closet gay or a drug user." This seemed a bit like media censorship in action to Rowley, but it also seemed reasonable; and they came to an agreement that he would draft a story and send it by email within two hours, and then Velma would send the photograph.

He began writing a story focused mainly on the judge's reprimand to the police. The aim was to highlight the "dubious and perhaps illegal" methods used by the Redfern Regional Police in collecting evidence in criminal investigations. There was a similarity to the non-disclosure of evidence in this case to the case of Guy Paul Morin. The Crown prosecutor had been severely criticized for having a determination to obtain a conviction rather than a determination to find the truth. He cited that case in his report, but he knew that it was the York and Durham forces that had been found wanting in the Kaufman Commission of Inquiry into that wrongful conviction. He also knew that the Crown Attorney's office had been chastised in the report for having a cozy relationship with all of the regional police forces.

He knew that there were corrupt officers in all police forces and that the Redfern ones were far from the worst. But he instinctively loved exposing corruption everywhere, except in journalism, and it provided natural great headlines. He had received an award for coverage of the Morin case years before. He could already envision the headline: "Redfern Police Reprimanded by Judge: Attempted Murder Charge Dismissed." He could also see the caption for the photograph: "Controversial 'One-in-a-million piece of photographic art' has its day in court."

On the way home from the court, Velma drove, as Leslie pondered what he might be able to do to repay his rescuer. "Do you think the media will now stop insinuating that I am a gay drug user?" Leslie asked.

"It all depends on how that reporter words his story. If he wants the picture badly enough he will be careful. And I am going to get a professional photo shop to touch up and frame that picture. It will be a great conversation piece. Where should we hang it? But don't you dare to show up to cheer at the Toronto Gay Pride parade in June."

Leslie laughed.

Rowley's story was quickly accepted without any changes by Velma and Leslie and by the editor. The photo was duly sent to him as promised.

On the way back to his office, a pleased Paul Albright realized that his client was still being held in a medium security institution. In accordance with Corrections Canada policies, Eric should now be moved to a much more relaxed and pleasant prison, since he had been cleared of the charge of committing a violent crime.

As soon as he reached the office, he asked his assistant to make out an application to Corrections Canada to have Eric Clouser transferred to either the Frontenac Institution or the Pittsburgh Institution, both minimum-security prisons near Kingston. That would at least limit his client's exposure to the teachings of the crime school veterans at Collins Bay, he reasoned.

12

religious dogs

On a warm and breezy April evening, Velma taught Leslie how to prepare a simple pasta and oysters entree followed by a chocolate mousse. As a nutritionist, she doubted the alleged aphrodisiac properties of oysters and chocolate, but she would test that theory. She set up candles for their dinner together. She then persuaded him to watch a movie with her on TV, suggesting *Ghost*, saying that she had seen it and she thought he would also like it. As they cuddled and chatted on the sofa, she began to rub his thigh. As they watched the pottery scene with Demi Moore massaging the phallus-shaped clay moulding, Velma startled him by whispering in his ear "Guess what?"

"What?"

"Do you think your Arnold could—"

A stunned Leslie finished her sentence for her, "—rise to the challenge?"—glancing down at his crotch. "Well, he's a bit out of practice, but I think he might be able to with your help. But what brought this on? First, cooking lesson, then candles at dinner, then cuddles, now this. Are you really Velma, or am I dreaming?"

"Yes, this is the real Velma, not the stressed-out Velma. Maybe the oysters and chocolate worked, but when you were in the ICU, I forgot to take the paroxetine for a few days and realized I didn't need it. I think that it helped me a lot at one point, but then it seemed to have the opposite effect and made me grouchy later. I sure don't need it anymore, now that I have no business to worry about and I have you back. This is the new and improved Velma— or the old, old Velma from thirty years ago. We don't really need to see how this movie ends. Let's go to bed." She was sporting the impish grin that he had once loved.

Afterward, it was obvious that Arnold had performed extraordinarily well, and that Velma eagerly anticipated many repeat performances. As a tsunami wave of the love hormone oxytocin and the pleasure hormone dopamine flooded the lower compartments of his brain, Leslie really hoped there was a God—he really needed to have someone to thank for his perfect happiness at that moment. Lying beside her, as the hormonal tide ebbed a bit, Leslie mused to himself that his many years of celibacy had led him to exaggerate his memories of the joys of sex, but he was nevertheless thrilled that Arnold had obviously been able to satisfy his loving wife's desire.

"Let's try it in the hot tub next time, for old time's sake," he suggested. As Velma turned over and began to snore softly, he spooned up to her and fell into a sound, peaceful, deep sleep.

Velma realized from reading numerous spy novels that a man in a post-coital state of disinhibiting blissful hormonal intoxication is very vulnerable to telling secrets that he would never relate in any other circumstances. Just after one of several repeat Arnold performances over a few weeks, she stated rather than asked, "You staged it all, didn't you?"

"Staged what? That was a real orgasm; wasn't yours?" Leslie inquired.

"Yes, but you staged Friday the 13th. You planned to kill yourself that night."

Startled, Leslie replied truthfully, as far as he knew, "No, I would never do that."

"Well, whatever. It doesn't really matter. But, honey, if you did plan it, I am sure glad you didn't succeed. I can live without solving the mystery of what happened that night. And I love you."

He reflected on what she had said, but could not believe that he would ever try to kill himself. *My life is far too enjoyable to ever do that*, he thought.

In late April, as a gift to his devoted Velma, Leslie told her that he was ready to take her up on her long-standing desire for a trip to Peru to see the ancient Inca ruins at Macchu Picchu and learn more about their diet. Velma had long wanted to visit Macchu Picchu and mentioned it to Leslie several times. She had submitted a term paper while attending the University of Guelph years before, dealing with the dietary habits of ancient civilizations. She had included the Australian aborigines, Greeks, Romans, Druids, Maori, Mongols, and the Inuit and Natives of North America. But because she had ignored the Maya, Aztec, and Inca peoples, she had gotten only a "C" on the paper. The deficiencies with respect to the Aztec and Maya had been corrected when she visited Mexico with Leslie while he attended medical conferences at resorts there. There was little about the Incas that could not now be gleaned from Internet searches, but she wanted to visit their home. Specifically, how did they prepare their meats of llama, alpaca, guinea pigs and human flesh? And did they ever have to deal with an obesity epidemic on their subsistence diet? Did they prefer their human steaks rare or well done and did their preparations of human flesh differ depending on whether the source was one of their own or an enemy? Once she rounded out the essay with this juicy information, she might submit it to some nutrition journal, or just post it on a blog.

After researching on the Internet, reading reviews, and talking to friends who raved about it, he suggested the rather leisurely five-day Llama Path Tours hike from Cusco to the summit. This was a compromise between his need for adventure and Velma's need for stable predictability. He would have preferred a more vigorous two-day hike, and she would have preferred to take the train from Cusco to the ancient sacred ruins.

Leslie realized that he needed to have his gall bladder removed at some point, as it was full of stones that could create a need for emergency surgery, and he worried a bit about that happening when they were in Peru. Furthermore, Velma, with her propensity to avoid risks, insisted that he have the surgery before they went. She, like most Canadians, worried about the financial ruin that might ensue if they got sick while out of the country, and noted that they could not get any reasonably priced travel medical insurance that would cover a pre-existing condition. They arranged with one of the surgeons Leslie knew to have the surgery in early June. In spite of finding a slightly low serum sodium level on the preoperative blood tests, his gallbladder was removed uneventfully. Thereafter, they worked vigorously together to get physically fit for the hike (although it was described as one of the less strenuous treks), going for longer and longer strenuous walks around the neighbourhood and along the Beaver Trail.

In early May, Leslie and Velma accepted Barb and Lyle Knott's invitation to visit them in Baltimore. Barb, whom Leslie barely recognized, introduced her father to the son-in-law he did not recall meeting at all, although Lyle had visited him in the ICU, and he immediately liked Lyle. They discussed the latter's work as a recruitment officer for the Peace Corps and his travels to universities to recruit new grads for the Peace Corps' local economic development programs around the world. He also was a registered lobbyist for the Peace Corps and related hilarious tales of meeting with D.C. politicians in that role, including one famous congressman who had propositioned him in his congressional office. Velma doted on the newest member of the Turle family, three-month-old Leslie and they looked after him one evening so Lyle and Barb could go out for dinner and a movie.

After Leslie junior, Velma, and Lyle had retired for the night, Barb and Leslie sat in the library and chatted long into the night. He commented on her extensive collection of books on moral philosophy, and picked up Robert Buckman's *Can We Be Good without God?* They agreed that it was great food for thought, and Barb told him about her assignment for her masters students in philosophy that was based in part on it. Leslie, thinking of himself as an amateur philosopher, asked for the assignment, and would work on it and send his essay to her as an email attachment when he was done. She agreed to mark it as harshly as if her father was actually a master's student in her class, grateful that they seemed to have a new bond based on moral philosophical dilemmas.

Barb said, "You know, the vast majority of people live their lives from cradle to grave without thinking about what philosophy they are following at all. At least you have moved beyond the brainwashing you got as a kid and are interested in the big questions."

"What big questions?"

"I think the most enigmatic profound question anyone has ever asked came from a female pop singer in the sixties, not from a philosopher at all. I don't have the answer to that one, but I am still searching for it."

"What question is that?"

"I am not going to tell you. You will have to do some home-work and tell me." Barb was enjoying the chance to treat her father like one of her students. "But unlike Richard Dawkins, I think that not exposing children to different religions and letting them choose for themselves is a big parenting mistake. You never made that mistake with me."

"You never gave me much of a chance to influence your educa-tion in religion or in anything else."

"Well, your namesake upstairs," Barb replied, "will get that exposure, and I'll accept whatever option he chooses. We will encourage him to read the Christian Bible, the Koran, the Book of Mormon and the Talmud at least, to increase his understanding and tolerance of others. Giving children no exposure to anything but atheism is just as big a mistake as teaching them only one set of doctrines. That makes them vulnerable to being lured into some really dangerous radical sect."

"Hadn't thought of that. But you are right. Maybe if my par-ents had done that for me, I would have developed more tolerance for all kinds of religion than I did."

Barb then shifted seamlessly into full philosophic orator mode. "Almost everyone seems to need some spiritual anchor to guide their lives, and if you give them no options, it can lead to disas-ter. If the neuroscientists who insist that evolution has hardwired the need for religion into our brains to provide some survival advantage are right, it is just wrong to dismiss religion entirely. But I think the scientists are wrong to say that it is unique to the human species. Almost no attribute except our bodies is absolutely uniquely a human trait—not even tool-making."

"Are you suggesting that other species have religious beliefs? Now I am beginning to think you have hung out with philoso-phers for too long!"

"Well, aren't modern dogs and wolves howling at the full moon just a bit like our primitive hunter-gatherers 50,000 years ago praying to the moon goddess for success in the hunt or the battle with their neighbours? And some modern dogs, especially police dogs, will risk their lives to follow the orders from their masters just as our forbears risked their lives in battles because they were following the perceived orders from their gods. Those dogs must in some foggy-brained way believe that their masters are gods who warrant sacrifice and worship."

"Hadn't thought of that, either, but it is an interesting thought. Maybe you should write a paper on religious dogs and submit it to some philosophy journal."

"Well, you have just heard part of a lecture I gave a few months ago at the local Humanist Society meeting, honouring the late Dr. Robert Buckman. So, Dad, what kind of religious beliefs do you espouse now?"

"None at all. I am what they call a celestial trolley car agnostic; that is, there might be amongst the millions of galaxies and billions of planets a remote planet in some galaxy with a perfect replica of a San Francisco trolley car ferrying people around a city like San Francisco, but I think the odds are about the same. You know, I was raised in one of those fundamentalist sects, but their beliefs in the literal truth of the Bible, with the creation story, the virgin birth, the resurrection myth, and so on are not compatible with science. Have you ever heard of Occam's Razor?"

"Of course. William of Occam's razor principle of parsimony says that for any observation, the explanation requiring the least number of assumptions should be accepted until proven wrong."

"Right, and if you apply that to modern observations of anything, there is no need to postulate the existence of a deity. Scientific endeavours can provide a more plausible answer to any puzzle in the universe, with fewer assumptions needed, than can the postulate of a Supreme Being. And what about Pascal's Wager?"

"You mean the wager that a prudent person should bet that there is a God even if the odds are extreme that there is not, because there is little to lose in doing so?"

"Exactly. Well, I can't think of any pleasures I would give up to please any deity, so that is meaningless to me."

"You seem to be quite the philosopher, Dad."

"Well, since retirement I have read a lot of philosophy, hoping that it would help to reconnect with you. And it worked. Never understood a word that Kant wrote, though."

"Well he enshrined two words that are abused in almost every philosophical debate to this day, but I don't understand much of what he wrote either."

"What two words?"

"I am not going to tell you. You need to do some digging for them and then tell me." She was once again enjoying treating her father like one of her students, but was becoming more and more impressed with his grasp of philosophical issues.

"But crazy, syphilitic Frederic Nietzsche had it right: A glorious fatalism is one of the only isms worth embracing." Leslie asserted.

"You're right. But you can't act on fatalism. That is why I am a humanist. You can act on that."

* * *

Velma and Leslie usually walked the Beaver Trail to the north from their home, often sighting deer in the woods along the trail and along the Beaver River. On one occasion, however, Velma accompanied him southward on the trail toward Beaver Park. As they approached the site of his near-death experience, he paused and stood motionless for a long time, then slowly walked over to the Little Beaver Trail and stood peering down into the Beaver River. Peculiar emotions overtook him and tears welled up in his eyes. Velma held on to his arm, but he didn't move.

Finally he spoke. "I guess I did do it, and I think I must have planned it, but I honestly don't remember," he said softly. They moved on back up the trail.

"Just as I thought," Velma replied. "But let's not dwell on it. We don't need to come back here, and I am so glad that you did not succeed. There is no point in living in the past, and we have a lot of living in the present still to do. And we don't need to tell anyone what really happened here, as you now recall it. This will be our secret."

The next morning, Leslie awoke to find that he was totally paralyzed. His body and his brain were once again out of sync, his body in the paralyzed state of REM sleep, but his brain wide awake. Then he saw himself lying on the ceiling above him. His left hand was writing a list in his handwriting in blood-red ink on the ceiling.

Crossword, Sudoku

Garbage
Goodwill
Car appointment
Hospital Visit
Beard
Call Velma

He suddenly jerked upright in utter panic. His heart was pounding and he was sweating profusely as he called out loudly to Velma. Velma, asleep at his side, awoke, startled and alarmed as well, and asked what was wrong. "I think I just had a bad dream," he said nonchalantly, trying desperately to conceal the sheer panic that he had experience just seconds before.

"Tell me about it, honey," Velma implored.

"I can't recall any of the details," he replied. He realized that he had just had his first, and hopefully only, episode of the phenomenon known as sleep paralysis that he had read about, complete with an out-of-body experience, and was alarmed at how frightening it had been.

13

disasters

Inge read the Toronto Star report of the preliminary hearing with great interest. She was relieved to read that her former idol had denied being gay or being a drug user, but was still puzzled and a bit miffed about why he had deliberately deceived her. But she reflected that she had already misjudged him once and was now determined to keep an open mind about his motives for doing so. And she was living with her own set of lies and deceptions, so perhaps he should be forgiven. *Perhaps he had a legitimate explanation,* she reflected. *I will likely find an answer some day,* she thought. And she wondered how he was coping with the unfounded media and gossip insinuations about having been lured out into a snowstorm for drugs or sex. He had indeed been shunned when he attended the Critical Care Interhospital Grand Rounds on one occasion. And at one point a nurse from the ICU who clearly saw him approaching in the Square Ten mall had quite deliberately ducked into a men's clothing store and turned her back to the window to avoid meeting him.

As Inge read the Toronto Star report, she recalled her involvement in the "dubious and perhaps illegal" fingerprinting of John Doe a.k.a. Dr. Leslie Turle. She concluded that a nurse should not be expected to know all the legal technicalities of such a situation, and in any case she had carefully documented the episode in the patient's chart. And the formal consent had come from the hospital administrator. Then she cynically reflected: *No one ever reads nurse's notes anyway.*

In May, Inge found and bought a condo in the Appleyard area of Redfern. Ken and Carol Creek, Father Kevin Wulff, and Joe

Glacier all helped with the move that Saturday. Inge had called Joe a week earlier when she was desperate to find someone who could fix the plugged kitchen drain and a leaky faucet in her apartment, after finding that Ken Creek was out of town. Joe had quickly come to her rescue and solved the problem. When she had told him about her impending move, he insisted on coming to assist with the move, using his pickup to haul the few larger pieces of furniture. After the move, which did not take long, as her worldly possessions were meagre, the whole party except for Joe went out for dinner. Joe begged off, citing an AA meeting that he needed to attend that evening. All of the others remarked on the dramatic transformation that they had witnessed in his demeanour and outlook. He had even impressed the skeptical Ken Creek with his caring and attentive attitude toward Inge, and he had profusely apologized to the priest for not listening to his advice earlier.

In early July, a disaster of sorts struck Inge. Her family doctor was the first to discover a distinct hard three-centimetre lump in the upper, outer quadrant of her left breast and he strongly suspected it was cancerous. She had worried about developing breast cancer, as her mother had died of it at age 70, and a paternal aunt had died of the same disease at age 48, but her mammogram a year earlier had been negative. Her doctor, on hearing the family history, referred her to the specialized breast cancer centre at Princess Margaret Hospital in Toronto, known for their very quick responses to referrals and prompt institution of treatment. Within 48 hours, she was walking into the Rapid Diagnostic Centre there and had an ultrasound-guided biopsy of the lump and some blood tests.

Five days later, after a call from Princess Margaret, she was back and was directed to their Familial Breast and Ovarian Cancer Clinic. A kind and diminutive female Oriental oncologist, Dr. Ling Li, examined her breasts, armpits, and abdomen and explained that she did indeed have a high-grade breast cancer and that she also carried the most common mutation of the still uncommon BRAC1 gene associated with some forms of familial breast and ovarian cancer. Dr. Li gave Inge a detailed pamphlet and discussed treatment options and the uncertain prognosis. At a minimum, Inge would need to have a mastectomy and possibly lymph node removal, and likely some follow-up chemotherapy, depending on what the pathologist reported. And she would need some screening for ovarian cancer at a later date. The oncologist carefully explained that since BRAC1 gene mutations accounted for only a small proportion of cases of breast cancer, there were no definitive practice guidelines for her situation. It was too rare to have had enough women to conduct a rigorous, controlled trial comparing different treatments.

"Sometimes those who recommend that all medical decisions should be 'evidence-based' are simply wrong," she stated. "If we followed that rule in your case, we would be paralysed into doing nothing." She recommended that Inge undergo a mastectomy as soon as possible, and then they would discuss the adjuvant chemotherapy options again, after the pathology was reported.

When Inge returned home and began an online search for more information about her cancer, she found that some guidelines suggested the treatment should include removal of the non-cancerous breast as well, because of the high risk of a cancer developing there at a later date. She recalled reading about Angelina Jolie undergoing a double mastectomy although she had no cancer at all, just a high probability of developing one because she carried the same BRAC1 gene mutation that Inge had. *If Angelina Jolie can do without breasts, I can, too,* she thought. There was never going to be a man in her life to admire or fondle her breasts, and she concluded that it was only her vanity that made her reluctant to part with both of them. She would wear a carefully padded bra after her surgery, and reasoned that it would not droop; her native endowments were already well past their starting points on their inevitable, slow, gravity-powered, southward migration toward her waist. As she looked down at them, they both now symbolized only danger.

When she met with a surgeon at Princess Margaret Hospital a few days and many tests later, she raised the possibility of removing her right non-cancerous breast as well, and he agreed that such surgery would be a wise precaution. He also discussed the new advances in breast cancer surgery with sentinel lymph node biopsy replacing the standard removal of all the lymph nodes in the armpit. The sentinel node would be found as the one to be far most likely to be involved with tumour first and, once identified, if it was normal, she would be spared the more extensive axillary lymph node dissection. However, when he examined her he found a definitely palpable and very firm node under her left arm, and he concluded that the new lesser surgery would be unwise for her; she would need the full dissection, as well as postoperative chemotherapy.

He discussed doing reconstructive surgery at a later date, and she flatly refused to consider that. The operation on the left breast would include removal of the lymph nodes under her arm, and the one on the right would be a simple mastectomy. Even in this, she found something positive to focus on. *At least I am right- handed,* she thought, *so I will not be troubled as much by the arm swelling that complicates axillary lymph node dissection.* The surgeon also gave her a pamphlet outlining the surgery and the possible complications, including the arm swelling problem, and booked her surgery for the next week.

* * *

Disaster struck the Turle family on July 30. Lesley was at home when he got the call from the emergency room at the Redfern Hospital. A doctor whom he did not recognize related that Velma had been in a serious car accident on Redfern Road at Youngman Street. According to a tearful Carol Creek, who met him at the door to the ICU and accompanied him to Velma's bedside, a deer had jumped over the railing onto the road, landing on the hood of her old Smart Fortwo Passion, causing it to swerve directly into a utility pole at high speed. Leslie quickly realized the extent of Velma's head injuries when he walked into the room and saw her on the ventilator and motionless. She had no signs of trauma at all on her head or face except for a bruise on her forehead, but apart from the breathing tube in her mouth, she looked like she was lying in a coffin and not in a hospital bed. His medical instincts led him to pry open her eyelids and he immediately saw what he most dreaded; her pupils were dilated and did not constrict to the bright lights of the ICU. He remained stoic, sobbing softly, determined not to create the kind of scene in the ICU that he had frequently witnessed in individuals in his situation. Glenna Bass came into the room and put her arm around Leslie, but she knew she didn't need to go into any details about the situation.

"She's brain dead, isn't she," Leslie stated.

"We are not sure yet," Glenna replied. "I am running mannitol to reduce the brain swelling, but it certainly doesn't look hopeful. And we are getting an emergency CT scan. The only positive thing I can tell you is that her right pupil was not fixed and dilated when she first arrived in the ER."

When the CT scan was completed, Glenna Bass pulled the images up on the bedside computer screen and reviewed them with Leslie looking over her shoulder.

"She has coned, hasn't she," Leslie commented, breaking into tears. The scan showed that there was a huge hemorrhage in the right side of Velma's brain with compression or coning of the base of her brain against the rigid bones at the base of her skull. Dr. Bass confirmed his observation, then suggested that they could transfer Velma to Sunnybrook to see if there was any possibility that a neurosurgeon could operate to decompress her brain and drain the clot.

Leslie was not hopeful and had been in that situation many times, where the temptation is to stall on delivering the inevitable bad news of a hopeless situation, but then, also grasping at straws, suggested that a neurosurgeon should be able to review the images online and give them an opinion. Glenna Bass commented that the new computer system was designed precisely to allow this kind of sharing, and went to the desk to call the Neurosurgery Department at Sunnybrook. When a neurosurgeon called back a few minutes later, after collecting the detailed information needed to bill for a telephone consultation, he told Glenna that he could not do anything to save Velma's life. Glenna asked him to speak directly to Dr. Leslie Turle and handed Leslie the phone. The surgeon then changed his message slightly. "There is at best a 10 percent chance that she would even survive surgery. And even if she does, the best outcome would be that she would spend the rest of her life in a deep coma, attached to a ventilator and totally paralysed."

"Thank you for being so honest. She would not want to be kept alive in that state." Leslie hung up and went to the waiting room to call Isaac and Barb.

When Nancy relayed the message from her father-in-law to Isaac at work, he immediately went to the summer camp to pick up Adam, and then drove home. Adam, at six, was too young to fully understand the concept of death, but knew from his parents' sombre discussion and tears that something dreadful had happened to his nanna. They drove to the Redfern Hospital and met Leslie in the ICU waiting room. When he confirmed that Velma was brain dead but still on a ventilator, Isaac eschewed going to see her, and stayed in the waiting room with Adam while Nancy and Leslie went to the bedside. Like Leslie, Nancy thought that Velma looked like she was in a coffin, with the pillows propped up and her hands folded over her waist.

Leslie sent the family back to his home and returned to Velma. A few minutes later, Dr. Bass, a social worker, and a nurse asked him to join them in the quiet room. Another lady sporting a badge he did not recognize joined them and introduced herself as an organ donor coordinator. Leslie recalled the several occasions when he had been on the opposite side of the conversation and knew was coming; he pre-emptively said he knew what they were going to request. When Dr. Bass confirmed that Velma was indeed brain dead, he immediately said, "Take whatever you can use; she has signed her driver's licence organ donor permission, and often asked that they take whatever organs they could after she no longer could use them."

The donor coordinator thanked him and said that it would take a few hours to assess what organs were useable, and asked after Velma's medical history.

"Any history of heart, lung, liver, or kidney problems?"

"No."

"Any diabetes or high blood pressure?"

"No."

"Any prescription medication or allergies?"

"She has had a severe systemic reaction to a bee sting." Leslie related.

"That is interesting. There are case reports of that kind of allergy being transmitted to recipients with organ donation. We will make a note of that for the recipient coordinators. Any known hepatitis B, or C, or HIV or risk factors?"

"Not as far as I know."

The coordinator produced a paper for Leslie to sign, then thanked him profusely for his generosity, and expressed her condolences to him. Dr. Bass indicated that before organ retrieval could be booked, they would need to notify the coroner and get consent from him or her, since the "sudden and unexpected " clause in the Coroner's Act required that formality. Then they would book an OR time and allocate the organs based on the provincial distribution of donated organs algorithm they followed. They could not legally reveal any identifying information about the recipients to Leslie, but she indicated that they might be able to use all of Velma's transplantable organs, including her heart, liver, both lungs, both kidneys, both corneas, and her pancreas, perhaps even her small bowel. The social worker asked if Leslie wanted to have a member of the hospital clergy team visit Velma before organ retrieval, and Leslie declined.

Leslie spent a restless night trying to sleep in the guest room outside the ICU, visited Velma one last time, then completed the forms, indicating that arrangements would be made for cremation, as per her wishes, and that Smyth's Funeral Home would be in charge. Then he drove home to update Isaac and Nancy.

Leslie called and then visited the assistant funeral director at the Smyth Funeral Home and confirmed the arrangements for a single memorial service on August 2nd with a scheduled one-hour visitation to precede that. When Pauline Pike, the assistant at the funeral home asked about a reception, Leslie opted to hold a catered reception for attendees after the service, at the funeral home. He indicated that he expected about 75 people to attend, but the experienced funeral director pointed out that many more were likely to show up, even if they had not known Velma, as they would come primarily to show support for the family. She ordered enough finger food and refreshments for 150. They agreed that there would be no clergy involved in the service and no prayers, but the funeral director would invite the attendees to lay a hand on the urn containing Velma's ashes at the end of the service as a gesture of a fond farewell. Leslie picked out a wooden urn and signed the papers for the cremation and the agreement with the funeral home.

At the Turle home, Nancy was assigned the task of finding appropriate pictures of Velma for display at the visitation. Isaac called Velma's only brother, Stephen, in Calgary but was not surprised when he expressed no grief and indicated that he would not be able to attend the memorial service because of some prior commitment. Relations between Velma and her brother had been strained since childhood, and they had not spoken to each other for many years.

When Barb called that morning, they agreed on the wording of an obituary to be placed in the *Toronto Star* the next day. Leslie tried to persuade Barb to stay at home with her five-month-old Leslie Jr., but she insisted that she wanted to be at the memorial service. She would fly to Toronto and back the same day, if possible. Nancy, Isaac and Adam decided to return to Kingston and would return without Adam for the memorial service two days hence. Leslie asked about eulogies and it seemed that only he and Isaac would deliver any at the service; it hardly seemed appropriate to ask Barb to do so, given her previous estrangement and long-standing strained relationship with Leslie and Velma.

* * *

On the first day following Inge's double mastectomy, Carol Creek came to visit her in Princess Margaret Hospital. After inquiring about how she was doing, she handed Inge that day's Toronto Star, opened to the Notices section with an obituary circled in red ink.

Turle, Velma Louise. Suddenly as a result of an accident, on July 31, Velma Louise Turle, of Redfern in her 61st year. Beloved wife of Dr. Leslie Turle and loving stepmother of Isaac Turle of Kingston, and Dr. Barbara Turle-Knott (Lyle) of Baltimore, Md. Doting step-grandmother to Adam Turle and Leslie Knott. Predeceased by her parents, Lorne and Victoria Pickerel, and her sister, Marie. Survived by her brother, Stephen, of Calgary. Friends may pay their respects at a visitation from 1 to 2 p.m. at the Smyth Funeral Home, 424 Highway 5 E., Redfern, on August 2. A memorial service to honour her life will follow at 2 pm. Cremation following organ donation has taken place. In lieu of flowers,

please consider donations to the Ontario Trillium Gift of
Life Foundation in support of organ donation.

"Oh, my; as though that family has not been through enough
grief," Inge exclaimed. "If you are going to the service, please give
Dr. Turle my condolences."

"Will do," Carol replied.

Inge, too fatigued and foggy to realize that there were more
details that Carol could relate to her, then drifted back to sleep
under the influence of the narcotic analgesics she was receiving
through an intravenous pump.

* * *

That Saturday, Leslie was left alone in his home, and answered a
few calls from friends and acquaintances calling to express their
condolences, having read the obituary. He made up a list of topics he wanted to cover in his eulogy, revising it several times.
He called the number for The Humanist Society Of Ontario, and
the lady who answered checked and then called back to say that
unfortunately there was no officiant registered with the society
who would be available to officiate at the service.

The assistant at the funeral home called to ask if he had any
requests for music to be played as people gathered for the memorial service. He was not sure what Velma would have wanted, having never discussed it with her but suggested Frank Sinatra's *My
Way* and Gloria Estefan's rendition of *Everlasting Love*. The caller
suggested that they play two more songs, as they would start the
music 45 minutes before the service. He knew that Velma considered Terry Jacks' *Seasons in the Sun* to be a bit sentimental and sappy,
but requested it anyway. The other song he suggested, noting that
Velma had gorgeous brown eyes was Van Morrison's *Brown-Eyed
Girl*. The caller was a bit surprised by his unusual selections but
agreed to find them online and play them.

On Sunday morning, Faisal Al Taqi came to the house with a
huge package of frozen foods from M&M Meat Shops and explained
that it was from the hospital team that Leslie had worked with. In
reality, Faisal had collected donations from only three individuals

and had spent more than $100 of his own for the generous gift, knowing his friend's total lack of culinary skills.

As more than 150 people crowded into the funeral home room, and as Terry Jack's line "it's hard to die, when birds are singing in the sky" faded, the funeral director introduced Dr. Leslie Turle. He managed to maintain his composure very well, frequently glancing at the list of subjects he wanted to cover held in his hand, and closed by looking directly at the urn, and thanking Velma for a wonderful life well lived and for her devotion to him "particularly over the last few months."

Isaac rose and, trying to lighten the mood, started his tribute to Velma by quoting a line from Garrison Keillor, "They say such kind things about people at their funerals that I am sorry I will miss mine by a few days." This got only a few chuckles. He then said that he could not recall anything unkind that he could think of to say about Velma in any case, a lie that he knew would not be challenged in this setting. He went on to note how tirelessly and valiantly she had stood by and fought for Leslie in the dark days since that fateful Friday the 13th.

As he sat down, Barb rose and said she wanted to say a few words. Isaac and Leslie both winced, unsure about what she would say. But she had learned from giving countless lectures to think things through before speaking and had an engaging habit of ad libbing in full paragraphs, as she did on this occasion. Without notes, she started off by saying that it was no secret that her relationship with Velma had been strained over many years, the understatement of the day. Then she said that she realized that she had caused Velma and her father a lot of mental anguish. Wiping tears from her eyes, and looking first at her father and then directly at the urn she said simply, "I'm sorry." After sobbing for a full minute, along with most of the audience, she regained her composure and went on to describe her awe and admiration for Velma's support, forgiveness, and kindness in the dark days of the last seven months.

At the reception after the service, Carol Creek made a point of delivering Inge's condolences to Leslie and the family, saying that Inge was sorry that she could not come to the service because she had just had "some minor surgery."

"Nothing serious, I hope?" Leslie asked.

"Oh, I don't think so" Carol lied, sensing that Inge would not want Dr. Turle to know that she was facing an uncertain future and had just undergone very major surgery.

After the service, Leslie took the urn and the certificates of death and of cremation home and then drove Barb to Pearson airport for her return to Baltimore. As he drove, Leslie asked her why she had felt obligated to say anything at the service. She replied in her usual paragraph form. "A religious person in that situation would probably have remained silent, as would an existentialist, but as a humanist, I felt obligated to go one step further and make my apology and admission of my role in the estrangement from Velma in public and I am glad I did. If it makes the members of the audience look on Velma and you more favourably, that is a good consequence that I'd gladly accept, regardless of what the attendees think of me for saying it."

That led Leslie to ask "By the way, why did you give me an F on that essay I submitted as a response to your class assignment?"

She replied after a full minute pause to compose another full paragraph in her head. "Your spelling was British and not American in a couple places, but more importantly, your scenario of the runaway trolley car was blatant plagiarism, and we at St. Andrews have a zero tolerance policy for that. One other student used that very overworked dilemma as well, but cited the original description of it by Phillipa Foot in the psychology literature. If you had cited the source or of any variation of it, I would have given you a top mark."

"Do you think you maybe had a bit of a bias in giving me that if-only top mark?" he asked, and then related that he didn't even remember exactly what he had written or how the scenario at the funeral home related to philosophy at all. Her reply was simply to suggest that he think about it over in the next few days.

"Your example of Guy Paul Morin working for the Association for the Defence of the Wrongly Convicted after serving time for a murder he did not commit was a great example of the humanist response to being wronged, and I used it to discuss the assignment. He must be a humanist even if he doesn't know it. And I think you are too. You should check into some of the humanist societies and see if you agree with their outlook. I am a member of the American Humanist Society and have given a talk at one of their meetings."

He dropped Barb off at the Air Canada entrance and asked her to give his regards to Lyle when she got home. When Leslie returned home he asked himself what Velma would want done with her ashes, but realized the decision did not need to be made right away. Nancy and Isaac left later that evening, leaving him alone and sad. He looked at the guest book of the attendees at the service and recalled most of them only as a blur of faces whom he had met for the first time, and could not recall what many of them had said to him. He decided to start to make up his list of people to whom to send thank you notes. There were some that he did not even recall from that day. One name stood out among the latter. *Who was Paula Kaufman,* he wondered.

Later that night, unable to sleep in their big bed, he got up, went to the computer, and googled The Humanist Society of Ontario. Realizing that he generally agreed with the broad, vague tenets of various humanist groups, he narrowed his search to their specific position statements and ethics statements. He found that he agreed with their one-school funding position, their support for same-sex marriage rights, abortion access rights, and family planning, and their opposition to the proposed Quebec Charter of Rights. But he had reservations about their opposition to fracking, the development of oil sands and the Northern Gateway pipeline development. He felt that he didn't know enough about the energy industry to know whether or not these projects and practices were better or worse than any alternatives. But since Prime Minister Stephen Harper strongly supported them, he concluded that opposing them must be reasonable. He registered as a member and paid his $20 annual membership fee with a cheque.

Back in bed, he was restless and began to have second thoughts about the new group he had just joined. He dreamed about moral dilemmas that humanists might be unable to resolve. He thought that in the near future someone would develop a pricy Prozac-like medication for pregnant women that would, like Prozac, cross the placenta and could permanently alter the neuronal wiring of the embryos to make them happier offspring. Perhaps this had already happened to depressed women who took Prozac while pregnant. Welcome, Brave New World. If so, how would a humanist society decide who should get said pill- pregnant women in the west who could afford it (dangerously close to the position of eugenicists), or poor malnourished African women who might reap more benefit? Then there was the Ivy League education fund he had built up for his grandson Adam, now to be shared with Leslie Knott. Should he, as a newly minted humanist, donate this to Malala Yousafzai's charity to support the education of many disadvantaged girls in the third world instead as many more people would stand to benefit? Where would that leave kin loyalty?

* * *

Just over two weeks following her surgery on July 31, Inge returned to Dr. Li to be assessed for further treatment. Dr. Li reviewed the pathology report on the breasts and nodes that had been removed, and told Inge that she had about a 70 percent chance of full recovery with no recurrence for at least five years, but only if she could tolerate a full course of chemotherapy. She also related that the right breast had contained a small focus of the same cancer that had been found in her left breast, and that there was only one node that was positive for tumour in her left axilla. Dr. Li commended Inge for deciding to have the right breast removed. But chemotherapy of some type was an absolute necessity in her situation.

In response to Inge's question about the possibility of late recurrence after more than five years, she reassured her that this was rare in BRAC1-induced breast cancer, unlike the situation in women who develop the sporadic form of the disease. Inge also enquired about the risks of her developing ovarian cancer, and the oncologist indicated that she would be wise to undergo removal of her ovaries at some point to reduce that substantial risk. In the interim, they would do an ultrasound of her ovaries to be sure that the ovaries appeared to be normal at that point in time. They then discussed the options for various forms of chemotherapy. After discussing five different "recipes," Dr. Li suggested that she opt for a standard combination of doxorubicin and cyclophosphamide for at least four cycles, at three-week intervals, all given by intravenous infusion in the outpatient clinic. This would be followed by the oral administration of tamoxifen for four years.

The side effects of the chemotherapy that Dr. Li outlined sounded horrendous, including anorexia and vomiting, weight loss, lethargy, an increased risk of serious infections, hair loss, and possible, but rare, irreversible heart muscle damage. Inge felt that she had little choice, and she innately trusted Dr. Li's good judgment. She was given lengthy information pamphlets about the drugs she was about to start, and she promised to read them carefully. She also discussed the regimen with a friend who had undergone a course of chemotherapy for breast cancer two years earlier. After Dr. Li weighed Inge and measured her height to allow accurate calculation of the appropriate dosages, Inge pointed out a definitely reddened area on the scar over her right chest. Dr. Li prescribed cephalexin and delayed the first infusion of chemotherapy until September 2.

The first cycle of chemotherapy infusion was uneventful. By the time Inge drove home, she was already nauseated, but that soon passed. She did a few yoga exercises in the afternoon, ate a nutritious supper, and retired early. She planned to do some shopping the next day, but by the evening was confined to the condo by persistent diarrhea. She had taken the precaution of buying several cans of a nutritional supplement in case the expected weight loss became excessive or she became dehydrated. Now she wished that she had bought some adult diapers, as the hourly diarrhea precluded her going anywhere far from the porcelain throne. The nurse practitioner in the oncology outpatient clinic promptly responded to her email about the diarrhea and advised her to take generous amount of loperimide, lots of fluids, and a bulking agent. She called Carol Creek and Carol agreed to bring the loperimide, adult diapers, and Fibre1 cookies. At the door, Inge broke down in tears at the kindness, generosity, and understanding that her dearest friend had shown.

On day three, the nausea and vomiting returned, and persisted for several days, in spite of liberal use of the ondansetron that Dr. Li had prescribed prophylactically for these side effects. By the end of the first week of the first cycle of chemotherapy, Inge felt vaguely human again, but was still nauseated and anorexic, and she ached all over. But she noticed that her urine had turned to a distinct red hue and again emailed the outpatient nurse practitioner about that. The immediate response was reassuring. "Sometimes that is an early side effect of doxorubicin therapy, but at this stage, it is more likely an effect of the cyclophosphamide on your bladder lining. Keep well hydrated and never delay any urge to empty your bladder. And abstain from sex."

I hardly needed that last advice, Inge thought. At that point, there was nothing more unappealing to her than the thought of having sex—even the thought made her nausea worsen perceptibly. But she was grateful for the accessibility of the nurse practitioner's advice and wondered how others in her situation had coped in the days before the Internet. By the time she was due to return for her second cycle of chemotherapy, she felt almost normal, but was still fatigued; and she had lost twelve pounds. She still had little appetite. The nurse said that her lab work was "satisfactory," but her white blood cell count was getting quite low and she gave Inge a paper facemask to wear whenever she was out in public to prevent any transmission of airborne infections. She then administered an intravenous dose of ondansetron before giving her the doxorubicin and then the cyclophosphamide. This time Inge just managed to reach home before the intense nausea and vomiting set in. She did not develop any diarrhea in the next few days, and the nausea, anorexia, and aches were more tolerable now that she knew what to expect.

About a week later, as she was starting to feel better, she developed an intense burning pain extending across her lower back on the right, into her right groin, and two days after that, a distinctive blistering rash appeared in the same area. After two more days of intense pain, she took a selfie and emailed it to the nurse practitioner in the outpatient clinic, hoping that the NSA was not intercepting her rather unflattering photo of her right groin and labia. The response was immediate and far from reassuring. "Please come in this afternoon. Dr. Li wants to assess the rash first-hand."

When Inge showed up at the clinic, Dr. Li looked at the rash only very briefly, confirming the self-diagnosis that Inge had already made of shingles brought on by the effects of the chemotherapy on her immune system. What was most important to Dr.

Li, it appeared, was her desire to get a few good photographs of the rash for teaching purposes. After Inge signed a consent form, she lay on the examination table with only a green surgical towel covering her pubic area while Dr. Li took several pictures of the rash from different angles. In discussion, she indicated that no topical treatment would likely change the course of the rash, as all treatments had to be started very early to be effective, and advised Inge to contact her nurse immediately if a similar rash appeared anywhere else in the next few days. She postponed Inge's third cycle of chemotherapy by two weeks to give the shingles time to heal, much to Inge's consternation. When directly asked if this would increase the risk of cancer recurrence, she stated "There is no evidence one way or the other on that, but the important factor is that you eventually complete the full four cycles of therapy."

By the date of Inge's appointment for her third cycle of chemotherapy on October 24, she felt well, and the rash had almost completely disappeared, but she had lost twenty-eight pounds. Feeling very well, with only mild pain over her groin, she questioned whether the further treatment cycles were really a worthwhile price to pay to very slightly reduce the risk of her cancer returning, but decided to persist. She now considered herself to be an expert in controlling the side effects in the first few days after the infusions. It seemed to help that Dr. Li, a bit concerned about the excessive weight loss, had prescribed oral nabilone for Inge, explaining that it was a pure cannabinoid similar to the main active ingredient in marijuana and was an appetite stimulant and mild sedative. Inge joked to Carol Creek that she was going to pot.

She had been told about and had noticed the clumps of hair falling out when she combed her hair, but was hardly prepared for the sudden and complete loss of all of her hair a few days after this cycle. All of her pubic and head hair suddenly fell out, but she was more alarmed when she looked into the mirror and saw someone that was barely recognizable, with no eyebrows or eyelashes, a completely bald head, and sunken dark cheeks. The nurse once again reassured her that the deepening skin pigmentation was a reversible side effect of the medication. After conferring with her friend who had been through this and being reassured that her hair, eyebrows, and eyelashes would grow back, she decided to look for a wig. Her friend suggested that she go to a beauty supply store in the Highway 5 West Mall.

She felt she was through the worst of her ordeal, could tolerate one more round of chemotherapy, and headed out to buy a wig. Her final cycle of the intravenous chemotherapy would be given on the 14th of November, and thereafter she would only be on oral tamoxifen. She would also likely be giving up her ovaries sometime in the next year, but that would involve a simple one-day visit to the hospital, and would be done through the laparoscope. It might yet be a Merry Christmas.

14

saintly seizures

Leslie Turle spent most of August in various appointments to clean up Velma's estate. His lawyer noted that since the will left everything to Leslie and the only bank accounts were joint ones, there should be no need for probate of Velma's estate. Their financial advisor/accountant found a few legal means of minimizing the taxes that would be owed on the estate and agreed to prepare the final income tax return for Velma's estate when all the statements came in. The insurance company could not contest the double indemnity clause in Velma's life insurance, and after a long delay, with lots of requests for more documents, issued a cheque to Leslie for $300,000 as well as a separate one for the wrecked car. He considered what to do with this unwelcome windfall. At the suggestion of the accountant, noting that it would barely impact his net worth or his tax status, Leslie directed $200,000 to the Beaverbrook Hospital Foundation, with the stipulation that the funds be used for the continuing education of professionals in the ICU or ER. He considered calling it the Dr. Leslie Turle Education Fund and would welcome the free goodwill from that. But he wondered what a real humanist would do, and finally stipulated that the source of the funds remain anonymous at least until after his death. He took Velma's clothes to the Goodwill drop-off store.

His good friend Faisal Al Taqi and his wife A'Idah took him out for a proper halal dinner at the Zaytoun Halal restaurant, and they reminisced and chatted. When Faisal reminded left-handed Leslie that it was *makruh* to eat with his left hand, the conversation segued quite seamlessly into a general discussion of religion, as it often did when they were together. They seemed to have a common bond in their skepticism about any organized religion. Coming from very different backgrounds, they both had arrived at a similar position with respect to religion, although Faisal was not openly agnostic and still professed to be a very liberal Muslim, confiding only to Leslie that he did not believe much of Islamic dogma. Leslie knew that Faisal regarded him as a radical atheist, almost evangelical in his denunciation of religions of all types, and often tried to push him to express ever more outrageous opinions on religion. Leslie was always happy to oblige. He was always interested in foreign cultural and religious traditions and said that he had read an English translation of the Koran, but did not recall reading anything about handedness.

"You are right that the Koran does not say anything about eating with the left hand. That and a lot of other things in modern Islam are either hadith from the sayings of the prophet from later *fatwas* or even just traditions And there are so many English translations of the Koran that you could readily interpret Islamic laws and traditions any way you want, depending on which translation you choose." Faisal then remarked that he was very disappointed in the Canadian Muslim leaders' mild condemnation of the radical elements in their religion that interpret the Koran as a call to armed conflict.

"Well, Faisal, if you want religious excuses to do horrible things, look no further than in the Old Testament. In Deuteronomy somewhere, the God common to our religious backgrounds orders us to commit genocides and rape. It's not just Muslims that can be radicals and quote their scriptures to justify cruelty."

Faisal related that he had attended a wedding at a Unitarian church, and had found their embrace of inclusiveness to be very attractive. He said that he was not yet ready to completely abandon Islam, but if he ever did get to that point, he would look into humanism or Unitarianism in more detail.

"I was married by a Unitarian minister and their outlook in many ways is similar to the humanists, except that they don't accept complete atheism," Leslie said. "But I don't think ... I am not sure ... I don't think that being a liberal Muslim is at all incompatible with also being a member of the Humanist Society of Ontario that I have joined.

"To make you think more about your religious beliefs, consider this. A while ago, I watched a BBC show about religious revelations that caused quite a stir. This idea is not at all new. I wish I could take credit for thinking about it first, but I can't. There have been scholarly expositions written about it for years.

Anyway, a neuroscientist speculated about whether or not St. Paul suffered from temporal lobe epilepsy. Almost certainly Joan of Arc and Fyodor Dostoevsky did. I remember seeing a very religious patient with that type of seizure disorder, who, during seizures, would relate sudden religious revelations and hear voices giving her directives that she believed to be coming from God. It's not that the revelations are less interesting, real, or important. It is just that they may all have come from within a human brain. And the prophet Mohammed had the same kind of sudden dramatic revelations, supposedly from Allah. What if all of those revelations came from within his temporal lobes? Would you still believe them?"

The more devout A'Ida piped up, rather upset with Leslie's heretical reasoning. "Well, while you are in the business of blaspheming religious leaders, what about Jesus. Did he have epilepsy, too?"

Leslie pondered that for a long time, having learned well from Barb to think out paragraph answers before responding to difficult questions.

Finally, he responded. "No. He never had sudden revelations from another world apart from the Mount of Transfiguration scene, which was probably mythical. I think he was just a very cunning, aspiring politician and the leader of a minor Jewish sect until St. Paul made him into a god, as a result of the revelations in *his* seizure, or epiphany, depending on what you choose to believe. Jesus may have been a bit delusional or even psychotic, but not epileptic. And it was as a result of St. Paul's sudden revelation that Jesus became the posthumous leader of a powerful political and religious party. Witness the political clout of the Catholic Church to this day. And it wasn't until late in the fourth century when the bishops and emperors stopped their fratricidal massacres long enough to agree on the wording of their various creeds that the identity of Jesus with God was widely accepted."

Faisal interjected. "Do you think that there were other leaders who had temporal lobe epilepsy?"

Again, Leslie thought through his response carefully. "Well, I don't know enough about Hinduism, Buddhism, Sikhism, or any of the other eastern religions to comment on them, but yes. What about Noah, Moses, Abraham, Jacob, Job, Isaiah? Some of them were certainly mythical figures or composites of several people, but for others, you can choose to call them true prophets, epileptics, or psychotics or some combination of the three."

"How can you tell the difference between psychosis and religious seizures?" Faisal asked. "Especially in someone long gone that you can't test for a seizure disorder?"

Again, Leslie considered his response carefully. "I am not sure, but it seems to me that psychotics, once they recover from an episode, no longer believe the delusions they had. On the other hand, religious epileptics carry their delusions or revelations over into their everyday lives and continue to believe them. And the other characteristic of religious seizures is their sudden flash-like appearance supposedly from another world. Which reminds me—we should include Joseph Smith, the founder of Mormonism in the list of suspects."

"What about the writer of the book of Revelations? I actually read that trying to understand the belief in a coming apocalypse and it made no sense to me."

"I agree. I think that was the disconnected writing of a complete lunatic—likely someone we would now consider to be a schizophrenic. If it appeared for the first time on the internet today, the security guys would hunt him down and lock him up until a shrink determined that he or she was a harmless schizophrenic. But there is nothing like the flash of a seizure there. But philosophers will say there is no way to distinguish reality from delusions. We know that all of our senses can deceive us and lead us to hold contradictory beliefs about reality without even recognizing the contradictions. You need to ask my daughter that kind of question. She is also the philosopher who thinks that dogs have their own religion! Are you ready to order dessert?"

As they parted, Leslie thanked them for an interesting dinner and for being open-minded about religious thoughts.

"Just be thankful that we are in Canada. In many parts of the world you would be stoned to death or beheaded for what you said tonight," Faisal replied.

When he returned home, Leslie added: "Audit a university course on comparative religion" to his bucket list, then, on reflecting, decided that he didn't really have much interest in learning more about any religion and deleted it.

Over the Labour Day weekend, Leslie visited Isaac, Nancy, and Adam. He had made up a list of points to discuss if or when he met the man who had saved his life, keeping it in his jacket pocket, and began the search while in Kingston. When he called the Collins Bay Institution, the guard said that Eric Clouser had been transferred to the nearby Pittsburgh Institution. Calling there, he was informed that Eric Clouser had been released on parole.

When he returned to Redfern, he called the Hook Line and Sinker tackle shop. A man answered the phone, calling the store the Hook Line and Sinker Fly Shop. When asked, the man said that Eric Clouser worked at the store but that it was under new management. He also commented that the name was changing, as they were going to concentrate exclusively on fly-fishing equipment, flies, and guiding fly-fishing excursions. Leslie got directions and decided to pay a visit.

On a sunny September afternoon, Leslie walked into the Hook Line and Sinker Fly shop. Tom immediately recognized him from his appearance at the preliminary hearing, as did Eric Clouser, sitting at a fly-tying table, tying a black and yellow bumble bee imitation bomber fly from spun and clipped dyed deer body hair. After an awkward silence, Leslie, pulling his list from his pocket, explained that he had come to thank Eric in person for saving his life that fateful Friday.

"You're welcome," Eric replied. "But you know, I really only did what any decent human being would have done in the same situation."

"Well, maybe so, but what you did had some pretty nasty consequences for you, did it not?"

"Not at all. I got free room and board for seven months, and the drug rehab program I went through changed my perspective on a lot of things. And Tom here took over this shop and knows how to run a business far better than I do, and it is doing well. And in the lockup they let me tie a pile of flies and teach some of the others how to tie flies as well. Take a look at that rack of flies over there, all courtesy of Her Majesty. I was almost disappointed when they kicked me out early just because I finished that drug rehab program. But I still have to report to my parole officer."

Leslie looked into a drawer full of tube flies, and, seeing his puzzled look, Eric explained how to fish them. He picked out a few tube flies for Leslie and showed him the appropriate-sized hooks to use with them.

"Is there anything at all I can do to help you?" Leslie enquired, glancing at his list.

"Nothing at all, sir," Eric replied.

Tom was more forthcoming. "You know that photograph of us that you referred to in court? If you still have it, I could certainly use it on the website for the shop."

"I do have it and I'll bring it in for you."

"Do you have any interest in fly-fishing?" Tom inquired.

"Learning the technique is on my bucket list, thanks to you guys," Leslie replied. "But it's away down near the bottom, as I figured I could do that after I turned eighty."

"We might be able to work something out that would be good for both of us," Tom stated, and then paused. "If you want to take some lessons and a guided trip or two, we could arrange that for a bargain price, or better still, we could employ you here in the shop. We have had to close the shop for a day on two occasions when both Eric and I are out guiding, and if you could fill in occasionally we could teach you how to run the till, and, in return, we'll sell you some tackle and give you some lessons at bargain prices or maybe free. All completely above-board, of course. What do you think?"

"As long as I would be able to keep it flexible, it sounds like a good deal." Leslie replied. He gave Tom his email address and phone number, and began to look over the rack of fly rods, asking what a newbie to the sport should buy first. Tom picked out the nine-foot, seven/eight weight rod that he had just built from a St.Croix blank, a Cortland weight-forward sink-tip line, a case containing a Grey reel with four interchangeable spools, some tippet

and weights, and a small sampler box of flies. He tied the backing
onto the reel and the fly line onto the backing cord. He picked out
a couple of weighted Kaufman golden stonefly nymphs and told
Leslie that the salmon would hit them year round.

"Once you have held the fort here in the shop for a couple of
days, these are yours," he told Leslie. "And you will need pliers to
remove the hook from a fish without harming them and to crush
the barb on hooks if you are fishing where only single, barbless
hooks are allowed. And be sure to check the Ontario MNR fishing
regulations before you fish anywhere. They're online."

"I was barbless for far too long already." Then Leslie had to
explain the double entendre meaning of the word "barbless" for
him, but was pleased to realize that his facility with quick comebacks and quips had resurfaced. "No. This tackle is mine, and I am
paying full price for it right now." Leslie moved over to the check-
out stand. "And I will be back to get some lessons in how to man
the shop for free and in fly casting, for your usual fee. Just let me
know when you need me."

"We don't apologize for this, but you know that Eric and I are
partners in more than business. I hope that doesn't stop you from
joining us and helping us run this business," Tom asked hesitantly.

"I know that and it doesn't bother me at all. Just don't expect
me to make it a threesome," Leslie joked. As he was leaving with
the equipment for his new hobby, he noticed a book called *Fly-fishing for Dummies*, and Eric said he could have a copy of it for free
if he promised to study it diligently before coming back for his
first lesson.

* * *

Leslie had cancelled the trip to Machu Picchu shortly after Velma's funeral but in early September he began to reconsider. He
was frequently reminded about Velma's longstanding keen desire
to travel there by the urn sitting on top of his computer desk. He
called Isaac and Barb to ask what they would think if he took her
ashes to scatter them at Machu Picchu near the big ancient sundial. Both thought this was a great idea and both said they hoped
to go there someday and would find it more compelling to do so

if they knew that Velma was, in some sense, already there. After checking online about regulations regarding transporting of ashes, he became discouraged. The rules seemed to indicate that he would need to have a funeral director in Canada to contact a funeral director in Peru to make the arrangements. He would have to notify the airline he was travelling on to check their policies. The funeral director at Smyth Funeral Home gave him some encouragement and indicated that his plan was in keeping with Canadian laws, but that he would have to avoid any stopovers on American soil to avoid the nasty rules imposed by the Transportation Safety Board. He suggested that Leslie not contact the airline in advance and simply take the ashes with him in his luggage. But he warned that Peruvian authorities would frown on scattering the ashes of a foreigner on what was considered sacred ground, and he could do so only with some deception as to what he was carrying.

Leslie found a flight from Pearson to Lima with a stopover only in San Salvador, and booked this for October third, returning on the tenth. He would try to get answers to Velma's questions about the Incas' dietary habits and rituals and perhaps he could then complete her review and send it as a posthumous contribution from her to *Nutrition Reviews*. The urn, being wooden, would pass the security scanning and he would take the death certificate and the certificate of cremation with him. Getting the ashes from Lima to Cusco and then to Machu Picchu would be more problematic, but he would devise some plan to do so.

Picking up the urn, he said, "Come on, honey, we are going on your dream adventure." He thought that if he had to abandon her somewhere along the Inca Trail to Machu Picchu, he could take multiple pictures of the site from different angles, so that future family visitors could locate her. Ideally she would be surrounding the sundial atop one of the pyramids within the ancient city.

His plan went beautifully until he passed through customs at Lima's Jorge Chavez International Airport. A customs inspector checking his baggage inquired about what was in the peculiar square wooden box inside the green velvet purse-string bag. When Leslie related that it was an urn containing ashes, the inspector informed him that he would have to dispose of that before he got to Machu Picchu. Leslie tried the usual trick of flashing a ten Nuevo Sol note at him, but he would have nothing to do with that. Instead the agent checked Leslie's itinerary, called the hotel that Leslie had reserved in Cusco and apparently gave them Leslie's name and reservation number, all in Spanish.

When he arrived at Plaza de Armas Hotel Cusco, the check-in clerk explained to him in broken English that he would have to dispose of the urn before embarking on the guided hike up the Inca Trail the next day. Alternatively the hotel would keep it for him and return it to him on his return from Macchu Picchu. At his request, she let him check in and he promised to return the urn to her within an hour. In his room, he devised a plan to overcome this little snag in his quest to take Velma to the place she long had dreamed of visiting. He fashioned a funnel from a sheet of paper, took the 10-litre plastic water bag out of his Camelback back pack and opened the urn.

"Honey, we have to change vehicles here," he explained, carefully pouring the ashes into the funnel, and thus into the Camelback bag. Pouring some tap water into the urn and swishing it around, he funnelled this into the Camelback as well, repeating this process three times. Placing the empty urn in a laundry bag, he returned to the front desk clerk and showed her the urn. The very helpful clerk then explained to him that there was a Catholic church within walking distance and, if he wanted to, he could take the ashes there. The clerk said that a priest would want to conduct a rite of some sort—Leslie could not understand the Spanish word she used—but Leslie knew how to deal with the clergy. He thanked her profusely in his limited Spanish, got directions, and headed out carrying the urn in the laundry bag.

Finding the immense Cathedral of Santo Domingo, he mingled with the tourists and carefully placed the empty urn on the floor behind a statue of St. Mary when no one was looking. As he passed back through the hotel lobby, he threw both arms in the air to show the clerk that he had disposed of the urn. Now if he could persuade the guides on the trail to let him keep his Camelback, Velma might yet reach her final destination. Later, in his room, he turned on the television news, entirely in Spanish that he could not understand.

But he suddenly understood the picture of police officers and men in hazmat suits surrounding the statue of St. Mary in the Cathedral de Santo Domingo.

The next morning, before the group of hikers left on the hike, they were all held up for more than an hour by a group of Peruvian soldiers. It appeared that someone had forgotten to grease the appropriate palms in the bureaucracy, and until that oversight had been taken care of, no one could move. Fortunately no one searched the backpacks and small bags the hikers took with them. From there on, things went exactly as planned. The guide thought it was peculiar that Leslie had hauled a Camelback water bag that was only half full up the trail and offered to fill it. Leslie replied that the water tasted stale and that he wanted to save it in case he became desperately dry, so the guide gave him some fresh water in plastic bottles.

Leslie changed his mind about where to put Velma to rest when they reached the Hut of the Caretaker of the Funerary Rock in Machu Picchu. Walking into this magnificent old structure, he waited until no one was looking and then opened the Camelback and drained the ashes onto the rock floor, then poured some of the fresh water into it, swished it around and poured that out, repeating this process three times to clear it of any residual ashes. A couple from Ottawa that had befriended him along the trail became worried about him when they found him sitting and sobbing on the rocks below the Hut, but he said he just found the scenery very overpowering. They agreed to take several pictures on his camera of him as he stood in front of the ancient ruin. When he got home, he emailed the pictures to Isaac and Barb with the note: "Velma's final destination."

Both on the trek and at the ruins, Leslie asked visitors and guides about the Inca's diet, food preparations and their cannibalism. Most of the visitors seemed to be unaware that they were visiting the site of a cannibalistic "civilization" at all. The guides were very keen to point out the carvings of pot-bellied stoves and related a lot of detail about their diets. But they uniformly either denied that the Incas were cannibals or pretended that they did not understand the word. He guessed that they did not have a big problem with starvation, as they were said to have kept a seven-year supply of dried vegetables and meats in vast storehouses, but his inquiries about obesity were greeted with blank stares from the guides. In the end, he didn't think he'd gotten enough juicy details to complete Velma's essay.

On his return trip, he decided to have some fun in disposing of his empty Camelback water container. He filled it with water at the Cusco airport then left it with no identification on it in a deserted departure lounge, imagining another frantic deployment of the Peruvian police to check it out.

* * *

Leslie knew that some of his medical colleagues and coworkers regarded him with some suspicion even after the report of the preliminary hearing had appeared to clear his name. That report had received much less media attention than the earlier reports insinuating that he had been a drug user or a gay sexual predator—or a victim of a gay sexual predator—and he was still uncomfortable going to continuing medical education conferences. But if he was to maintain his licence to practice and his standing with the Royal College of Physicians and Surgeons of Canada, he needed to keep up his continuing medical education credits. He needed to maintain his licence if he was ever going to work as a physician at the Canadian High Arctic Research Station, as he hoped to do. He thought he would be more anonymous at the Canadian Critical Care Forum at the Toronto Sheraton hotel on October 30th to November 2nd, and old friends from across the country might not have heard about the John Doe found in Beaver Park that Friday the 13th. When he registered for the conference, some old friends did indeed greet him warmly, but others seemed to shun him.

As he was chatting with Faisal Al Taqi at the conference mid-morning break, Faisal said, "You have to see poster Number 81. It's in the trainee section." Faisal would not say anything more about it. "Just go and see it," he urged. When Leslie found the poster with a small Vietnamese trainee standing beside it, he almost choked. The poster title was *Hypothyroidism Protects the Brain from Injury Due to Hypothermia*. The authors were Dr. Winki Pham and Dr. Glenna Bass, and they had accurately presented the case of the anonymous hypothermic man with coexisting hypothyroidism. In the discussion, the authors speculated that induced hypothyroidism might also be appropriate treatment for other forms of brain injury.

Winki did not immediately recognize the elderly bearded physician who was carefully reviewing her poster until he turned to talk to her and she saw the scars on his nose and cheek and then introduced herself, very embarrassed that the subject of her poster was now reviewing it. She would be forever grateful that Dr. Bass had insisted that the only identifier of the patient had been "A 64-year-old male."

Leslie pointed out that they had his age wrong, and Winki replied that the error was deliberate, at Dr. Bass's insistence, to protect his anonymity. "If anyone thinks it is about you, just point out the age discrepancy. And very few people know about your hypothyroidism."

After Winki Pham related her role in his early ICU stay, Leslie complimented her on a well-designed poster, and thanked her for her treatment of him. Then, as he moved on, he muttered to no one, "They could at least have made me a co-author."

* * *

By the end of October, Leslie felt lonely and sad in the big house and decided to move to smaller quarters. He listed the house for $20,000 below the $569,000 price the real estate agent recommended and it sold within three days at the price the agent had suggested. He had to scramble to find an apartment or condo before the closing date of December first, and finally settled on a penthouse loft in a new condo development still only half a kilometre from the Beaver Trail that he loved to walk. Faisal Al Taqi, Isaac, and Nancy helped move the smaller items, delivering others to the Goodwill charity shop. He hired a professional mover to move the larger items. He had made up a list of items that he thought Barb or Isaac might want, including six of his Bev Doolittle camouflage prints, but kept his favourite, *The Forest Has Eyes*, and Velma's favourite, *Sacred Circle*, to hang in his new home, and donated *The Sentinel* to hang in the ICU at the Beaverbrook Hospital. He worked hard to get everything in place at his new abode and invited Isaac, Nancy, Adam, and the Knott family to spend whatever time they wanted with him over Christmas. He knew that his culinary skills were very limited and tried to cook a turkey with online directions as a practice for that. He ate nothing else but very overcooked dry turkey for about a week, but was proud of his accomplishment.

The next week, to take a break from unpacking, Leslie visited the Hook Line and Sinker fly shop again, with a list of items he realized he still needed to begin to fly-fish, including chest waders, a fishing vest or chest pack, a wading stick, nippers, and a stringer. Tom chose RedHeaded Bone Dry booted chest waders and a Fishpond chest pack. He suggested a steel stringer, and said that Cabellas Canada online store would be a better place to find a wading stick. He told Leslie that he didn't need nippers, as a nail clipper would work just as well, or he could use his teeth to cut tippet as long as he didn't tell his dentist. Then he sat Leslie down and tried to teach him a few basic fishing knots he would need to learn. He quickly learned to tie an improved cinch knot, a blood knot, and a surgeon's knot but had difficulty tying a nonslip mono loop knot and the nail knot, even with a tube in place of a nail.

Tom, who prided himself in knowing everything about knots, suddenly looked at him and asked, "Are you related to Major Greer Turle?"

"Not as far as I know. Why do you ask?"

"Well, there is a knot named after him—the Turle knot—and it's easy to tie. Let me show you how to tie it."

Leslie found the Turle knot indeed easy to tie and vowed to try it. Tom referred him to the online Orvis app that would teach him how to tie all kinds of knots and would describe all kinds of flies. Tom then suggested that they go together for a two-day fishing trip to Pulaski, New York, in January, to fish the Salmon River for steelhead and salmon. They would hire a local guide to drift fish the river for the first day. Eric would be unable to cross the border because of his criminal record, but might take Leslie fishing in the Beaver River later. Leslie had never considered fly-fishing as a winter sport, but found the thought of it somehow appealing. Tom assured him that he did not need a fishing licence for fishing in Ontario, as he was over sixty-five.

15

hair

On December 12, Inge went shopping for a lymphedema sleeve for her increasingly swollen left arm. As she entered the Square Ten Mall, she was startled to see Dr. Leslie Turle sitting in the barbershop near the entrance waiting to get a haircut and beard trim. He was wearing an odd combination of clothes, including unmatched red socks, above which were black long johns under blue biking shorts, and a heavy yellow biking jersey. She was sure he did not recognize her with her bald head wrapped in a scarf, sunken dark cheeks, and sporting a paper facemask. She wore the mask partly for protection against infections in her vulnerable state, and partly to hide the cheeks with bone outlines almost showing through her skin. She hurried to the drugstore in the mall and got fitted with the compression sleeve. As she passed the barber shop again, Leslie was now lying back in the chair getting his beard trimmed. Old memories and emotions flooded into her consciousness. She bought a coffee in the nearby food court and sat down on a bench where she could watch him in the mirror in the barber shop, pulling the mask up to sip the coffee. She carefully adjusted her new sleeve until it was comfortable. As Leslie walked out of the barber shop, donning his blue gortex biking jacket that at least matched his shorts, she stood up, walked toward him and nonchalantly greeted him. "Hi, Dr. Turle."

He stared at the source of the greeting and at first did not recognize the gaunt and plain woman; her emaciated appearance immediately reminded him of the anatomy lab cadaver that he had dissected many years before. Then he saw the distinctive tan fibroma, completely exposed by the absence of eyebrows.

Her stare met his and he exclaimed "Oh, my God, Inge, what has happened to you?" immediately regretting his impertinent inquiry.

"Come on over to the food court. Let me buy you a coffee and I will tell you all about it," she replied. He declined the coffee, but told her how glad he was to see her again as they walked to the food court. He sat down across a table from her and apologized for his inappropriate question, saying he was shocked at how much weight she had lost. Inge proceeded to tell him about her ordeal with breast cancer, surgery, and chemotherapy, concluding by saying that she hoped the worst was over, and that the oncologist had quoted her a 70 percent chance of a cure. After he wished her a speedy recovery and Inge conveyed her condolences to him on his wife's passing, they sat in awkward silence. Leslie realized that he was more upset by the news of Inge's ordeal and uncertain future than he had been about anything since Velma's death. He expressed his sympathy to her and commented that the next year could only be better for both of them.

Then he tried to lighten her mood "Have you found that rich older widower that I hear you have been looking for?"

This was Inge's chance—it was now or never. She recalled that he had always ignored the clues about how she felt about him, including the most blatant one on that fateful Friday almost exactly a year before. But there was no turning back. She also knew that she was possibly about to commit a terrible social blunder, and might well be rebuffed, but she had to know whether or not he had any affection for her.

"Well, I think so, but I haven't seen him for almost a year, and I have no idea what he thinks of me now." She hesitated. "And the last time I saw him, he was in a coma." she added, her heart pounding.

"Well, do I know him?' Leslie asked.

Realizing that he still didn't get her hint, she hesitated again then said "And the last time I saw him, he wasn't a widower either, but he is now."

"Well, who is he?" Leslie asked innocently.

"Leslie" she replied, having never called him by his first name before. "You still don't get it? I dream of being with him all the time. Now I am staring into his eyes."

Leslie still took a second to realize what she was saying, and returned her stare. He stood up to give her a hug, and she also stood. As they hugged, he said, "Inge, I never had a clue what you thought of me, but I feel the same way about you and have for years. I am thrilled that we have met again."

Impulsively pushing caution and her face mask aside, she gave him a short passionate kiss on the lips, oblivious of the stares of the startled passing shoppers who had never seen such an unlikely pair of lovebirds. Then they sat down, and looking around a bit embarrassed, held hands across the table and began to talk.

"You certainly never gave me any clue how you felt about me until now, Inge," Leslie began. "We have a lot of things to discuss. I'm not sure what you will think of me when you find out about all the skeletons in my closet. I am not sure where this is going, and I certainly don't want to hurt you."

"Well, I did give you lots of subtle hints, but you always ignored them, and I knew you were a happily married man then and you probably thought I was a happily married woman."

"Well, Velma was unhappy, and I was married," Leslie joked.

"And Joe was happy, and I was married. Maybe there are some skeletons in my closet, too. Right now I have a bit of brain fog from the chemo. When I first saw you sitting in the barber shop, I thought my brain was playing tricks on me. But there is no escape from the feelings I have now. The oncologist tells me that the brain fog will go away, but I know my feelings won't. I promise to be completely honest with you if you will do the same for me. We have deceived each other for long enough."

"Fair enough. Now that we have both made complete asses of ourselves in public here, where can I take you for lunch where we can talk without the stares?"

"How about Panera Bread, just down the street?" she suggested.

They walked down the street together chatting like old friends, but a bit awkwardly as both were uncertain about whether they really were going to share a future of some sort, or be rejected when their lies and deceits were revealed. They shared a roasted turkey and avocado BLT sandwich that Inge chose, and reminisced. To be cautious, and lighten the conversation, he joked that they could not possibly get serious with each other until at least after their first big quarrel. They agreed that they would meet again and then swapped contact information.

After she gave him another hug back in the parking lot, she stared after him as he unlocked his Marinoni road bike and rode down the street without a helmet, marvelling at how well she suddenly felt. She knew that there would be gossip about her new relationship, coming as it did so soon after Velma's death and her own divorce. But for the first time in many years, she didn't care what others thought of her- this felt too right to be wrong.

For his part, as he rode away, the word *limerence* re-emerged into his consciousness, and he realized that he had once again lost control of the state of his mind. But he was determined to go slowly into this new territory, and wait a discreet few days before calling her for their first real date.

The next week, feeling happy but cautious, Leslie decided to try fly-fishing on his own for the first time, the day after his Cabellas wading stick arrived in the mail, but he then forgot to take it with him. He had spent hours practising fly casting in the backyard, much to the amusement of his neighbour. He was confident with his technique and aim.

He drove to Beaver Park on the warm, cloudy Tuesday, got into his waders beside the truck, assembled his rod, reel, and line, and tied a Kaufman golden stonefly on using a Turle knot. South of the Highway 5 bridge, he cautiously stepped into the shallow water along the side of the river. A young man was standing twenty feet from shore and casting repeatedly out about twenty feet. He studied the man's sequence of movements, standing motionless. Suddenly the line jerked tight and the rod tip bent. The man lifted the tip and the line sang out as a huge fish jumped in front of him. After about ten minutes, the exhausted fish was reeled up close, and the man backed up toward shore. Seeing Leslie, he pulled a net off the magnetic holder on his vest back and handed it to him, asking him to help net the fish. Once the hook was removed and the fish was weighed, the man held it gently by the tail in the water then slowly released it. Turning to Leslie, he introduced himself as Mel Caddis. Leslie, showing his ignorance, asked what species it was and was told it was a brown trout. Mel added that he never kept them in the interest of conservation. "New to the sport, are you?" Mel asked.

"Yes. First time out, but it looks like a lot of fun," Leslie replied.

"Well, you really shouldn't be out here alone at this time of the year if you don't know the river and can't even identify the species. But I can give you a few tips, if you want. Always keen to introduce a newbie to this fine sport."

"That would be great, and much appreciated. Where do I start?"

"Listen. That boy will likely go right back to that pool and there are others there, too." Pointing, Mel guided him to a spot to cast from and pointed at a spot upstream from a seam in the river below some rapids near the far bank. Leslie thanked him and tried to cast, but several casts were well off the mark. Mel offered to make a cast for him, flipped the tip of the rod to mend the line for a proper drift of the fly, and handed the rod back to Leslie. Suddenly the line tightened and the rod tip bent. "You got him! Now set the hook!" Mel shouted. Leslie jerked the rod tip up.

"Now let him run." Mel advised, as he checked the drag tension on Leslie's reel. There was a huge splash as the fish jumped four feet into the air away downstream.

"That's not the same fish!" Mel shouted. "That one's fighting like a salmon and must be at least fifteen pounds. Just keep some tension on him until he gets tired, and then be prepared for some more runs even when he seems to be beat."

Mel kept giving instructions as the fish jumped three more times. After twenty minutes, the exhausted fish was directly beside Leslie. Mel held his arm and guided him back toward the shore, and then expertly scooped the fish into the net. Leslie was as exhausted as the fish, but more excited and undoubtedly happier. Mel weighed the fish at 16.5 pounds, and announced that it was a very fresh king salmon. He asked Leslie if he wanted a picture, and took one with Leslie holding the fish in front of himself, then jotted down Leslie's email address on the back of his hand to send the picture to him.

"Can I keep him?" Leslie asked.

"Sure. But if you want to eat him, best to bleed him out now." Mel produced a knife from his belt and expertly cut the gills on both sides. Fresh blood spilled onto the sand.

Mel then sat down, lit a small cigar, and handed Leslie a business card describing himself as a fishing guide and taxidermist. He pointed out that Leslie should never go wading in a river without a safety belt, and offered to book a date to take Leslie out on a guided trip. Leslie thanked him and said that he knew another guide that he owed a big favour. When Mel asked whom that guide was, he replied. "Eric Clouser."

"Not the ex-con with the new shop in Shacletown?"

"Yes, that would be him. He may be an ex-con, but he is a great guy, and I owe him big-time."

When Mel asked if he wanted to try for more, saying that there were some salmon in the river almost twice the size of the one he had just caught, Leslie declined and said he was already tired. He could not imagine fighting a bigger fish. He picked up his fish and walked to the parking lot. He deposited the fish in the back of the Escape, realizing that he should have brought along a garbage bag to put it in, and, returning to Mel, handed him a twenty dollar bill. Mel thanked him for his generosity, saying it wasn't necessary but it was appreciated.

At home, Leslie deposited the fish in the kitchen sink and washed the sand off of it. He downloaded instructions from the internet on how to fillet a fish without gutting it. The finished product was far from perfect, but he had two large slabs of boneless fish in the fridge. Later that afternoon, the picture appeared in his email and he forwarded it to Inge with the note: "My first fish on a fly rod." He knew at that moment that he was hooked on both fly-fishing and on Inge. He sat down and made up a list of further items he would need to buy at the fly shop: a filleting knife, net, safety belt, fingerless fishing gloves, some more weights, and a bigger selection of flies. A few minutes later, the phone rang.

"Hi, Inge."

"Congratulations. What did you do with the fish?"

"I have two huge salmon fillets in the fridge." Leslie boasted. "Not sure what I should do with them, though."

"Why don't you bring them over and I'll cook them up for you?"

Inge greeted him with a big hug, and noting the size of the fillets, wrapped one in tin foil and put it in the freezer for later. She showed him around her modest condo, and he sat down on the sofa in the living room while she prepared the surprise meal. She was confident that he would like her favourite recipe for preparing salmon fillets, entirely ignorant about his peculiar lack of taste sensation. She asked him to stay in the living room as she prepared the feast in the kitchen. She cut two generous portions from the least mangled part of the fillet and mixed a slurry of mayonnaise, yogurt, and mustard, diced onions, dried dill weed, and pepper and spread this over the flesh side of the fish. She preheated the oven to 450° F and placed the fish in the oven on a greased baking tray. As it cooked, she grated parmesan cheese and some old cheddar and added a dash of paprika. When the fish was cooked, she added the cheeses and paprika and broiled it for two minutes. She served it with roasted green pepper slices and some capers over a bed of red quinoa with a slice of lemon. Dessert was a homemade blueberry pie with vanilla ice cream. When she returned to the living room, Leslie was sound asleep sitting on the sofa.

"Hey!" she admonished. "Not a good sign when you fall asleep on our first date. Am I that boring to you?"

"Oh, come on! Fighting that fish exhausted me ... and you're not boring; you just have a way of making me totally relax."

"Okay. You're forgiven. But does this qualify as our first quarrel?" she teased.

Sitting down to a delicious meal that Inge could not finish, Leslie complimented her on her culinary skills. "I could get used to your cooking. My skills in the kitchen are nonexistent."

Teasing him again, she asked if he had better skills for other rooms in the house.

"Whoa, there! We need to discuss a lot of other things before we get to that," he admonished.

"I agree. But I couldn't resist that question."

"So what is the biggest skeleton in your closet?" she asked.

"My accident a year ago. I've hidden what that was all about from almost everyone, although Velma did apparently figure it out. And she told me details about it that I have no memory of at all."

"You planned it all, didn't you," Inge stated firmly.

"Yes. I guess I did. But how did you find that out?"

"Well, it was the only explanation that made any sense to me, and you lied to me that Friday." She explained the visit to the hospital and his lie to her about the reason for the visit and how she knew he had lied. He vowed that he had no recollection of those events at all, and begged her to believe him, apologizing for lying to her.

"I'm glad that you didn't succeed, but why did you try?"

He tried to explain. "I think I was depressed, and I was sure I had Alzheimer's disease, and I felt trapped in an unhappy marriage and a meaningless existence. I felt that I was as useless as the tits on a bull. And I completely missed the obvious symptoms and signs of hypothyroidism. They tell me that when I hit the ICU, I was jaundiced, so I suspect I misdiagnosed myself as having a cancer of the pancreas—so much for my differential diagnostic acumen!"

He went on to relate that he was at that time already infatuated with her but was sure that she was happily married and had no feelings for him. By this point they were both teary-eyed sitting on the sofa with his arm around her shoulder.

"But Velma was a changed woman after my ordeal, and became a wonderful, loving, and considerate wife, and I miss her terribly. Maybe it was me who changed—I don't think I have ever been easy to put up with, and you had best remember that. But I even forgot about you for a while, until we met the other day. Have you discussed your conclusion about that Friday with anyone?" he asked.

"No. And I won't if you don't want me to," she replied. "I am pretty good at keeping secrets, and this will be our secret forever."

She broke the silence by saying that she, too, had some skeletons. She related that she had lied and hidden from almost everyone the abusive relationship she had endured with her husband, and then said simply, "I also have a son."

"Well, what is so bad about that?" Leslie enquired.

She explained that her son had been born when she was 17 and had been given up for adoption.

"That is hardly something to be ashamed of or worry about these days."

"I know that it is no big deal these days, but it sure was back then for me. At least I am glad that I gave him up for adoption rather than having the abortion that I considered."

"Do you have any contact with him?"

She explained that she had found her son and that he was a Catholic priest in St. Catharines.

"That is hardly your fault. I don't have a lot of love for any clergy, but I think I am pretty tolerant. But he will probably look dimly on your seeing me. Are you a practising Catholic?"

"Not at all. I do go to Mass occasionally, but like many church-goers, I'm not sure I believe much of anything in the creeds any-more. I guess that makes me a bit of a hypocrite, but I enjoy the experience. Father Kevin Wulff—that's my son's name—is pretty liberal, and I think he would be pleased with anything that made me happy ... and you sure do that."

Leslie replied, "I don't think there is anything terribly evil about going to Mass even if you don't believe in the doctrines of the church, and you are certainly not alone in that. I joined in in repeating the Lord's Prayer in church long after I stopped believ-ing in a personal God who had any influence or interest in our lives." He ventured a guess that at least 50 percent of the clergy he had met have major doubts about the doctrines they are paid to instil into others.

"But if you are trained for nothing else, it must be hard to find another job when you lose your faith and your flock."

"Well, I don't doubt Kevin's sincerity in what he preaches. Aren't you being a little harsh?"

"Well, maybe. My father also was a sincere clergyman. You and I were lucky that we could change our religious beliefs with-out losing our jobs. But the possibility of losing the only job you are trained for is a powerful disincentive to expressing any doubts. I guess maybe most clergy are sincere, or else switch into a related field and become convincing con artists like Jimmy Bakker. Or else they become pastorpreneurs like Jimmy Swaggart and Oral Rob-erts. Much the same as con artistry really."

"Pastorpreneur? Is that even a proper word?"

"Well, I don't know, but I heard it somewhere and it should be even if it isn't. There are at least a dozen multimillionaire pastors that fit the description."

They chatted long into the evening and then parted with a hug and a kiss. As he was leaving, she reminded him that he would have to return to help her eat the other salmon fillet. But he said

that their next date would be at a quiet restaurant, and promised
to call her the following week.

On December 22, Leslie took Inge to an Italian eatery near both
of their homes. He had been there several times for pharmaceuti-
cally sponsored continuing medical education events. He hoped
that there would be no such event involving the Beaverbrook hospital doctors that night, as he was not yet prepared to make his relationship with Inge known to his former colleagues. She ordered a
glass of white wine, the first that she had had in several months,
and he had a Merlot. She ordered the linguini alle Vongole, and he
the Spaghettini pescatore, as it sounded vaguely like spaghetti and
he knew he could eat that. And pescatore must be something to do
with fish, he reasoned from his knowledge of Latin. He was quite
surprised when the plate arrived loaded with oysters but no fish.
He did not want to admit that he really had little idea what any of
the foreign-sounding items on the menu really were.

He cautiously pulled a list of things he wanted to discuss out
of his pocket, but Inge said, "Please put that list away. You need to
learn to enjoy this occasion without a defined agenda." He apologized and put the list away but managed to steer the conversation
to cover most of the topics on his list anyway.

They agreed to keep their friendship a secret from family and
friends for the present, although neither thought knowing about it
would particularly upset their relatives or friends. But there would
be gossip, what with it being so soon after Velma's death and Inge's
divorce. They discussed hobbies and interests they could share,
and he was disappointed that she did not want to travel with him
to any of the exotic locales he had in mind. They agreed that there
would be no arguments over religion. She encouraged him to try
to learn to play duplicate bridge and curling, but he agreed to only
try either if they did it together. She refused to even consider playing bridge with him as her partner, as she was sure that it would
lead to serious strife. He indicated that he might try to learn to
curl if she would try to learn to fly-fish with him, confident that
she would refuse. She compromised by saying that she did a lot
of needlecraft and knitting and would be willing to try tying flies
if he would fish with them. They never discussed living arrangements or finances at all, both recognizing the need to be cautious

about that; this fragile relationship might yet fall apart. Then he asked what she had meant when she asked if he had better skills in other rooms than he did in the kitchen.

"Oh, I was only teasing you. But I am a woman and you are a man and—" He interrupted her to say that he didn't think she would ever want to see his old carcass in the buff. She said, "And you would hardly be thrilled to see this skinny, boobless body in the nude, either. And at present my libido is nonexistent. But we could turn the lights off. And if you can't do the manly thing or need a little green pill, I can live with that, too. It is not that important."

"Well, I'm sure I could for you and without any pills. It's not that I have erectile dysfunction; it is just that I have not found anyone in the past six months who cares whether I can perform or not."

His answer reflected more confidence than he was feeling. He recalled an encounter that had been an embarrassment. It occurred in his days between marriages when he was not even dating. He was at a medical conference and had imbibed three glasses of Merlot at the pharmaceutical company cocktail reception. He had been invited back to her hotel room, allegedly to review some data, by a sexy, tall, blonde company sales representative in a short skirt. He had just met her.

She promptly lay down on the bed and asked him to give her a "full body massage"; then said that entertaining the doctors was the best part of her job. Even Leslie, consistently and reliably clueless in dealing with women and sex, got her message, but his unreliable Arnold only assumed the posture and rigidity of an overripe half-peeled banana. Even the lady's expert efforts at resuscitation failed to revive Arnold. As Leslie quickly put his clothes on, he said apologetically, "Well, the spirit is willing, but the flesh is weak." He never saw her again.

Although he blamed the Merlot for Arnold's disobedience on this occasion, the memory of that evening made him realize that his partner would always need to be someone not only athletic and eager, but someone he also loved or at least respected. *But with Inge, Arnold really will obey orders, because I love her so much.*

He told her that he, too, did not consider sex important at this point and said his Arnold was a bit out of practice but would try hard to please her if she wanted, apologizing for the pun.

"Arnold?"

"Well, every man has a name for his favourite appendage," Leslie replied lamely.

They agreed that their relationship would be platonic for the foreseeable future, but she said that she was not a prude. "Before Joe started drinking heavily, we had a pretty normal sex life. But then his libido seemed to increase but his ability just dwindled to nothing, and my enthusiasm also dwindled to nothing."

"Well, Shakespeare knew about that phenomenon. To quote Falstaff to MacDuff, I think. Alcohol 'provokes the desire but takes away the performance.' Known now as 'brewer's droop.' Joe certainly abused alcohol—he abused you as well?"

Tears welling up in her eyes, she confessed to having been beaten many times. "That's one of the many reasons I felt I had to leave. I would have been unhappy to live with a jovial drunk, but I wouldn't have left him, if not for the beatings. While I'm in confessional mode, I might as well tell you that he also accused me of having an affair with you, and when I denied it, that led to more beatings. I wish that he had been right. We should have been a couple years ago. But I knew that, when I first identified you in the ICU, he would sooner or later find out about that, and I feared for my life. I really had no choice at that point. Joe is now a member of AA and a changed man, but I haven't been able to forget the beatings."

"You identified me?"

"Yes. It was on that Monday morning. Did no one ever tell you about that?"

"No. I thought that Velma was the one who identified me but I can't ask her now. How could you identify me when no one else could?"

"Let me see your neck."

He opened his shirt collar and she ran her fingers across above his clavicle. "It's gone now. But, like I said, there was a very distinctive growth there on your neck, and you showed it to me on that Friday the 13th. So when I saw it again on the Monday, I knew it was you."

He ran his fingers over the spot. "I don't recall any of that. But I do vaguely remember that the barber commented on something there when he was giving me a beard trim once."

"Did you ever suffer any abuse?"

"Physically, only once. In an argument, I held her by the shoulders, and she then kneed me in the twins. I think I spent that night in the car. But Velma was not a happy person, and I was always to blame for anything that annoyed her. Before she changed, she certainly caused me a lot of mental torment. On one occasion, when she was mad at me, she cooked up a big meal, ate it all herself, and then hid the car keys so I couldn't go out to eat. This was meant to be torture, but with my anorexia, it was more of an annoyance than what she meant it to be. And to answer the next question before you ask it, I never beat her but I probably said a lot of cruel things to her. But she could always upstage me in sarcasm."

When he dropped her off at her condo, they agreed to spend New Year's Eve together and she offered to cook up the remaining salmon fillet for that celebration. Before leaving his car, she said "And no more lists. You really need to learn to live life without constantly referring to an agenda."

They hugged and parted. They both had plans to spend Christmas with family, and would not meet again until New Year's Eve. As he drove home, he vowed that he would never again show up on a date with a list, but realized that she could not prevent him from using a memorized one to steer the conversation. Then he realized that he had not even bought a card for her for Christmas and tried to think of something that would be appropriate.

The next day he went back to the Hook Line and Sinker. After he explained that he had a friend who had never fished but who wanted to try fly tying, Eric picked out a vice, bobbin, whip finishing tool, various thread spools in different colours, and a few bags of rabbit and possum fur along with glue, scissors, and several different kinds of feathers, tinsel, and chenille, and different-sized Mustad hooks. Leslie added three different books on fly tying, including *The American Fly Tying Manual*. Eric told him that he was glad to get rid of the books, as most fly tiers now simply looked for patterns to tie on the Internet and followed the video instructions on U-Tube. Leslie paid full price for the merchandise but Eric insisted on giving him the books, and added two more. Then Eric said that Tom was running a fly tying course for beginners in January and February. Leslie promptly enrolled Inge.

As they chatted, Tom announced that he and Eric were planning to get married and that Leslie would be getting an invitation. When Leslie congratulated them and asked about details, Tom said, "The details are still sketchy, and we have not picked a venue or a clergyman to officiate," adding that Eric was an agnostic and he was a member of the United Church of Canada. Eric wanted a civic ceremony, but Tom preferred a religious one.

That gave Leslie an idea. "Why not have the best of both worlds and have an officiant from the Humanist Society to officiate?" he asked. "They can do weddings and when they officiate, it is considered as a religious ceremony even though they are almost all agnostics or atheists; go figure that out. And if you can wait a few months, I am taking training to become an officiant with them and would be glad to marry the two of you. There should not be any rush, as I doubt that either of you is pregnant."

Leslie even had the temerity to suggest the Toronto Board of Trade golf course clubhouse where he had been married to Velma many years before as an appropriate venue, and a chance to thumb their noses at the elite. Tom and Eric promised to discuss his suggestions.

When he got home, Leslie did his best to wrap the materials and books up, and delivered them to Inge, advising her at the door to not open them until Christmas Day. Hardly a romantic gift, he thought, but it might do something to keep her interested in his new hobby. She apologized for having not gotten him anything, and he noted that in her vulnerable, debilitated state, she had a good excuse and said that he really didn't want her to go out into the crowds of Christmas shoppers to get anything. She also hoped that whatever he had wrapped up for her would not be an embarrassment when she opened it in front of Kevin on Christmas morning. When he left, she went to her computer and bought him a membership in the American Contract Bridge League, asking them to send the notification of that to him by email the next day.

salted crème brulee

Leslie spent Christmas Day and Boxing Day with Isaac, Nancy, and Adam and did not have to cook a turkey after all. They reviewed the eventful year, and several times Isaac and Nancy commented on how well he had recovered and on how happy he seemed to be in spite of losing his wife and coming close to losing his life. He showed them several more pictures of Velma's final resting place and described how he had gotten her there, and talked about the awe he had felt in seeing Machu Picchu. They vowed to visit Velma there when Adam was a bit older.

Leslie described his new obsession with fly-fishing and described his first catch, neglecting to mention the help from Mel. He asked if Isaac and Adam would like to try it in the spring, and Isaac agreed. Leslie offered to outfit them and buy their licences, and Isaac pointed out that Adam would not need a licence. When Isaac protested that it would be quite an expense for Leslie, he rejoined that he could afford it and that he would much prefer to spend money on them now, rather than make them wait until he was on the brown side of the sod somewhere. They agreed that he would book a guided fishing excursion somewhere for the May 24th weekend, and they would come wherever that was to take place. He knew which guide he would hire.

Nancy interrupted the father-son conversation to ask what he had done with his first catch.

"A friend cooked it up for me and it was delicious."

"A lady friend? Is that why you seem so happy now?"

"Oh, no. Not what you think. She's just a friend, not a girlfriend."

Barb, Lyle, and Leslie Knott joined them later in the afternoon, having spent Christmas morning with Rachael and Edgar Jacks in Shacletown. Leslie Jr. seemed fascinated with Leslie Sr.'s beard and kept everyone laughing as he crawled on the floor with his grandfather. After the children were in bed, Lyle, Leslie, and Isaac all got into the bottle of Scapa single malt scotch that Isaac had gotten from Nancy for Christmas, and became quite tipsy. Leslie, realizing that he was a bit disinhibited by the alcohol, was nevertheless determined to keep his promise to Inge to keep their relationship a secret. This was not easy after the other two disinhibited men began to tease him about being a good catch for some gold digger, asking him how many women were chasing him. Nancy finally came to his rescue, saying that he had a right to some privacy, and if he wanted to have some fun with any number of women, he didn't need to tell them all about it.

Barb agreed, siding with Nancy, but warned, "Just don't get caught by a gold digger. I am sure there are lots of them out there, and we don't want you to get stung."

"Being freely translated, you mean you don't want me to spend all of your inheritance," Leslie retorted.

"Well, I don't really care about that as much as I care about your welfare. We can all support ourselves, but we are not keen on supporting you after some high-maintenance dame takes everything that you have," Nancy interjected.

"Don't worry about it. I am not dating anyone," he lied. "And I don't know where you think those hordes of horny women are. Let me know if you find them."

* * *

Inge spent Christmas with Kevin in St. Catharines. In his Christmas Eve address, he prayed for her without mentioning her by name, noting that the Lord had sent some of those present through some severe trials in the past year and then had given them the strength to carry on. Afterwards, at his home, he complimented her on her positive, accepting attitude after a year of turmoil. She replied sincerely that he had been a tremendous help in getting her through the tough times, and then lied by saying that she was sure that his prayers for her had been a big help, adding that she was grateful for the support of a lot of good friends as well.

Inge cooked one large and one small turkey on Christmas morning at Kevin's home and they took the larger one to the Out of the Cold food program to share with the less fortunate. They returned to his home and had a delicious late Christmas dinner with another priest and a couple from the parish. They all remarked on how well Inge looked after suffering through her Annus Horribilis. Inge insisted that she had not suffered greatly and was just grateful for the support and prayers of the people who had helped her. When asked what she most looked forward to in the New Year, she hesitated and then said, "Simply being healthy and energetic again."

On December 28, Carol Creek called Inge to ask if she had any plans for New Year's Eve, as they had none and would be glad to take her out for dinner. Inge hesitated, and then said simply that she did have plans.

"What kind of plans, if I can be so nosy?" Carol asked. "Are you entertaining that rich older widower you have been looking for?"

"Well, as a matter of fact, I am."

"Wow! I am so excited and glad for you. Tell me all about him. This is great news."

"Well, we are not serious at all, and we agreed to not talk about it yet, as we don't know if it will last, but let's just say he is a fisherman who brought me a great salmon fillet and we are having that on New Year's Eve. I know you can't imagine me with a fishmonger, but he has just taken up fly-fishing as a hobby. I have known him for years." She was enjoying keeping her best friend in suspense. "I don't even know if he is rich, but he is intelligent, witty, and very compassionate, and I don't care about his money."

"When can we meet him?" Carol asked.

"Why don't I check with him and see if he would mind having you over to meet him for New Year's Eve dinner? There is certainly enough fish for four, and it's not as though we would be spending the evening in bed. He is just a good friend." She could now envision a great evening of surprises for Leslie and the Creeks, and hoped that Leslie would not object.

She called Leslie, and he had no objections to inviting two of her friends to share the evening together. He pressed her to tell her who would be coming, but she refused, saying that it would be more fun if it were a surprise to him. He agreed, saying that anyone who was a friend of hers could be a friend of his as well. He agreed to show up at 6:30 p.m. and she called Carol back to tell them to come at 7:00.

Leslie arrived promptly at 6:30 and handed Inge a dozen red long-stemmed roses.

"Oh, those smell so sweet."

"Actually, I can't really smell them."

They discussed the gifts that they had exchanged for Christmas, and he commented that he would now have to take duplicate bridge lessons and get serious about the game. For her part, she said that she had already tied a few simple flies for him to try, and had found the hobby time-consuming and intricate but a lot of fun. She commented that she might have to try fly-fishing to fully appreciate the finer details of fly tying, but she would certainly wait until spring for that. She said that they planned to eat at 7:30 and then they could perhaps play some bridge, as her friends who were coming were very good players. She had planned a sumptuous meal with her recipe for salmon fillets, a Caesar salad, and mashed sweet potatoes, followed by a her best dessert, homemade Mississippi mud pie. She had her best china and silverware on the dining room table. She trimmed and added the long-stemmed roses as a centrepiece. When the doorbell rang at 7:05, Inge pretended to be busy in the kitchen and asked Leslie to answer it. When Carol Creek met him at the door with Ken right behind her, she was stunned.

"Why, Dr. Turle, so nice to see you again ... "

"Inge just invited me over for dinner tonight," Leslie replied lamely to her confusion.

Inge appeared from the kitchen with a mischievous grin as she looked at her stunned friend. "I believe you know each other."

"Oh my God, Inge, you pulled this off so beautifully. What a surprise! I'm speechless. No I'm not, but I'm thrilled. I'm—I'm—flabbergasted and so happy for you!" She gave Inge a big hug, and then turned to her husband to introduce him to Leslie. Leslie shook hands saying that they had met before at some hospital function, but he could not recall when. Ken was a bit perplexed by Carol's wild reaction to the discovery of the fourth guest's identity, not knowing much about Inge's long-standing infatuation with Leslie. But he recalled vividly how upset Inge had been the day she had identified John Doe.

The men sat in the living room, and Inge asked for drink orders. Both men chose a beer. Carol chose a white wine to pair with the fish and after a while joined Inge in the kitchen. The men made some small talk and then heard the ladies whispering, and shouted out that it was impolite. Carol could not stop expressing her amazement and pleasure at the discovery of Inge's new man friend. Inge asked her to tone it down, pointing out that they were just old friends who had renewed their acquaintances at a purely chance meeting, but Carol winked at Inge, and whispered to her that she knew better. Inge worried for a moment that the rumours would start flying at the hospital and made Carol promise to not say a word around the hospital about how she had spent New Year's Eve.

Both Ken and Carol complimented Leslie on his new hobby and Inge on her cooking skills. After helping Inge clear off the dinner table, they all sat down to play some bridge. Leslie asked them to go easy on him, as he was not very good at it. They agreed to keep it informal and to discuss the bidding and play after each hand, as a learning experience, but to bid and play the hands as though they were in a duplicate league and not just playing contract bridge. Ken refused to play with Carol as his partner, saying he had been cut off for weeks by doing so and playing poorly, everyone knowing what he had been cut off from. So the men played against the ladies. Leslie had been hoping to play with Inge as his partner. He thought it was likely that he would mis-bid or misplay a hand and she would get upset with him, enabling him to assess how she reacted when he did something really stupid, but Ken insisted.

Leslie did manage to mis-bid a hand. He was staring off into space thinking about how boring bridge was when Carol, on his left, dealt and then bid a pre-emptive three diamonds. Ken bid four diamonds, a Michael's cue bid indicating 5–5 distribution in hearts and spades, and Inge passed. Unfortunately, the three diamonds bid had not registered in Leslie's memory centre and, with only two high-card points and two small diamonds, he passed the cue bid. Carol was too clever to double, and so Ken had to play four diamonds with no diamonds in his hand, going down seven. It was Ken who berated Leslie for his inattentiveness, but Inge said nothing. On a later hand, Leslie opened the bidding with one no trump, and Ken with twenty-two high card points, including all the aces, jumped to seven no trump. Leslie managed to strand two good diamond spot cards in his hand, going down three, much to Ken's annoyance. It was Carol who came to his rescue this time, noting that if the heart suit had broken 3–2, as the odds were, Leslie would still have made the grand slam.

Leslie kept watching Inge throughout the evening and, noting that she appeared to be tired, suggested that they could leave before midnight, but she insisted that she was fine. They stopped playing at 11:00 and sat down to watch the show from Times Square. Ken asked Leslie what plans he had for the New Year, and Leslie replied that he had a whole list of adventures in mind, but that Inge did not like to live by lists. He related that he hoped to do a lot of fly-fishing and wanted to raft down the Columbia River through the Grand Canyon at some point. Inge looked at him in horror and Carol also asked why he would ever want to do anything that dangerous.

"Well, how about bicycling around the Cabot Trail, then?"

"You can bike it if you want," Inge said. "I wouldn't mind seeing it and I have a brother that I haven't seen in years who lives out there somewhere in Cape Breton. You could do the bicycle ride while I visited him, if I can find him and if you are willing to drive there in decent weather."

"That sounds like a great plan for the two of you," a slightly tipsy Carol interjected, trying hard to help the lovebirds find common interests.

"There isn't a lot to do in Cape Breton," Ken observed. "What does your brother do?"

"He works for some green energy company installing small wind turbines and solar energy systems for the locals, I think, but I haven't even talked to him for at least three years. He couldn't stand Joe."

Midnight ... the ball dropped, and there were hugs all around. Shortly thereafter, the guests left. Outside the door, a now very tipsy Carol gave Leslie a hug and told him how happy she was for him and Inge, admonishing him to take good care of her best friend.

* * *

In early January, Tom called Leslie and asked if he could come in and spend a day learning how to tend the fly shop as they had discussed. Both he and Eric had inadvertently booked charters to guide two different groups for the same day later that week. They would like him to keep the store open. He gladly accepted and spent a pleasant training day tending to customers, watching Eric tie flies, and learning the specialized vocabulary of fly fishermen as they told tall tales about the one that got away. He learned how to use the credit card reader and learned the names and features of some of the merchandise. He was given a key and asked to open the store at 10:00 a.m. the next Thursday and to close up at 5:00 p.m.

His first day as a retail clerk went well. Before he opened the store, he hung a professionally framed copy of *The Fisher* on a wall of the shop between a mounted muskellunge and a mounted Northern pike, and left a memory stick with the photograph under the counter. He managed to sell two fly rods, one tube fly kit, and one set of expensive Simms chest waders with the cleated boots to go with them, along with lots of feathers, hooks, thread spools, tinsel, and furs. He chatted with customers as they discussed fishing experiences and tying techniques, never letting on that he found most of their vocabulary as foreign as Swahili. The following day, the weather turned cold, and Eric advised Leslie to stay well away from the river for a while; the river was running high, the fishing was poor, and the ice made it quite dangerous.

Inge was feeling much stronger and looking much better by mid-January, having gained a few pounds and a few strands of hair. Leslie took her to a movie and dinner, and then he invited her to come for dinner at his condo for their next date. But his culinary skills really were nonexistent. He regarded food in the same way that he regarded fuel for his car: necessary but not worth wasting time over. He had always relied on Velma to ensure that his nutritional needs were met. Ever since internship, reinforced by his years of being on call, he had been a fast eater, ready to fill up in a hurry in case he was called to an emergency.

But his peculiar relationship with food had started long before that. He recalled an experiment by one of his physiology professors in medical school testing thresholds for detection of different flavours. He was told after that experiment that his threshold for detection of mint, chocolate, salt, sweetness, and bitterness was between fifteen and thirty times higher than the class average. Even earlier, his mother had told him that as a toddler, he would frequently refuse to stop playing to eat, and at times she had to use bribery to get him to eat at all. However, she said, he would quickly eat prodigious amounts of anything she offered him when he was bored. He mused that perhaps he had a genetic syndrome to account for his unusual eating habits, defective taste sensation, tone deafness, and maybe even his highly selective erectile function. He was often embarrassed when eating at formal affairs after realizing that he had finished his main course before others had gotten halfway through it.

As he reflected on his peculiar relationship with food, he realized that he also had a defective sense of smell. The nose clips used in that old physiology experiment to reduce any olfactory clues had not been necessary for him—he seldom detected any odours and could not understand all the fuss about the need for scent-free work environments. He was always more amused than upset by the looks of bewildered disgust and held noses when he silently released noxious colonic gases into the environment in a crowd.

He could barely taste the difference between beef and lamb—or camel. During a brief locum at Hamid Hospital in Doha, arranged by Faisal Al Taqi, he had been taken out into the desert for a traditional Qatari midnight meal. On tasting some meat off an unidentifiable carcass on a long table, he asked his host if it was lamb, and was told that his question would be considered an insult to any self-respecting camel!

After reading *Fat Chance*, he realized that he could never succumb to the supposedly addictive power of high-fructose processed foods. He regarded his body as simply a vehicle to convey his mind from one thought to the next or to deliver enough

adrenalin and cortisol from his adrenals to his brain to thrill to
some new adventure. He knew he would never be susceptible to
any addiction other than to risky adventures. Was this lack of sus-
ceptibility to hunger and to any addictive substance also a defect
in the wiring of his nervous system?

He seldom felt hunger, usually eating only because he knew he
should. He was always slim except when he had developed that
undiagnosed thyroid problem. When alone, he often ate nothing
all day then pigged out on salted Kraft Dinner or cold cereal late
at night, realizing that he needed calories to stay healthy and salt
to stay lucid. His weight had decreased dangerously between his
marriages. Velma, trying to impress him at work, had expressed
her concern and asked him to weigh himself, then calculated his
body mass index at 17.6—well below the healthy range of 18.5 to
24.9; she then insisted on giving him daily high-calorie snacks and
encouraged him to eat more regular meals after they started dating. His weight was now again declining, but he never weighed
himself. In the past he had overheard coworkers speculating about
the possibility that he had anorexia nervosa. He tried to stimu-
late his appetite by increasing the dose of his thyroxin, but was
sternly lectured by Dr. Turbot about adjusting the dosage himself
when the lab reported that his TSH level was well below the reference range, indicating that he had overdosed on the thyroxin. His
serum sodium level was also low once again, but no cause for this
was found.

Leslie mused about his problematic relationship with salt. *This
is the third time my sodium level has been low. It was low when my classmate did the test three years ago. I wonder if that weighed on my mind
when I made that foolish decision on Friday the thirteenth? And when
they did my gallbladder surgery, it was low. Whatever the cause, it can't
be too serious or I would be dead by now.*

That first time that he was found to have a low serum sodium
level was after the 40th class reunion formal dinner, three years
earlier. He had been seated beside a classmate who specialized
in genetics. She had noted that he ate the meal fast and that he
seemed confused about the multiple utensils in front of him. When
he began to add salt to the crème brûlée, she had become alarmed
about his mental state. To her inquiry, he had related that he had
forgotten to add salt to the entrée and he knew he needed extra

salt. "When I don't get enough salt, I get all confused and can't think straight. I've been like that all my life."

"But what does salty crème brûlée taste like?"

"Well, I don't really taste the salt." He told her about the results of the old experiment on taste thresholds in their physiology class and his peculiar eating habits going all the way back to infancy.

"Maybe there is a genetic basis for that," she mused. You may have a salt-wasting syndrome like SIADH. Have you ever been tested?"

"If you mean the Syndrome of Inappropriate Anti-Diuretic Hormone secretion, the answer is I don't know. And I don't really crave salt; I just have learned that I need a lot of it. But if it's genetic, it may be X-linked. My father and my son both use piles of salt on everything; I don't know about my daughter." He was fighting back tears as soon as he said that. "And I have other problems that might be connected."

"Such as?"

"Well I am apparently completely tone deaf, and my sense of smell is almost nonexistent, too." He hesitated. He had devoured two glasses of wine and was a bit disinhibited. "And unlike any other man I know, I can never get an erection unless I am with or fantasizing about a woman that I at least respect and admire if not love. I guess I am more like a woman than a man in that respect. I certainly could never rape a woman, no matter how beautiful she was, or even be seduced by a stranger."

"Now I am sure that you have some genetic defect. But you are wrong. You didn't get any X chromosome from your father. If your father and your son have the same syndrome, it must be on your Y chromosome. You are one weird dude. Can I get a sample of your DNA to analyze and a serum sample to check your sodium level? When I find the defect, we'll publish the findings and call it Turle's syndrome. And your son must have it, too. If he is really your son, he must have your Y chromosome. Can I get some of his blood, too?"

The next day at the homecoming football game, he had handed her two vials of his blood that he had arranged to have drawn earlier that morning. A week later she had emailed him and reported that his serum sodium was a bit low at 129.

To ensure that he made a good impression on Inge when she

came for dinner, he spent hours watching The Food Channel to learn how to cook a respectable meal, but the recipes all seemed hopelessly complicated and time consuming, and he had no idea where to look for most of the ingredients in the confusing maze of aisles in the local grocery store.

He ended up making a lumpy, salty, and undercooked French onion soup and the only entrée Velma had ever taught him how to prepare. It was that pasta and oyster mix with Rotini, substituting canned baby clams for the oysters, Béarnaise sauce (finding no Béarnaise in his kitchen, he used Hollandaise instead) and the clam juice, milk, butter, and grated pepper, mixing in grated parmesan cheese at the end. He knew that Velma added some other ingredients, but he couldn't remember what they were. Dessert was a simple apple pie from Costco with vanilla ice cream. He was quite proud of his concoction, and Inge complimented him. She refrained from making any suggestions that she knew would improve the dish but thought addition of some thin slices of roasted red peppers, and some caramelized onions or some diced mushrooms would improve the colour, texture, and taste of the entrée, and even the aroma. And she would add some finely chopped parsley topping. She realized that Leslie really needed someone to give him some guidance in food preparation—and in clothing selections.

As she looked around his sparely decorated abode, she realized that he could also use some help in interior decorating. The parked Marinoni road bike did nothing to enhance the décor of the front hall; the The Forest Has Eyes and The Fisher needed to change places on the living room walls, and the latter needed to be enlarged and mounted in a much darker and wider frame. And while contemplating the meaning of life may be best done in a sitting position, the oversized Sacred Circle was definitely out of place on the blank wall of the guest washroom directly in front of the toilet.

On their outings that month, both Inge and Leslie began a covert game of testing each other out to find common interests and values. He kept his bucket list off paper, but had it memorized and asked if she would like to try the items on it one by one as the appropriate occasions arose. She was horrified when he said he wanted to learn how to solo pilot a glider plane, scolding him about acting his age. He refrained from telling her that he had already done one glider plane flight. A few years before when Velma was away for few days, he had visited the York Soaring Association outside of Arthur and taken a silent flight over the fields and farms of West Luther Township. The instructor had even let him take the controls until he came close to crashing the glider into a large manure pile outside of a pig barn and had then taken over and expertly caught the updraft from the rotting pile. He had told Velma after that experience that he had had the most fun he had ever had with his clothes on. She never even asked where he had been.

He indicated that he had already joined the Humanist Society of Ontario, and Inge encouraged him to attend their meetings, saying that it would provide great intellectual stimulation. She was equally supportive when he revealed that he would like to audition for a contestant spot on the quiz show Jeopardy! She bombarded him with answers and questions for him to study that she randomly downloaded from the online archives of past shows. She discovered that he did extremely well if the topics were related to any science, literature or history, but he was hopeless if they related to sports or anything to do with Hollywood. But he had a habit of pausing before answering, a fatal error in a contest like Jeopardy! When she pointed this out, he responded that his brain was too cluttered with trivial facts to ever retrieve any one of them quickly. She suggested that with his precision in language, he might fare better on the show Wheel of Fortune, but he did not like the show at all, and commented that it was very easy to rig such a show and that there was far too much phony applause.

At her urging they both enrolled to take bridge lessons later in the spring and spent an evening playing bridge with Ken and Carol Creek. He never mentioned to Inge his desire to do a distillery tour around Scotland, thinking that he might be able to do that on his own. They tentatively agreed to visit her brother in Cheticamp in June and he would bike the Cabot Trail and perhaps fish the Northeast Margaree River if he could find a guide there as he passed through the area on his bicycle.

One evening, Inge invited Leslie for an evening of bridge practice. She reasoned that if she could get him to sense the exhilaration of bidding a disruptive DONT (Disturb Opponents No Trump), defeating a slam contract with a Lightner double, or cue bidding the opponents' suit in various conventions to get to the best contract, he would be as hooked on duplicate bridge—and on her—as he now was on fly-fishing. They would dedicate the evening to agreeing on what systems to play by filling out a convention card together. When she greeted him with a tight hug, he managed to cup his big hands over her slimmed-down rump. When she showed no objection, he joked, "I guess we can no longer call you 'The Out-of-Bounds Lady.'"

"You and who else?" she asked, pushing him out to arm's length and staring into his eyes. "I have heard a few others at work call me that. Was this a sick joke that you started?" Her quick feigned anger didn't fool him.

"Well, maybe I was involved, but I didn't start it, and we never intended the label to stick."

"You and who else?" she repeated.

'Well, Faisal was the main culprit, and we were just having fun tossing around labels and nicknames for different people."

"Well, what other labels did you try to stick on me?"

"Well, we both knew how stylish and modest and proper—and beautiful—you always were, so we imagined some others. But I am not going to give away Faisal's little jokes. It was all just in fun as we were driving to a meeting, and as I said, we never meant for the labels to stick."

Over the course of the evening, she kept returning to the labels, and he finally revealed the three labels and their placement on her dress that he and Faisal had concluded fit her best.

"Some boys just never grow up," she concluded with a smirk.

As a way of finding out something about her political views, on a later date, he dropped a hint that he might apply for a two-month summer job working as the camp physician at the construction site of the Canadian High Arctic Research Station at Cambridge Bay, above the Arctic Circle. He deliberately and provocatively stated that Prime Minister Stephen Harper had been promising to develop this since 2007, saving face as he was at the same time attempting to close the Polar Environment Atmospheric Research Lab even farther north in Eureka, Nunavut. He pointedly told Inge that it seemed that Harper was ready to restrict any significant research that might question the wisdom of oil exploration in the far north. The first construction crews were just getting started on the Cambridge Bay project.

He got no reaction from her. He was amazed that Inge had no objection to this, and she even asked if they were also looking to employ a nurse as a temp there. He did not tell her that he wanted to do this because working in a remote location was a requirement to joining Doctors without Borders and being sent to some other remote location to help out, perhaps in a disaster area or even a war zone. He still did not know much about her political views, and was being deliberately provocative to see how she would react.

On that same evening, he did find out more than he wanted to know about what he considered her irrational political views. In the car, a radio report prompted her to reveal that she had signed a petition to the Redfern Liberal MPP to cancel the two planned gas-fired power plants in the area. It was now Leslie's turn to be irate, pointing out that there was far too much NIMBYism in that action and that everyone should be prepared to make some concessions in the interest of green energy development. Inge indicated that she usually voted for the Conservatives, but had voted Liberal in the latest provincial election because of that issue. He became even more irate, pointing out that Tim Hudak's Conservatives and the NDP under Angela Horwath's leadership had also promised to cancel those projects if elected, so her reason for voting Liberal was irrational. He had voted for the NDP candidate in the latest election in June and she revealed that she had voted for the Conservatives, telling him about the struggles she had experienced with the nurses at work as they tried to form a bargaining unit.

His politics defied party labels and defined inconsistency. He leaned toward the Greens or the New Democrats but agreed with the libertarians on the need for smaller government. He took his right to vote seriously and researched carefully before voting, but was not attached to any one party and distrusted all political promises. He had a habit, when living in his house, of asking the first politician who came to the door begging for his vote to erect a sign on his front lawn. He explained to his puzzled neighbours that it acted like insect repellant in keeping the other candidates from pestering him. He had, on three occasions, deliberately named the least likely candidate when contacted by pre-election polling firms, to decrease the accuracy of the results they would publish.

After a heated political debate, Inge had simply asked, "Can we agree to disagree without being disagreeable?" They had finally had their first big argument and he was satisfied that she had found a way to defuse it without holding a grudge.

For her part, Inge showed some enthusiasm for fly-tying and playing bridge and hinted that she would like to someday travel to Gatlinburg, Tennessee, the mecca of duplicate bridge, to play in the annual week-long Mid-Atlantic Regional Tournament. She said they could play Knockouts, Swiss Teams, Gold Rush or Stratified Pairs, and he wondered what language she was speaking. She hinted that she would like to do some classical ballroom dancing but he said he totally lacked any sense of rhythm, as his guitar instructor had informed him.

She frequently reminded herself that they both needed activities that they didn't share. She would like him to try curling even if they joined separate leagues and played at different times, but he was noncommittal, saying that it looked somewhat tame and repetitive. He said unkindly that what little curling he had watched on TV looked about as exciting as watching grass grow. He did not understand some of the arcane rules or the strategies used by the skips. And he secretly thought that he would never start a new endeavour where he would be at the bottom of the pack. She hinted on two occasions that she had never been on a cruise, but he never seemed at all interested and made no commitment. He thought that would be even more boring than curling.

By late January, they had had that major argument that he said was a prerequisite to getting serious about each other, and agreed that it was time to fill the families in on their secret. Leslie invited Isaac, Nancy, and Adam to spend a weekend with him and casually said that he had someone that he wanted them to meet. He invited Inge for dinner on the Saturday night and introduced her as "a friend and a bridge partner." Inge and Nancy seemed to strike up a friendship immediately, and the whole evening was thoroughly enjoyable.

After Inge left without so much as a hug for Leslie, Nancy closed the door, turned to Leslie, and started to deliver a speech she had carefully rehearsed in her head. "Look, you can't deceive us forever. That lady is more than just a friend to you. Isaac, did you not notice the looks they were exchanging all evening? It's okay, and I'm glad for you. She seems like a very nice lady, but don't try to tell us that she is just a friend and a bridge partner. I thought you didn't even like playing bridge. What else does she do with you, if I may be so nosy?"

"Oh, no, and she isn't even my bridge partner. We usually play against each other. And our relationship is strictly platonic, if that's what you are being so nosy about. It almost certainly always will be. But you are right in one sense. We have known each other for many years, and have always been good friends, but it seems to have somehow gone a bit beyond that now. I play bridge with her because I owe her big time. She is the one who first identified me when I was out cold, so to speak. If it had not been for that, I might well have died before anybody even knew who I was."

Both Isaac and Nancy were apparently satisfied with his answers and were pleased that he had found someone who would put a damper on his adventurous, reckless nature that had almost cost him his life at least twice before. He belatedly handed Isaac a requisition to have some blood tests done for his geneticist classmate, explained the peculiar traits that they suspected were related to a Y-chromosome mutation, and suggested that Adam should be tested as well. He added, "My friend is holding off on the expensive genetic testing until she gets your sample to compare with mine."

"But if it is on your Y chromosome and Isaac's Y chromosome, it has to be on Adam's as well," Nancy reasoned. "And he should not be officially tested, as it would label him with a genetic disease. He does not need to go through school with that hanging over him." Leslie made a mental note that Adam showed no unusual fondness for salt and did not seem to particularly resemble Isaac. He considered the possibility that Adam might not have the defect and that finding this would raise questions about his paternal lineage that Nancy would find embarrassing, but he said nothing.

The next evening, Inge called Leslie to enquire about what the conversation had been like after she left the evening before, and he related that she had been a big hit with his family. Isaac had even called Barb late that night and they discussed the calming influence Inge would have on Leslie, saying within earshot of Leslie that he was "pleased that someone would be finally able to rein the old man in."

Inge decided on a different forum to introduce Leslie to Kevin, taking them both out for a late evening dinner at a nearby French restaurant, telling Kevin only that she wanted him to meet a friend whom she had known for years. Leslie found Kevin to be cool and affectedly polite at first, but after a glass of wine, he loosened up a bit. But Leslie knew from the start that he would never develop much of a friendship with any priest. In spite of considering himself to be very tolerant, and having had a clergyman father, he never could relate well to any clergymen. After they parted, Kevin called his mother to relate that he was very pleased that she was happy with her new man, but advised her to go slowly as she was very vulnerable and he did not want to see her get hurt again. He sensed that Leslie would never warm up to him but thought that if Leslie made Inge happy, he would do his Christian duty and try his best to be civil and polite to Leslie. For his part, Leslie reflected that, as clergy go, Kevin was perhaps one of the better ones, and he said nothing negative about Kevin to Inge.

17

dilemmas

In the second week of February, Leslie and Tom travelled to Pulaski, New York, and stayed two nights at Whitacher's Motel and Sports Shop. Leslie was a bit nervous, having never stayed in a motel room with a gay man before, but Tom was a perfect gentleman and they spent the two evenings tying flies on the fly tying station in the room. Their first day on the Salmon River was drift boat fishing with a guide that Tom had arranged, and it was rainy and cool. Although the guide worked hard and stayed on the river for an extra hour, they landed no fish, and only Tom even had one on the line briefly. The next day, Tom and Leslie drove to the Pineville pool and waded in, faring much better. Tom caught two steelheads and one salmon, landing two of them; and Leslie, with instructions from Tom, landed a 9-pound steelhead, marvelling at the fight it put up. He had another fish on for a while, but his Turle knot let go, and Tom then belatedly advised him to use a nonslip mono loop knot instead for steelhead, and tied one on for Leslie.

Late in the day, as he was trying to wade to a high, flat stone so he could cast to a small back-eddy where Tom said there would likely be fish, Leslie stumbled on some very slippery stones. He staggered backwards for about 20 feet and then fell into waist-deep water, but he kept a firm grip on his rod. He was soaked with ice-cold water from the waist up, and for the first time appreciated the importance of wearing a tight safety belt. He bruised his elbow when he landed and his hat flew off into the current and disappeared. Tom expertly helped him to his feet and guided him to shore and the warmth of his truck. But for Leslie, this incident only increased his enjoyment of fly-fishing. Reading the water, getting to the right spot to cast, picking the right fly to cast from an infinite variety, and assessing the riverbed were all part of the challenges of this new sport. And he would have to study the life cycles of aquatic insects and learn to identify them to improve his fly selections for differing conditions.

Leslie returned home happy, tired, and a bit ambivalent, thinking that he missed Inge but he also had had a lot of fun without her. He reviewed an email from his excited geneticist classmate saying that she had discovered the genetic basis for Turle's syndrome and had attached a draft manuscript to be submitted to the Canadian Medical Association Journal describing its features in an anonymous elderly male and his son. He reviewed this eagerly. She had found a heretofore unknown mutation of a few nucleotide sequences in what had been considered to be a noncoding or junk DNA region of his Y chromosome. The discussion section of the paper stated in part: "Since many genes are obviously involved in expression of these traits, this mutation must be a regulator or modifier of the expression of those genes."

Leslie added speculation that he, as the "index case," must have either the most severe manifestations of a common syndrome that others also had, or the mildest form of a syndrome that was usually fatal prenatally or in early childhood. He recalled seeing a patient who had "idiopathic SIADH" in his working days, and had concluded that he also had this to explain his low serum sodium level found on three occasions. He chose to believe the first possibility. *Even with purely genetic diseases, the manifestations vary from person to person, and I must have the most severe form of a disease that others have with milder manifestations,* he reasoned.

He hadn't seen Inge for a week and realized that he missed her. He knew that their relationship had gotten to the point that he could not break it off without hurting her horribly but he was worried that she seemed much less adventurous than he was. He was concerned that she would eventually, like Velma, nix many of the adventures that he wanted to indulge in. Perhaps they could continue to be just friends ... but that somehow seemed unsatisfactory as well. He fell into a fitful sleep but awoke early. He completed his brain exercises by doing the daily crossword and Sudoku then strode to the computer room and pulled up his bucket list. He had last revised it after his first fly-fishing experience, and now, realizing that it was Friday, February 13th, stared at it again.

1. Raft the Colorado through the Grand Canyon.
2. Learn to pilot a glider plane.
3. Learn to walk on tall stilts and to ride a unicycle.
4. Complete training to become an officiant of the Ontario Humanist Society.
5. Bike around the Cabot Trail.
6. Work at the Canadian High Arctic Research Station.
7. Join Doctors without Borders.
8. Go on a distillery tour of Scotland.
9. Try out for Jeopardy!
10. Fly-fish in every province at least once.
11. Take a snowmobile/ice fishing trip somewhere in Northern Ontario.

As he stared at the list, he realized that Inge would really only approve of two or three of the items, and there were none that he had specifically put on the list because of his infatuation with her. He thought that if this were truly his bucket list, he would have to get over his obsession with her.

The ongoing low-level intermittent subconscious skirmishes deep within his brain then engaged in one of the fiercest civil war battles to control his conscious decision-making that had ever taken place. There were many factions, analogous to the modern-day warring Syrians or Iraqis. Longing's and Love's strong army of neurons were from the populous but divided warmongering nation of Emotions located deep his dominant right amygdala. Under the command of Field Marshall Limerence, they sent a barrage of strongly worded petitions to his cortical reasoning centre pointing out that Inge was the beautiful, charming, tender, strong, and loving woman that he had dreamed about for years, and that he really needed her. Sexy Lust from the same centre sent a strongly worded email in support of Limerence, but had been so weakened by age and fighting losing battles that Leslie regarded all information from that source as suspect. Lust's misguided characterization of Inge as "a great piece of tail" was interpreted as an unfair ad hominem attack on her whole persona. Leslie filed it among the many reasons to break off the relationship.

Other factions weighed in. One, headed by Independence, with strong support by Prudence, Grief, and Guilt, convinced him that he had had a lot of fun in Pulaski without Inge and that it would be an insult to the memory of Velma to enter into a new serious relationship so soon after her death; he would be making the same hasty mistake that he had made when Rachael left him. Strong ruthless Freedom fighters convinced him that Limerence was a transient and unreliable traitor that he should not listen to; he had already won one battle against Limerence and could do so again, they pointed out. They also convinced him that he was enjoying the solitude and the freedom to pursue whatever adventures he wanted. His weak, uncoordinated, and widely scattered Risk Aversion and Fear guerrilla units remained neutral in this war. They had both been weakened by years of fighting losing battles. Reality's battalion argued that the object of his limerence was now known to be not the beautiful, perfect angel he had once pictured, but a scrawny plain human being with major human flaws. This same faction gave his consciousness a long detailed list of her flaws, including vanity, hypocrisy, deceptions, lying, and irrational political beliefs, with examples of each in supporting briefs. They also blocked all the signals from their own Reality checkpoint traitors who were trying to feed him thoughts that would have made him consider that Inge could find those same human flaws, and more, including his strident dogmatic pronouncements about religion and politics often expressed at highly inappropriate times, in her memory bank of him. A small platoon of unruly Self-Preservation neurons reminded him of the difficulty he would have dealing with his grief if Inge's cancer returned, and that he would be unable to bear to watch her die a slow and painful death as he had done years before with his mother.

With all of these neural battle groupings except Limerence lined up against her, Inge never had a chance in his decision as the CEO of his true self. After some reflection to consider the messages he had just received from the generals in his subconscious centres, Leslie stood up and said aloud to no one but himself: "I have to get outta this now, before it becomes impossible."

He had already decided that snowmobiling and ice fishing in northern Ontario were the next items to strike off of his bucket list, as that was the only one that needed the winter conditions prevailing that month. He called his former classmate who had been in practice in Timmins for 35 years and had just retired. They had last met three years earlier at that 40-year reunion, and Jeff had discussed the fun they could have if Leslie ever wanted to try snowmobiling or ice fishing with him. They chatted for a while; then Leslie said he was ready to take Jeff up on his offer to go snowmobiling and ice fishing, if the offer was still open. Dr. Jeff Whitlock was enthusiastic, as his wife had just left for a visit with her ailing sister in Langley, B.C., and he had no one to go out on some trails with.

Leslie packed up his van two days later, checked the weather forecast, and then headed out on the 401 and 400. He decided to take Highway 11 from Barrie rather than go through Sudbury, composing different versions of what he planned to tell Inge as he drove. At a coffee shop outside of Bracebridge, he bought a black coffee and pulled out his cellphone for what he knew would be a difficult conversation. He would pitch his decision to break off their relationship as being in her best interests and not the selfish act that he knew it was. But he knew that she would be disappointed. Hearing Inge's cheery greeting made it no easier. After he told her how enjoyable he had found the fishing in Pulaski, he enquired about what she had been doing. She only related that she had been to the tackle shop, had met Eric Clouser, and had bought some peacock herl to try tying a grey hackle peacock midge pattern for him to try. She said she had explained to Eric that she had never fly-fished but that her new man friend had given her books about fly tying for Christmas and that she had enjoyed keeping Eric wondering about the strange woman who tied flies but did not fish almost as much as she had enjoyed keeping Carol Creek in the dark about her New Years' Eve plans. And she said she had done some embroidering that he would be interested in.

"I can't imagine any embroidery that I would be interested in."

"Well, I came up with an interesting surprise for your friend Faisal. I have an old black dress that I was going to discard, and have embroidered three carefully placed labels on it. You can invite

Faisal for dinner at your place—you said you owe him and wanted him to know about, you know, you and me. I'll help you cook, then disappear into the bedroom and reappear in that dress after he has been there a few minutes."

He loved her plan but it made what Leslie had planned to say even more difficult—if not impossible. He quickly modified his carefully rehearsed speech, uploading a response fed to his conscious self by Independence and Freedom.

"But Faisal hates surprises."

"That can't be true for a guy who makes a living working in the ER."

Oops, I guess that was the wrong response, he realized.

Inge wondered why Leslie was not pleased with her careful plan. "Is there something else wrong with you?"

"Well, I am out of town and on another trip, and I was just wondering if I should expect you to put up with all my quirks and idiotic behaviour at all. You were doing fine before we met again and it was really just a chance meeting. I think you would be better off to forget about me. That way you don't have to put up with all my foibles and foolish adventures, and you will have one less thing to worry about."

"Are you saying you don't want to see me anymore?"

He could sense sobs coming, and his resolve began to waver.

"Oh, no. But if you think about it, you might decide that you don't want to see me anymore. All I am saying is that if you do decide that way, I will somehow respect your wishes and get over you." With a huge offensive attack from Field Marshall Limerence's units in his amygdalae, sensing a possible win this time, his resolve dissolved into mush. But with an even stronger counteroffensive from the combined forces of Independence, Freedom, Propriety, Reality, Grief, and Guilt, he was able to resuscitate it in a much-weakened form. "But it won't be easy," he added.

There was a long silence and then Inge said "That will definitely never happen. I will never forget you. Is there someone else?"

"Oh, no, I will not be with any woman, but this trip is something that I really want to do. And there will never ever be another woman."

"Promise me that you will call when you get back, or before if you want to, and take your cell wherever you are off to. And be careful, I couldn't bear to lose you. How long will you be gone?"

"Oh, I don't really know, maybe 10 days or so, and I promise I will call you when I get back, but I will be out of cellphone territory at least most of the time. I'm just off on another fishing trip with a medical school classmate."

Inge hung up and sobbed as though she had just discovered that her cancer had spread throughout her body. She was angry and confused. One part of her wanted to hurt him as much as he had just hurt her. *I could do major damage to his reputation as a mentally stable healthy man by leaking the truth about that fateful Friday the 13th to the gossips at the hospital. But I promised to keep that secret. I could start rumours without lying by telling mutual acquaintances that he had just spent a few days fishing with an openly gay man, sharing a motel room, leaving them to draw their own conclusions. But I am not going to stoop to revenge,* she told herself. *I'll just wait and see if he really will come to his senses. But he really had tried to dump me, had he not?*

On the road again, Leslie mulled over his botched attempt to free himself from limerence and now knew that it was going to be even harder than he had imagined. At Jeff Whitlock's house, he caught up on the gossip about their classmates and reminisced about sharing a cadaver in the dissection lab in the anatomy lab at Queens many years before. Jeff was a member of the Jack Pine Snowmobile Club, and they planned to go out on the C Loop part of the Gold Rush Tour to Mattagami and then to Shining Tree Lake for some ice fishing, staying at the Three Bears Camp and Outfitters. As they loaded up the two Arctic Cats the next morning, Jeff commented that Leslie would need to get into warmer clothes than the motorcycling gear he was wearing, as the temperature was to fall to –25°C over the day on the trail. For once Leslie took the advice seriously. He fit a bit too snugly into the dedicated snowmobile outfit belonging to Jeff's wife and donned her visor and helmet. After instructions from Jeff, they started out on the C trail.

Leslie did not get any thrill out of driving the snowmobile, but looked forward to the ice fishing. They stopped for a hearty lunch at the Mattagami Games and Restaurant in Gogama and then headed back out toward Shining Tree Lake. By the time they arrived, Leslie was shivering and thoroughly chilled, but they checked into a small cabin at Three Bears Camp Outfitters, and he slowly warmed up.

The next morning, with a wind chill of –42°C, they headed out to West Shining Tree Lake and set up Jeff's Outpost ice fishing shelter near a dozen other huts 200 metres offshore. The hut was soon warm and cozy thanks to the portable propane heater, and they drilled a hole through almost one metre of ice with the Canadian Tire electric ice auger. Jeff assured Leslie that there were huge lake trout down 20 metres. They dropped the portable fish finder probe down the hole, noting some large fish near the bottom, which was only about 14 metres below. They dropped their lines on the very short ice fishing poles, and waited. An hour went by before a slight tug jiggled Jeff's line and he quickly hauled up an ugly-looking, short, flat, silvery fish. Grunting in disgust, he took it off the hook and kicked it back through the hole. To Leslie's inquiry, he stated that it was a mooneye, the least edible of all the fish in the lake and a bottom feeder rumoured to be contaminated with mercury

After another 45 minutes, Leslie's line jerked and he began to reel in, but there was little fight on the other end. To his surprise, when the fish appeared in the hole, it was a 16-pound monster that Jeff identified as a lake trout. Jeff commented that fish in ice-cold lake water seldom put up much of a fight, unlike those in rivers and warmer summer lake water. After four more hours, they had two more fish, including a huge Northern pike that gouged two deep furrows on the back of Leslie's hand as he tried to remove the hook. Jeff belatedly cautioned him to always use pliers when dealing with pike, checked that the tendons were all intact and applied Polysporin cream and several Steri-Stips from their first aid kit to the injured hand.

The last, very colourful, fish of the day got Jeff very excited, although it was not big. "Holy Christ, that's an aurora trout! They're an endangered species, for Chrissakes! I didn't even know they were here. They were at one point only found in two lakes, but now the MNR has restored them to nine others, and they obviously have spread to this one, too. I've never ever seen a real one before!" He insisted on several pictures and measured its length and girth before releasing it. He explained to Leslie that with the pictures and measurements, he would get a taxidermist to do a reproduction to put on his wall. Jeff said he would send the pictures to a Conservation Officer buddy as proof that it had now reached Shining Tree Lake. They then headed back to the campground cabin.

Jeff asked if Leslie wanted to stay for another day of fishing but he was not thrilled with the experience, as his hand was really hurting. He suggested that they head back to Timmins the next day. By the time they arrived, Leslie was thoroughly chilled again and a bit disillusioned. The weather had turned sour, and they could not go anywhere by car the next day, but Jeff took him out on the snowmobiles again, to Casey's Bar and Grill. Leslie seemed to be quiet and preoccupied, and Jeff attributed that to being saddened by Velma's death. Jeff then began a search for taxidermists on line.

Trying to be helpful, Leslie said, "I met a taxidermist in the middle of Beaver River just a couple of months ago. I wish I could remember his name."

Finding multiple sites and locations—but no taxidermists in Redfern, Jeff read the reviews and scanned the pictures. He was most impressed with Lowry Taxidermy in Ottawa. Almost all of the pictures were of fish, and the reviews were glowing. It did not much matter where the fibreglass reproduction of his aurora trout was made, so he sent the pictures and measurements to Lowry Taxidermy, asking for a price quote and a time frame to do a reproduction, deleting the detail that he was a physician. "He will charge double if he knows that," he told Leslie. Leslie, looking over Jeff's shoulder, was intrigued by the variety of fish and the artistry of the mounts; *maybe someday I will catch a trophy fish and have it mounted,* he mused.

Within 10 minutes, an excited Gary Lowry called him. He said he dreamed of having an aurora trout photo on his website and maybe a reproduction for his booth at fishing shows, and would do two, and would keep one of them for himself. He quoted Jeff a bargain price of $20 per inch, and they discussed the background and the time frame—one year as a minimum, as Gary would need to make a custom mould. Jeff asked him to start the work as soon as possible and said he would pick up the finished product in Ottawa en route to his 45th reunion at Queens the next year.

The next morning, as the weather had improved, Leslie thanked Jeff profusely and headed home. On arriving late in the evening, after unpacking, he reconsidered his bucket list and pulled it up on the computer, deleting the "ice fishing/snowmobiling somewhere in Northern Ontario" listing. He had done it but would never try it again.

He looked around his computer room and found the perfect spot to mount a fish—the blank wall over his desk. He emailed Lowry Taxidermy saying that he wanted another reproduction of the aurora trout that Gary was preparing for Dr. Jeff Whitlock. He reckoned that he could get away with pretending that he had caught it, as he knew exactly where it had been caught. Then he went to bed and tried to sleep. But he was restless and heard the chimes of the grandfather clock every hour. At 2:00 a.m., he awoke with lyrics of a song recurring in his head. He grabbed his iPad and looked it up, then listened to Peggy Lee singing *Is That All There Is?* on YouTube. He promptly emailed Barb asking if he had answered her homework assignment correctly in finding *Is That All There Is?* Then he added, "As a bonus, are Kant's two over-worked words 'Categorical Imperative'?"

At 3:00 a.m., he decided to check his phone messages. There was no message from Inge, but a pleading, almost desperate message from Carol Creek from Inge's number asking him to please call Inge as soon as he got home. Carol said that Inge was too proud to call him herself, but was more despondent than she had ever seen her in all the years they had known each other. He thought he heard sobbing in the background. He stared at his bucket list again and the subconscious neuronal battles for control of his decision-making rose to a new fever pitch.

1. Raft the Colorado through the Grand Canyon.
2. Learn to pilot a glider plane.
3. Learn to walk on tall stilts and to ride a unicycle.
4. Complete training to become an officiant of the Ontario Humanist Society.
5. Bike around the Cabot Trail.

6. Work at the Canadian High Arctic Research Station.
7. Join Doctors without Borders.
8. Go on a distillery tour of Scotland.
9. Tryout for Jeopardy!
10. Fly-fish in every province at least once.

He sighed and then asked himself what a real humanist would do in his situation. Then he highlighted # 1, #2, and #3 and, deleting them, substituted

1. Learn to curl.
2. Take Inge on a bridge cruise.
3. Take Inge to Gatlinburg to play bridge.

He emailed Inge: "I have finally come to my senses. Miss you terribly. Please call me as soon as you get this. I can't live without you. Love you." He attached a picture of the aurora trout with the note, "Caught in Shining Tree Lake."

Damned limerence, he mused. *Not a fatal disease, but an incurable, serious, chronic brain affliction—or a maybe a chronic mental illness. Or perhaps it's more like Chinese water torture.* Then, to very slightly ease the distress of accepting the fate from which he now realized he could not escape, he added a further small item to the bucket list.

1. Rent *Ghost* and watch it with Inge.

epilogue

Sometime in the next year or two ...

Leslie watched *Ghost* with Inge, but they still did not see how it ended.

Leslie and Inge surprised Dr. Faisal Al-Taqi at a private dinner.

Isaac, Adam, and Leslie spent the May long weekend fly-fishing in the Beaver River, hiring Eric Clouser to guide them on the Saturday.

Leslie entered *The Fisher* in the Queen's University Alumni Review photo contest and won in the Nature category.

A double wedding took place at the Toronto Board of Trade Golf Course clubhouse with Dr. Leslie Turle officiating at the first one and Father Kevin Wulff at the second. Leslie and Inge chose a Caribbean bridge cruise for their honeymoon.

Leslie and Inge Turle joined separate leagues at the local curling rink.

Joe Glacier's AA sponsor found his body at the bottom of the stairs, still clutching a bottle of Bacardi. Father Kevin Wulff officiated at the private funeral. It was his last official act as a priest. He left the priesthood in disillusionment over the Church's unchanged stand on abortion, gay rights, clerical celibacy/marriage and its harsh treatment of America's liberal nuns. He joined a marriage counselling service in Elmsville. He became infatuated with the divorced daughter of the Creeks' after a carefully planned chance meeting arranged by his mother and Carol Creek. His newly revived libido made him quickly decide that his marriage counselling job required personal experience with marriage and sex, and his marriage proposal to her was accepted three months after their first meeting. They found two home pregnancy test kits from anonymous well wishers among their wedding presents.

At the Mid-Atlantic Regional Bridge Tournament, Leslie and Inge earned 1.8 Gold Master Points in the Gold Rush, 5.7 Red playing in the Stratified Pairs and 2.4 Silver in Swiss Teams playing with Ken and Carol Creek, who drove to Gatlinburg with them.

Leslie and Inge did some fly fishing in the Bow River near Calgary, en route to new temporary jobs in Cambridge Bay.

Inge Turle began frantic knitting of baby clothes for Leslie Jr. and in anticipation of a grandchild.

Dr. Faisal Al Taqi donated $200,000 to the Beaverbrook hospital Critical Care Education fund, insisting that it be called *The Dr. Leslie Turle Critical Care Education Fund.*

Dr. Faisal Al Taqi, supported by Dr. Turle, joined the Humanist Society of Ontario, but maintained his Islamic connections and was asked to speak about Islamic traditions at one of their meetings.

The *CMAJ* published a paper titled, "Sex-linked Salt Wasting, Anorexia, Defective Taste and Olfaction, Tone Deafness, and Selective Erectile Dysfunction. A New Syndrome." An accompanying editorial also speculated about the prevalence of this new "Turle's Syndrome" along the same lines as Leslie had.

Leslie Turle biked around the Cabot Trail while Inge visited her long-lost brother.

Leslie and Inge began to work with a Toronto-based film company on a planned 4-hour TV miniseries, a loose adaptation on this story. They hoped to cast Victor Garber as Dr. Leslie Turle, Angelina Jolie as Inge, and Travis Fimmel as Eric Clouser.

Dr. Leslie Turle, on a solo bicycling tour of Scottish distilleries, began writing his tell-all autobiography, tentatively entitled *Is That All There Is?*

disclaimer

The major characters listed at the start of this book are entirely fictional, and only passing reference is made to real people, such as Guy Paul Morin. Any resemblances of the fictional characters to real people are entirely coincidental, as is any resemblance of the institutions to any real-life institutions.

author's notes

This is not my first published book, but it is my first full-length novel, and I should be forgiven for not knowing how to categorize it. Is it a mystery, a romance, a suspense thriller, or even a disguised treatise in defence of humanist philosophy? All those elements are here, but I will leave it to readers and reviewers to decide what label to put on it and how to categorize it.

Readers may well wonder who the real people in my real life are that I have modelled the fictional characters after, but I can assure them that they are all entirely fictional. But most—or at least most good—fiction writers write about things they have experienced to some degree. I am no exception so I write about characters and actions that are somewhat related to personal experiences. Like the main male character, I am a retired nonreligious medical specialist circling 70, with extensive experience with the culture and routines of hospitals. And, like him, I have experienced the joys and disappointments of two marriages, although neither my ex nor my current loving wife shares any character traits with his two wives. I have enjoyed fly-fishing in many southern Ontario rivers. I have visited many of the locations in the story. Like him, I have been on many long bicycle rides and I have experienced the frustrations of playing bridge poorly on many occasions. Like him, my culinary skills are nonexistent and my wardrobe style and colour choices are often outlandish. And like him and many other health care workers, I have had the disturbing experience of misdiagnosing a fatal disease in myself. Having acquired one feature of the fictitious "Turle's Syndrome," I falsely concluded that I had a fatal cancer to account for it. All mere mortals make mistakes.

However, that is where the resemblances stop, and the story is in no sense autobiographical. I never considered the option he took to deal with his wrong self-diagnosis, and I have never even once smoked marijuana.

I definitely do not have a secret infatuation with any of the many nurses I worked with over more than 40 years. But after reading about all of the lies and deceptions that the fictional characters I write about live with, why should I expect anyone to believe me?

acknowledgments

So many individuals contributed their knowledge and help to me in writing this book that I hardly know where to begin. Some did so in minor ways without realizing the information they imparted would show up here. Such was Tom Dool's discussion of the varieties and market economy of British Columbia marijuana; John Coderre's discussions about the hierarchy and placement of Catholic priests; Sue Carlyle's discussion about the legal process for obtaining a certificate of death; and Bob and Mary Dore's discussion about their experiences on the Inca Trail to Macchu Picchu. Bob Dore also gave me hundreds of tips and informal lessons in fly-fishing that made the fishing stories herein more realistic. Dr. Nigel Paterson first expounded to me the meaning of trolley car agnosticism. My loving, supportive wife, Vera Simon, made many suggestions for changes in earlier drafts and critically read later drafts, making further suggestions for changes and rewording on all but a few pages. She also introduced me to the word "limerence," using it to describe our feelings for each other when we first started dating. And it still afflicts me. She suggested the most appropriate erotic movie for Velma and Leslie to watch together. My daughter, Dr. Andra Ghent, made helpful suggestions and corrections to make the characters and the plot more realistic. Her faint praise of an early draft with a casual comment that it was better than my first well-received book, *Medicine Outside the Box*, steeled my determination to continue writing on days when I was ready to quit.

My story was unbelievable until Lesley Wormold enthusiastically and meticulously made major corrections to make it fit with the local geography, institutions, and timelines. Jill Puffer contributed enormously in educating me about the routines and cultures of police forces, and did so with good-humoured tolerance of my ignorance of such matters. Without her help, no law-enforcement officer would ever read this story and believe that it could happen. My devoted sister, Lois Hibbert, made many suggestions for further changes in style, content, and formatting, even though I must have annoyed her greatly by sending her newer drafts while she was working on earlier ones. Jane Karchmar provided cheerful and meticulous copy-editing. These and the comments of yet others resulted in hundreds of revisions; the title alone was changed a dozen times. These reviewers should not be held responsible for any remaining errors or inconsistencies. Finally, Magdalene Carson cheered me on after a publishing organization that had contracted to publish this story suddenly closed. She also provided the ingenious layout and design of the final product. The irony in her clever depiction of the main characters, most in life-saving and soul-saving professions, wending their way toward a graveyard should be lost on no one.

Some readers will no doubt recognize the voices and ideas of other writers and speakers in both the narrative and the dialogue of the characters in this novel. The sometimes-divergent outlooks of many people whom I have never met but who have influenced my thinking to greater or lesser degrees are indeed here in some sense. They and countless others have continuously altered my brain's synaptic network into an almost infinite number of configurations over a lifetime of reading and listening. Perhaps surprisingly, none of them are classical famous philosophers and none are fellow novelists. I find it impossible to rank the importance of their enormous contributions, but among those to whom I owe a huge debt of thanks, David Eagleman (*Incognito: The Secret Life of the Brain*) stands out, and I have used his beautifully apt analogy of warring brain factions in subconscious decision making processes in several places; I thank him for developing it.

The long list of the others, in no particular order, include the late Dr. Robert Buckman (*Can We Be Good without God?*), Nicholas Wade (*The Faith Instinct: How Religion Evolved and Why it Endures*), Karen Armstrong (*The Bible: A Biography*), Phillip Zimbardo (*The*

Lucifer Effect), Francis Fukuyama *(The Origins of Political Order)*, Robert Lustig *(Fat Chance)*, Richard Dawkins *(The Selfish Gene)*, the late Christopher Hitchens *(God Is Not Great)*, Robert Green Ingersoll *(Some Mistakes of Moses)*, Richard E. Bernstein *(When Jesus became God)*, Thorstein Veblen *(The Theory of the Leisure Class)*, Lionel Tiger *(God's Brain)*, Yuval Noah Harari *(Sapiens)*,and any number of guests on Bob McDonald's *Quirks and Quarks* and Paul Kennedy's *Ideas* on CBC radio. I am sure there are many more whose names have been buried so deeply in my subconscious as to be inaccessible at this point.

about the author

Dr. Cam Ghent is a retired liver specialist from London, Ontario. Born and raised in the farming community of Mount Forest, Ontario, his medical training was at Western University in London, Ontario, and at Yale University School of Medicine. General Store Publishing House published his first book, *Medicine Outside the Box*, a series of critical essays on modern medical practices, in 2011. He can be contacted at **cghent6@rogers.com** or on Facebook.